LAST RESORT

By
JOHN E. CARSON

AMI™

An Aspirations Media Publication

An Aspirations Media™ Publication
www.aspirationsmediainc.com

Prose and Poetry Copyright © 2006 by John E. Carson
Cover by Darryl Taylor
Layout by Jennifer Rowell
Design: Jennifer Rowell and John E. Carson

LIBRARY OF CONGRESS CONTROL NUMBER: 2006930466

IBSN-10: 0-9776043-3-0
ISBN-13: 978-0-9776043-3-3

MANUFACTURED IN THE UNITED STATES

First Printing October 2006

Also by John E. Carson

Ramblin Rose and the Internet Newsletter

A review for *Ramblin Rose and the Internet Newsletter*

"...a unique and well crafted story..."

"Ramblin' Rose And The Internet Newsletter
is very highly recommended as an active and
fun read, particularly for children, for the
inventive and engaging story it tells."

-Midwest Book Review

The Making of Last Resort

It was a cold, rainy October day in St. Cloud, Minnesota. My wife and I had just sat down at a booth in The Copper Lantern and were waiting for our order. I had ordered their broasted chicken dinner, which was my favorite.

We sat, continuing our discussion of our recent success with the recording of *Deep of The Night*, a poem I had written which Charlie Roth had just recorded as a song. The conversation flowed between my future plans for writing and how it had all come about. I realized that without Marlene, I would have never kept writing.

Looking at the old, depressed houses across the street through the occasional gusts of dry, yellow leaves, I was struck with an idea. Why not incorporate my poetry with prose and set it in a ghost story? Using our collective family history and the mystery of my childhood, all the unanswered questions I had about my life could be put to work!

With a burst of inspiration, we framed up the story as we ate, weaving fact with fiction until a plot was born, eventually growing into the novel.

Broasted chicken is still my favorite food.

John Evan Carson
2006

Thanks for the memories...

Singer/Entertainer Bob Hope's classic song seems an appropriate way to open this book.

Music has long been a bridge between generations in all cultures, stepping stones that help link us with our heritage and this story makes use of a lot of song titles that help to link us with the world of 1934.

Many important things happened in that year and though it seems like long ago, it is only a generation or two away for most of us. For some of us it is our own past. Yet, today's world is a result of many of the events of that time.

Younger readers may remember the stories told by their own grandparents and realize that the past and present are not so distant. In fact, there seems to be more appreciation today than ever before of the link between the past and the present, rather than the "Gap" we used to hear about.

The everyday lives of the people before us have shaped the world we live in today. The unsung heroes who go about their lives and jobs creating the things we all depend on as we live our own lives.

And like the world around us, this book is the result of a lot of behind the scenes effort and I'd like to thank those people for what they do.

Some of them are listed in the credits; Darryl Taylor, who did the wonderful cover art that draws us in, Jennifer Rowell for the great layout, Patricia Stively and E.D. Easley of Creative Editing Solutions for their valuable expertise and appreciated comments and Lee and Chad Corrie who pulled it all together.

To all the dear readers, friends and family who encouraged me I say again

Thanks for the memories!

And tell all the stars above

this is dedicated to the one I love.

— The Shirelles, 1961

for

Marlene Rose Carson

PROLOGUE

We were seated at the front table of the Grand Hotel in New York. Guests of Honor at the Best Seller celebration of Royal Blue Publishers new hit *Stepping Stones*.

We had made the New York Times Bestseller list and looked like we could climb to No.1!

I could hardly believe it was happening!

"Why do you think it couldn't happen to you?" Marianne asked as she sipped wine from the fine crystal glass.

"Your mother must have put that in your head when she was drinking!" She continued, reminding me of my mother's two personas.

"Guess you're right." I said. "When Mother wasn't drinking she was always telling me I could do anything! But when she was drinking I think she was talking to my father when she said I'd never amount to a hill of beans."

"Well, it's not up to her. It's up to you. Your background has nothing to do with what you can accomplish if you want to. I've been telling you that for years." Marianne said with a little too much attitude.

"Well, I know one thing," I replied, " you are the reason that book was written. I could not have done it without you!"

"I wish you hadn't insisted on naming me as co-author, though. Sometimes we have to split up to promote the book or do talk shows. I hate traveling without you!" Marianne said.

Before I could respond, the announcer's voice boomed over the microphone.

"Ladies and Gentlemen! The Grand Hotel and The Big Band are pleased to welcome the guests of honor, the authors of the best-selling book *Stepping Stones*, Christopher and Marianne Evans for the Spotlight Dance of the evening. Please clear the dance floor for the lovely couple."

A round of applause found us blushing under the moving spotlight as we stood up from the table and walked to the floor.

In the darkened room under the big light we danced as the band played the old classic, *You Belong To Me.*

"I don't like traveling alone either." I said as we danced. "I don't like doing anything without you."

"Sometimes I worry about other women, now that you're rich and famous, especially!" Marianne confessed.

"You have nothing to worry about," I said, as I pulled her close, "I promise. We started this together and we'll finish together."

After the accident on the way home those words would come back to haunt me.

ONE

I never really believed in ghosts. That is until last summer, when I rented the Zimmerman house in Minnesota. My publisher had given me three months to deliver the last book on my contract. It had been three years since my last best-seller and a year since my wife's death. A part of me had died with her. *The writer.*

Marianne was my silent partner. She was the writer behind Christopher Evans, the one the public did not see. Without her ideas and encouragement, I would not have been able to complete my first real novel, *STEPPING STONES*, which made the New York Times bestseller list for five weeks and allowed me to become a full time writer.

Until then I had been writing poems and short stories in little cracks of time while I worked in middle management at a local supermarket chain in Minneapolis. I began to have some success here and there; a contest won, a poem or two accepted in magazines.

The type of things a lot of writers go through.

Marianne kept encouraging me, and together we hammered out *Stepping Stones.*

It was simply the story of my life told as a mystery that led me to the truth about my family's secret life and their escape from the fringe of organized crime in the Thirties. I convinced her to take the credit she deserved and the book listed us both as the authors.

Now she was gone. In three seconds. The truck driver never even saw us...some cartage company from Annandale, Minnesota.

The writer in me left with her. I was contracted to deliver one more book by the end of the third year. The book signings were the hardest. Though the story sold well this last year, partly due to sympathy I suspect, I had left my job and the funds, though still considerable would not last forever.

The second year without Marianne took its toll. I had no one to share my success with. No children, no pets, no house; just an empty apartment and my computer.

One day, my publisher called.

"Look, Christopher, you need to get away. I know a realtor in Annandale, who has a house available for the summer. He needs someone to rent it and will cut the rent in half if someone would clean the place up a bit. It's across the lake from the Last Resort. It's been empty for a while. He wants to turn it into a bed and breakfast someday...it might be just the thing for you. Lots of atmosphere; you might get some ideas. What do you say? I need that book, and you are a good writer. You could be a great writer. You can take it on Monday. You can spend the summer there. If nothing else, you can help my friend."

Ed Harris could be pretty convincing. He was the owner of Harris Publications and Royal Blue Publications was his leading imprint.

"Okay, Ed. I'll help you out. I'll deliver your book, too. But don't expect much."

I accepted the offer as a sort of last resort also. If I couldn't make a comeback, I would quit writing forever.

Though I wouldn't let on to Ed, he had lit a spark of hope in me. Maybe the old house could do it!

The Last Resort was somewhat famous. Set on Zimmerman Lake, it was home to many vacationers, mostly businessmen and even some gangsters in the Thirties and Forties, but I did not want to be reminded of my family's history or the connections I wrote about in my first book. Both of my great-aunts had gotten involved with the wrong crowd. Minneapolis was not far from Chicago then, either.

Minnesota was a sportsman's paradise with its many lakes and good hunting. I never had the chance growing up to do anything like that with my father; he had left when my mother became pregnant. Marriage wasn't his thing. I never saw him. But I heard plenty about him when Mother hit the bottle!

Growing up in the city, I had always felt like a fish out of water. I had to join the Navy to learn how to swim!

But I wasn't staying at "The Resort". I was staying in the house across the lake.

"Atmosphere; Clean the place up a bit?" I said as the headlights lit the overgrown brick pillars at the front of the driveway. I wasn't prepared for The Zimmerman House! It looked haunted! Must have been sixty years since it was lived in! As I eased my little Mercury into the driveway, I thought about turning around. If I had a cell phone I'd call Ed...

I had to stop the car just inside the old stone gate and get out of the car to clear the brush blocking the path. At one time this had been a rustic brick drive. Now there were weeds growing in every crack. The stone walls were crumbling, the irregular shaped blocks separating from each other. The lilac bushes had gone wild and grew across the drive to meet each other.

Strange too was the bed of petunias along the inside wall, wild but still looking recently tended. Marianne once told me that petunias had to be planted every year.

Though the summer sun was still in the Western sky, there was a haze surrounding the old two-story house. A big house, though. It must have five bedrooms at least.

The realtor said there was some furniture left in the house; I could only imagine what it looked like.

"There are tools in the shed and cleaning products in the kitchen. I've arranged to have a phone put in and my number is on my card. Don't hesitate to call if you need anything." Phil Hanson's words echoed in my mind as I pulled the car up to the front porch counting the six steps I'd have to climb with the computer.

Wishing Marianne were here, I touched the gold, heart shaped locket that hung from the rear view mirror. It had been my mother's and I had presented it to Marianne after we were married, hoping she would hand it down to our child one day.

Shaking off the memory, I gave it a little push and left it swinging back and forth as I opened the car door and got out, trunk key in hand.

I stood on the porch with my suitcase, looking out past the old stone gate. The lake was visible across the road. A flight of old wooden steps led to the remains of a dock. At one time the beach must have been sandy and clear and the Zimmerman's pontoon must have hosted many parties. Now the dock was buried in silt.

I tried to see the Resort on the other side of the lake, but it was too far.

The words "last resort" echoed from my lips in a whisper and I turned to the house.

A chill ran down my spine. Did I just see the curtains move?

TWO

"Come on, Christopher! You don't believe in ghosts!" I told myself out loud, re-assured by the sound of my own voice.

I looked at the window again. Through the dirt on the glass I could see the yellowed moth-eaten drapes, were they white at one time? They hung motionless, as still as the air and the eerie quiet of this place. There was a sense of timelessness here.

Maybe it was just me. I was used to the sounds of the city. Cars and people rushing around from place to place, as if they had somewhere important to go. I used to watch them in the store agonizing over the little purchases that seemed so urgent as they went about their lives all wrapped up in themselves. I used to think they were so self-centered, thinking only of their own little world.

That was until my own world was shattered. Now the little things Marianne and I used to do seemed very important and I would have given anything to have them back.

I shook off the feelings and memories and the chill that had fallen over me. I was here for a reason. I had something important to do. I had a book to deliver, and this old house was going to help me do it!

I walked across the old painted floor of the porch to the front door. The house was big, but not a mansion. It was a lake home and not as opulent as it might have been.

Still, the tall spires and gabled rooftops spoke of modest wealth.

The front door was tall and rounded at the top. There were three little panes of glass across the front, dusty and needing cleaning. The doorknob was tarnished, as was the brass plate behind it and I imagined what it must have looked like when it was new.

Turning the knob, I remembered the keys. The house was supposed to be locked.

I set the suitcase down and fished in my jacket pocket for the keys. There were six keys on the ring, front door, back door, garage, tool shed, basement and attic.

Which was which? The keys were old; Phil must have given me the originals.

I tried to match them by appearance and name on the lock, but there was no name on the doorplate. I would have to use the process of elimination.

Grasping the knob again with the chosen key ready, I was surprised when it turned and the door opened slightly, away from the key.

Must have been unlocked, I thought to myself. "It must have been." I answered back aloud.

I put the ring of keys back in my jacket pocket and picked up the suitcase. Remembering some old movie, I kicked the door gently and as it swung open on the old rusted hinges, and yelled out, "Honey, I'm home!"

Chuckling at my own humor I stepped inside. The musty, stale air assaulted me and I felt the oxygen being drawn out of my lungs. Gasping for breath, I turned and stumbled on the transom, almost falling down the steps.

"Well, that was graceful, Christopher!" I was still talking to myself as I recovered, leaning on the porch railing. I decided to leave the door open for a while.

"The first thing I'm going to do is open all the windows and doors and air this place out!"

No one disagreed with me, so that's what I did. Stepping back in I took inventory of the number of windows. There was a large picture window in the living room to my left, the kind with the stained glass corners and leaded across the top and two large double hung windows in the outside wall. To my right was the sitting room with a smaller picture window overlooking the porch and a smaller window in the sidewall by the stairway.

Above the picture window in the sitting room was a row of four smaller windows, which also did not open. All of them were framed in wide, dark woodwork.

The house was very masculine, heavy and dark. It needed a woman's touch, which the once white draperies and lace must have provided.

I walked across the old braided rug, each step raising little puffs of dry dust. The rug separated from the shock of being used again and I made a note to myself not to try and save it.

Reaching the first window, I pulled back the curtains, which tore in my hand and collapsed to the floor as if finally they could rest. I wouldn't be saving these either!

The lock on the window was made of brass, but now looked black with age. It was sticky to the touch and I prayed that time had not sealed the windows shut.

A little pounding with the heel of my hand broke the windows' sleep and a telltale *snap!* announced its resurrection.

One by one, in the dining room and the kitchen - wherever I could find one, the windows opened reluctantly, victims of my now perfected technique. The curtains came down in pieces and I retraced my path, scooping them up as I went and kicking the last ones onto the porch. I would find the trash later.

Whatever light came into the house through the now naked windows seemed to be eaten up by the darkness within. I wondered if there was a way to brighten this house up and still retain its original appearance. But I was only supposed to clean it up a bit, not restore it. I would only be here for three months anyway.

Yet, if I were going to work here, I would have to do *something* with it!

Leaving the curtains on the porch, I continued my tour, a few butterflies in my stomach as I started thinking of the project, and the potential this house had. They don't build them like this anymore!

"This would be a candidate for This Old House, or America's Most Haunted! What do you think, Norm?" I talked to myself aloud again, justifying the idea now taking shape in my mind. "No wonder Phil thought of the bed and breakfast! There must be a lot of history connected with this house, local history anyway."

I continued my tour, noting the house had already begun to inspire me; if not for a story, than as an investment. Maybe I could partner with Phil and I wouldn't even have to write...

The sudden slam of the front door shook the house. My heart jumped into my throat! The timing was coincidence, wasn't it? The house could not read my mind. A strong sudden breeze...of course it was, "Just the wind".

Resuming the tour though, I was careful with my thoughts. But I couldn't shake the feeling that something or someone was watching me.

THREE

It took a few minutes for my heart to slow down. I concentrated on slowing my breathing and telling myself again that I did not believe in ghosts. That's what I had always said and even though my stomach was telling me otherwise, I was determined to live up to my words. I couldn't let fear rule me.

Shields up, I continued my exploration. Recalling *STAR TREK,* I realized the opening theme from the original series did have a haunting quality. Was I Kirk or Mr. Spock? Boldly going...

Suddenly feeling silly, I shook my head and smiled. Here I was, all alone and thinking how I must look!

To whom?

I had always quoted songs, books and movies when I was nervous. It seemed to help me stay in control. I saw no reason to stop now.

Sherlock Holmes seemed appropriate. Hmm! The old wooden floor must have been polished once. Here and there I could see the evidence of furniture. Here was the dining room, the depressions in the floor revealing the clawed feet of a massive wooden table and it's attendant chairs. The dining room was separated from the living room by a half-wall about four feet in from both sides. On either side of the divider were glassed in shelves and doors. On the living room side they were meant to house books and display ornamental decorations. On the dining room side they became the china cabinets that held the formal dinnerware. Amazingly, the glass was intact.

On the inside wall of the dining room were marks left by a piano. Not a grand piano, but the straight-backed ones I had seen in pictures of old homes. I could imagine a young lady entertaining the guests at dinner. In this dark setting she would have been the life in this house. Her music would have been both light and passionate...

My mind traveled across the years, captured by the scene in my imagination. First I saw the table and guests and heard the sound of their conversations, then from somewhere came music. Turning my head to the piano, the others faded away and I saw the dark hair of a young woman, hands on the keys, playing with a passion beyond her years. I did not know classical music but the beauty of it was that one did not need to. The music was about life, tragedy, triumph, sadness and joy as her spirit expressed itself, the piano a voice for her feelings. I was enthralled.

As suddenly as the vision had come to me, it vanished, leaving only the stark silence of the empty house. Where had the music come from? My imagination was not good enough to write classical music...

Maybe I was going crazy. Crazy with loneliness for Marianne. Finally away from distractions my mind was releasing pent up emotions not yet dealt with...

Now I was Sigmund Freud! Sure I was. But the girl at the piano was not Marianne! Recalling the scene in my mind I almost expected her to turn around and look at me as she played, showing a skeleton face!

This was too much for me and still 'in control' I decided to explore the grounds. I could not deal with the rest of the house right now.

Turning back to the living room, my eye caught on an old yellow piece of paper lying on the china cabinet shelf. I bent down and carefully opened the glass door. That's when I found the first poem.

It was written in long hand on what looked like a page torn from a diary or journal. There was no date on it, but as I deciphered the graceful script, a chill went through me from front to back. It was titled *Catherine's Song*.

CATHERINE'S SONG

The piano played-
I did not
The notes not from
My hands were wrought...

I sat each day
Reluctantly
My fingers poised
Above the keys...

I played on
Just by ear
While I listened
For my prince to near...

To please my mother
I endured
My lonely life
'Till freedom neared-

Now at Midnight
It plays once more
Though no shadow falls
Upon my door.

Catherine Zimmerman

Now my heart was *really* pounding! My head was telling me that all I believed was about to change. My stomach was churning and the chills running through me convinced me I must have a fever.

"*You're traveling through another dimension-your next stop The Twilight Zone!*" Rod Serling's voice brought a smile to my lips. A little humor helped restore me. I must have been watching too much T.V. lately!

I welcomed the warm summer air as I walked out onto the old porch, dodging the remains of the old curtains I had yet to bury. For the first time, I noticed the old swinging bench on the North end of the porch. The chains were rusty and the paint long since worn off, but I needed a place to sit. I hoped it would hold 185. Pounds, that is. The doctor was happy at my last check up. Ideal weight for a six-footer! Blood pressure good. Lungs clear in spite of the smoking. Heart healthy. All of this reassured me as I tried to hold onto my perception of reality.

Would I stay? I was not one to back away from a challenge. I had signed on for the summer. But what would stop me if I changed my mind? No one would be the worse for it. I could write somewhere else.

Soon my justifications exposed my cowardice. I reminded myself that being brave was not about having no fear; it was about doing what you had to do in spite of it. And if I left with my tail dragging, could I face myself? That was the greater fear! Nor would I ever know who the girl at the piano was.

I let my mind drift with the wind through the treetops, their rustling branches playing a song of their own. They seemed to be telling me that this place would be here regardless of my beliefs. That, here things just *were* and like the trees, did not need to explain themselves.

I hadn't realized how long I had been sitting on the old swing. The sun was beginning to set and my watch told me I had been here for three hours already. It did not seem possible! *Was* this a Twilight Zone?

Before I could answer, the old chain gave way and my end of the swing landed on the porch, leaving its impressions on my behind!

Guess I'll have to fix that too! I thought as I stood up painfully. My Doctor's report now humbled by my sudden collapse!

I smiled at the humor of it and looked back at the house. Humphrey Bogart now talking. "Just you and me kid. Here's looking at you!"

FOUR

There wasn't time to explore the grounds. It was getting dark fast. I wondered again about my perception of time. There was a chill in the summer air and the wind had picked up. The trees were not gently swaying now. A storm was coming.

I felt another chill. Was the old house haunted? Who was Catherine Zimmerman? What really did happen in the dining room today? Could I spend the night here? I hadn't even finished my tour of the house and had no idea where I would sleep.

The lights! I would have to find them. I had lost the protection of daylight, though I hadn't felt any safer when the piano started playing...

Opening the door, I felt along the wall for a switch. Instead of the familiar plastic toggle, there was an old metal plate and two push buttons. These had been popular in older homes. I found the button sticking out and pushed it.

Instead of being bathed in light from the chandelier as I had hoped for, there was a dull yellow glow from an old light bulb hanging from the ceiling in front of the door. I looked up at the frosted tulip shade hanging from an old chain, the yellowed wire weaving in and out of the once golden links.

I sighed. Here I was in a vacant old house that I had agreed to spend the summer in and had promised to "clean up a bit". What had I talked myself into now?

"Well, Pilgrim, let's get to it!" I said out loud in a poor impression of John Wayne's famous voice.

The one thing I knew how to do was work. I had learned early in life that if I wanted anything I would have to work for it. I had started making money as a kid long before I was old enough to have a job. Mowing lawns, shoveling snow, delivering newspapers, going door to door selling everything from seeds to bobby pins and finally getting a real job when I was fifteen. At twenty I had received a medical discharge from the Navy and returned to Minnesota, landing a job at Carlson's Market; a small but growing chain of food stores. I had worked there eight years until the success of *Stepping Stones*.

So now I had a new job. I took comfort in the tasks before me. They kept me from thinking too much. They became my armor and reminded me who I was. I went from room to room turning on whatever lights I could find.

Some of the bulbs worked and some were burned out. I made a note to replace them all tomorrow. I had avoided the dining room, going to the living room first and turning on the three-tulip ceiling fixture. Two of those bulbs worked. From there I doubled back to the entry into the foyer or sitting room by the stairway. The single bulb worked there also.

There were six stairs leading to a landing and on the other side the steps led down into a large study or family room. Looking up from the landing to the left were the stairs to the second floor. Finding the switch plate in the wall I pushed the button and was pleased to see both the fixtures at the top and bottom light up.

Part of the stairway was open on both sides, a scaled-down version of opulence. This was, after all, a summer home and not a mansion. The years of neglect had made the woodwork darker with age, yet the quality showed through in the banister and the spindles for the railing. The amount of cleaning and polishing required to restore the oak was intimidating and I reminded myself that I was just to clean the place up a bit, not restore it.

The walls were also darkened with age and the wallpaper separated at the seams and corners, the glue now dry and brittle. Each lamp lit revealed cries for attention and I felt a growing sympathy for the once fine home.

My curiosity was also growing. Why had the house been empty for so long? Why hadn't the family passed it on? Homes and sites like these had always been prized in this part of the country. Perhaps some research would answer my questions.

I continued the trek, my bravery growing with every new light. As I moved from room to room I tried to ignore the urge to look over my shoulder, as if I was not alone. Distant rolls of thunder magnified the silence of the house and I tiptoed about as if I would wake some sleeper. The wisecracks and quotes that had helped me earlier were stifled now as I fell into an eerie trance, matching the stillness around me.

The thunder was louder now and I could hear rain falling on the roof and tapping at the windows. Gently at first, then louder as it was driven by the wind.

Remembering that I had left the windows open, I hurried back to the living room. The rain blew through the old screens in a mist, refreshing the stale air. With the rain and the lights for company the house seemed more alive. I broke out of the trance that had gripped me on the stairs and decided to leave the windows open. The moisture would do the old place some good.

Looking out the picture window in the living room I watched the storm. The rolling clouds were occasionally lit by spikes of lightning. There were no streetlights or neighboring houses, and as I stood there I felt a growing chill of expectation.

A loud *crack!* And a sudden bolt of lightning lit the grounds and in that instant I saw a girl bent over in the patch of petunias by the driveway wall. She seemed to be weeding the garden. I froze as she stopped and looked back at the house and right at me!

Another flash of lightning lit up the yard. She was gone! Was it the girl at the piano? Heart pounding in my chest, I looked for somewhere to sit. I felt faint. I didn't believe in ghosts! There must be a logical explanation! Where was that furniture that Phil had mentioned?

My fear was turning to anger now. Frustration grew in me as once again I was faced with something I could not explain.

"I've had enough of this! Keep your inspiration, Ed!" I said out loud as I fished in my pocket for my keys. I was ready to run. The car was waiting and I reached out and opened the front door...

That was as far as I got. My blood ran cold as I stared back at the ghostly face of a young woman standing on the porch! The girl from the garden, with not a drop of rain on her. Her hair was motionless in the wind, her eyes beseeching me not to leave. I thought I would have a heart attack right there!

I opened my mouth but no words came out. I felt incredible sorrow. And then she vanished.

In a daze I shuffled into the kitchen only to realize there was nothing to eat. I stayed in my trance and absent-mindedly climbed into the car, slowly and methodically starting the engine and driving out onto the dirt road to the highway and the local gas station convenience store.

The clerk looked at me as if *I* were a ghost!

"Long drive," I said as I paid for the bread, lunchmeat, and chips. "By the way, do you know anything about the old Zimmerman House?"

"Only that it's supposed to be haunted. Something to do with the banker that lived there. They say he was doing business with the Mob," he replied.

I looked at the kid behind the counter. Red hair and acne, maybe seventeen, I thought.

"The Mob? Out here?" I asked.

"That's what my grandpa says. "Course, he wasn't around in the Thirties. That's what *his* dad told him."

"Oh, and the Mob killed the banker?" I asked, skeptically.

"Not sure, but folks say the house is haunted," he was suddenly less friendly as he caught my tone and finally put the money in the cash drawer, closing it with a slam.

"Well, thanks," I said, picking up the plastic bag and turning away.

"Why you wondering about the Zimmerman place?" He asked as I reached for the door.

"That's where I'm staying," I said, stepping through the door into the wet summer night.

FIVE

Sleep Mode. Those two words were on my mind as I woke up late in the morning. I had crashed on the daybed after my midnight snack, too tired to care about ghosts or gangsters. Sleep Mode. My computer! I had to get it set up. I only had three months to write a novel.

I sat up, swinging my legs to the floor one at a time. Sleeping in your clothes in the summertime is not too comfortable! I wondered if the shower worked. There was a lot to do this morning yet. I had to get some furniture, clean the place up a bit and finish exploring the house.

I was proud of myself for not running away. If I had any sense, I probably would have! But I had an idea for a story! A ghost story!

This was the first time I had been excited about anything since Marianne had left. I had relied on her for inspiration, telling her all of my hopes and dreams since we had first met. After we were married she encouraged my writing, building my belief in myself. She was the first stop I made with every thought, every poem and every idea that came along. She became my crutch also. I would watch her as she read, or listened and read her expressions. If she didn't truly like something I would lose interest in it quickly.

I must have put a lot of pressure on her.

After the accident, I sank into depression. Keeping busy was my only therapy.

Not having her here to share the spotlight was hard to bear. I not only missed her, but the support she had always given me. She was my reason for living.

Part of the reason I hadn't run away at the sight the ghost was simply that I just did not care what happened to me anymore. Staying at this house was just one more distraction that kept me from facing myself. It was in a sense running away, after all.

I could not live like that anymore. I had closed my mind to any wonder or joy in life, feeling guilty that Marianne was gone and I wasn't. I felt disloyal if I got ideas without her or even thought about being happy again.

When I saw the ghost on the porch, I was surprised by my lack of fear and also that I did not immediately think of Marianne. Was she a ghost? Could she come back? Could I somehow hold on to her? No, none of these questions entered my mind, though I still loved her dearly. I sought only peace now.

Then again, had I really seen a ghost? Were the old house and the power of suggestion working on me? Was I still suffering from depression?

Real or not, the poem I had found awakened a curiosity in me. Who was Catherine Zimmerman? The girl I had seen on the porch? And she was a writer!

Her style was not unlike my own. I became aware of a sense of belonging here. As if there was a reason I had come. I felt a sense of purpose, to write her story, albeit in my own unique way...

For the first time in a long time, I felt butterflies in my stomach. Could I do it? Here was a challenge! My former success was fading due to a large part on Marianne. But it was a formula that worked. I could function alone, but I had always felt I was not meant to live alone. And living, for me, was not just surviving. Maybe her spirit was still with me.

Either way, I was going to tackle this project! Marianne would be proud if I could stand on my own!

With a new attitude came new enthusiasm and energy I had not felt in a long time. I made a list of things to do and in my excitement failed to notice that the old drop leaf table in the kitchen seemed a little brighter now. In fact, everything looked a little newer.

But I wouldn't notice that until later.

The first thing on my list was to bring the computer into the house. There was no place to set it up and I would have to go into town and get a desk. I would also have to get groceries. I needed to call Phil and ask him about acquiring some new curtains, and where *was* that furniture he had mentioned?

Finishing the tour of the house would have to come later; my desire to write was tugging at me now.

There was an old phone on the kitchen counter. It was an old desktop push button model, black with white buttons and an old, yellowed cord. Phil said I should call on the weekend, when his wife June was out of town. And everyone knows a realtor is never far from a phone!

I dug his card from my wallet, scattering the contents as I went. I needed to weed this thing out! I dialed the number.

"Phil Roberts. How can I help you?" Came the answer.

"Phil, Christopher Evans."

"Hello, Christopher! How's it going?"

"Well, I survived my first night. Listen, Phil, if I'm going to stay here I'm going to need some furniture. There isn't much here. And I tore down the curtains...

"I know, there wasn't much there, my wife, June, put up a little resistance about the budget. She is not too excited about my plan. I don't know why..."

"Well," I said, "I'm going to need a desk and chair and some new curtains, lamps and a couch. If money is a problem I can split the cost with you..."

Phil stopped me. "Tell you what, Chris, can I call you Chris? There is an antique store in town and some of the original furniture is there on consignment. I'll call the owner and arrange for you to pick up the pieces you can use for the fee...funny but not many of the pieces sold. Some have been there a long time. They will probably be glad to see them go. Anyway, I'll settle up with them. Unless you want new stuff..."

"No, I'll take a look at what they have. I'll need to have it delivered though. And I don't know a thing about buying curtains..."

"Okay, Chris. I'll arrange to have Pete at the furniture store deliver it to you. As for the curtains, that's going to be an investment. How about this, there is a gal in town named Betty Lou. She's a seamstress. Why don't we apply your "rent" to the cost and have Betty Lou take care of the downstairs windows for you? I'll give her a call and have her contact you."

"Sounds good Phil, I'll call you later. Thanks."

"Sure, Chris, I'll stop out at the end of the week. Good luck."

Phil hung up leaving unanswered questions in my head. What was the history of this place? Why was June reluctant to support Phil's plan? Why hadn't the furniture sold? It was antique and probably expensive, too. It would be good to have the original furniture back in the house. I hoped it was comfortable and clean...

The morning was disappearing fast and I brought the computer into the house, setting it on the floor. When it was all in I jumped into the Merc and headed into town. I had some shopping to do!

As I pulled out of the driveway I noticed the petunias were standing a little taller. They seemed brighter, too.

The curtains were still on the upstairs windows and as I looked into the rear view mirror I thought I saw one of them move...

SIX

I parked the car in front of the insurance agency. Downtown was only a block long. The antique store was across the street, next to the bar. Annandale was playing on its *Americana* theme and the "downtown" was recently remodeled with new wooden sidewalks and posts; the shops sheltered by the rustic roof over the boardwalk.

Traffic wasn't a problem and I jaywalked across the street. It felt a little like the old west and my shoes echoed on the wooden walk like boots.

Stepping into the antique store, I expected to hear a little bell at the top of the door. There wasn't one, but the atmosphere reminded me of the Zimmerman house. Or the *Twilight Zone*! It was like being in a time machine.

There were knick-knacks and old toys from wooden carvings to ray guns. It was every cliché from every generation going back at least sixty years. Dishes, books, lamps and furniture. Furniture was what I was here for.

A voice from behind the counter said, "Howdy! Can we help you find something?"

I looked up at a man in his sixties and a woman who was apparently his wife.

"Hi." I said, stretching out my hand. " My name is Christopher Evans. I'm here about some furniture."

"You're the fellow Phil called about, eh? I'm Ray and this is my wife Martha."

I smiled and said, "Pleased to meet you."

Ray returned the handshake but Martha declined.

"You're that fellow who wrote *Stepping Stones*, aren't you?" She asked.

"Why yes, have you read it?" I asked, pleased at the recognition.

"Ain't many around here who haven't," Martha replied without smiling.

"Didn't you like it?" I asked, puzzled by her tone.

"Some folks don't like to be reminded" She said, and then continued with "Now I suppose you'll write about the Zimmerman's and Annandale!"

"I know what you're looking for," Ray interrupted, "Come on downstairs with me and I'll show you the furniture."

Still puzzled by Martha's reaction, I followed Ray down the steps.

The store was bigger than it looked from the outside. The stairs leading down reminded me of a department store. They were wide and well lit and as we descended I looked up, noticing that there were two more levels above the main floor. A person could spend a day here and not see it all.

At the bottom of the steps Ray turned and said, "The bigger pieces are down here."

I continued to follow him to the far right corner of the "basement".

Set up like rooms were pieces from the Zimmerman house.

There was a leather couch, a matching chair, a double size bed with an ornamental brass headboard, a lamp, a nightstand, dresser with mirror and a desk. I tried to picture where they had been in the house, but I had not seen the bedrooms in the old mansion yet.

I had seen the study, though. What I thought was a family room must have been the study at one time! The double doors had been removed! As had the door to the kitchen and bathroom! The desk must have sat in front of the large window in the North wall of the room, where the daybed I slept on was. There were bookshelves built into the West wall. They were empty now.

I looked again at the couch. It was covered in dark red leather, dried by time and cracked just to the left of the center of the cushion. The old yellow batting was peeking out. The back was a dark wooden frame, ornamental and carved, swooping up and then curving down in the center. Dark brass upholstery nails studded the front of the arms where the material was secured. It was very masculine and the dry, cracking chair that matched it now placed itself in my mind, in the far corner of the room. The couch would have sat on the wall opposite the desk.

I was especially interested in the desk. I needed one for my computer. I wasn't interested in the prices so much because of my arrangement with Phil. Still, I wondered why they hadn't been sold? They were in good shape for their age and obviously antique. I looked around for the dining room table I had seen in my "vision" but there was none.

"Ray, how long have these pieces been here? Why haven't they sold?" I asked.

"This is all that's left from the Zimmerman house. Looters and family got the rest. Been here about five years now, since Phil bought the place. Don't know why they didn't sell. Some folks believe the old house is haunted."

"Wait a minute, five years? Why the house looks like it's been empty for sixty!" I could not believe what I was hearing.

"After the Zimmerman's died, the family decided to use the house and would come out in the summers. They never stayed long and would tell stories about ghosts... As the older ones died, the younger ones lost interest and eventually let the house go. Phil bought it for the back taxes. Hoping to get some money on the few things left, he consigned the furniture to us. Never sold though."

"Who were the Zimmerman's?" I asked, "And what happened out there? When did the family die?"

"1934, and I suggest you ask Granny Franny the rest. She has a shop down the street, a meat market and dairy and bakery. They have ice cream too."

Ray sounded like he was talking to a tourist. He started to walk back to the steps and I hurried behind him full of unasked questions.

Upstairs again, he steered me to the door with Martha looking on silently from behind the old glass counter.

"I'll tell Pete from the furniture store to pick it up and bring it out to you. Phil said he'd settle up with me. Have a nice day." He held the door for me and I stepped outside in a daze. The door closed and Ray disappeared back into *the Twilight Zone.*

I stood on the boardwalk and scanned the buildings looking for Granny Franny's shop. I spotted it at the end of the street just off the highway. I started towards it, feeling Ray and Martha watching me as I walked away.

I needed more furniture and might have browsed the shop had I not been "escorted" to the door.

"Here's looking at you, kid." Humphrey Bogart's famous line went through my mind as I listened to my footsteps. *"These boots are made for walkin..."* Nancy Sinatra's song faded as I reached the shop.

The sign on the window said "Franny's Meat and Sweets". It was painted on the window in old-fashioned white and underneath the lettering I could see the stretched gingham curtains of red and blue. It was very patriotic. *Americana.*

·

I opened the door and this time a little bell at the top *did* ring. I stepped through and stood on the old wooden floor, adjusting to the light. Another "time machine".

The walls were covered with old posters. The Coca Cola girls smiled at me as I looked at the Pat Boone albums and old 45 RPMs on the wall. Going back even farther, there were ads for old Model As and Chevrolets. Norman Rockwell's paintings added to the décor.

In front of the window were two metal tables and chairs painted white. Many a young couple shared sodas here no doubt. I wondered how old this shop was.

The smell of rolls baking had been vying for my attention and I finally breathed in the aroma. A young girl and an old woman were working in the little room behind the main counter, baking a fresh batch of something. In the back of the shop was a small meat counter and dairy cooler. There was no one at the meat counter and I stepped up to the old cash register and rang the bell.

They hadn't heard the doorbell, but now they looked up and turned toward me.

"I'll get it, Grandma," the girl said as she wiped her hands on a towel and turned her head, a wisp of long brown hair falling on her forehead.

When she walked up to the counter, her smile faded and she looked like she had seen a ghost! Her brown eyes were the only color on her face.

Sensing the silence, Granny called out, "Who is it Ginger?" She wiped her hands and retied her apron before turning around.

"Good Lord!" She said, looking at me and then above me to the wall over the door. "Good Lord!" She said again as Ginger turned to look at her. "Granny" looked like she was going to faint and I rushed behind the counter to help steady her. She motioned to the tables in front and we helped her into one of the metal chairs.

"What in the world…" I said as I looked at Ginger.

The color had returned to her face now and she pointed to a portrait above the door. It was a picture of a young man of about twenty, I guessed and it was signed, *Fran.*

If I had questions before, I had more now! I stood there staring at a portrait of myself at about that age.

As the chills ran down my back I realized I might not have found all of the *Stepping Stones…*

SEVEN

I sat across the table from "Granny Franny" as she was affectionately known. Ginger had gone to get some tea for her and a Coke and a roll for me. I hadn't had breakfast yet, and after seeing that Granny was recovering from the shock of seeing me I had accepted her offer, asking for a Coke instead of coffee.

Feeling like a long lost relative, I looked at Granny and smiled. Her hair was white, but abundant, her face wrinkled but still reflecting beauty. She was not frail looking as one would expect to see in someone in their eighties, but not overweight either. Time had been kind to her.

She smiled back; looking years younger than her numbers, blue eyes sparkling with memories.

"His name was Christian. He was my brother. I painted that portrait of him in 1934 when he was twenty. You look just like him," she said.

"Where is he now?" I asked as Ginger returned with the beverages and rolls.

"He died in 1934" Ginger answered as she set down the tray and poured tea for Granny. She placed the Coke in front of me and unwrapped the straw, leaving the top covered with the paper.

"Was he in the service?" I asked, trying to remember my history. It was before World War Two and I could not think of a major conflict, except the war with the gangsters. In an eight-month period between 1934 and 1935, most of the gangsters in this country were shot down or apprehended. If not the service, then maybe law enforcement or...

"He never got the chance to serve!" Granny answered, somewhat bitter. "Could have joined the Army or Navy, could of left this place, but he fell in love, hanging around for his high school sweetheart to catch up with him. No, he died in an accident, fell off a dock and drowned," Granny softened now and sipped at her tea.

"You say your name is Christopher?" She continued as Ginger took a chair from the next table and joined us.

"Yes, Christopher Evans. I am a writer. I'm staying at the old Zimmerman house for the summer, working on a new book," I sipped at my Coke and bit into the fresh sweet roll. It was still warm.

Ginger looked up and said, "Not *the* Christopher Evans! The one who wrote *Stepping Stones*? I loved that story!"

"Yep, that's me," I replied modestly, not wanting to talk about Marianne just now. "Apparently, some people around here didn't like it. It's nice to meet a fan."

"Who around here didn't like it?" Ginger asked, excited to meet a writer and ready to defend me.

"I just left the antique store, where I met Ray and Martha. I needed some furniture and went there to collect what was left from the old house. I would have gotten more, but they seemed anxious for me to leave and even held the door for me. I had questions but Ray said I should come here and ask Fran." I went back to the sweet roll and waited for the explanation.

"Ray and Martha!" Granny said. "Think they know everything about everyone around here because of their 'antique' store. Probably have the most to hide. Their family was more involved with the gangsters than most, her brother being one of them."

"Who was her brother?" I asked, expecting an infamous name, like Al Capone or someone of that status.

"No one you would have heard of. His name was Tom Baker. He brought them to us. Left Annandale after high school and went to work for the Mob in the cities. He never got past the outer circle though. "Mr. Big" used him as a runner."

"A 'runner'?" I asked, finishing the roll and looked for another.

"Yes. Mr. Big didn't trust the banks in the cities; with the stock market crash and the hold-ups. He kept his money out here in the Annandale bank where he thought it would be safe. Every week Al would drive to Minneapolis and pick it up. Money from protection rackets and payoffs." Granny's eyes were getting bluer as her anger increased with the memories.

"What do you mean, 'thought' it would be safe? In my research I never encountered anything about a bank in Annandale used by the mob." It was a double-edged question, asking two things at once.

"In those days, Annandale was a popular resort area. People came from all over the country for our lakes and the hunting and fishing. The old Annandale hotel was popular too and is now being made into a historic landmark. People are looking to their roots now and Americana is big." Granny stopped now and sipped her tea.

"So, was this Mob money?" I asked as Ginger got up to get another Coke. She had been drinking coffee while we talked, patiently waiting to ask me more questions about the book.

"No, the Mob knew nothing of Mr. Big's activities here. It was money he siphoned off for himself. He was a silent investor in The Resort out here. He wanted a place where his cronies could "take it on the lam"; hide out, for a couple of weeks in style. "Vacations", he called them. It opened in 1934, the same year Baby Face Nelson had a shootout with the law at a resort in Northern Wisconsin", Granny stopped again.

I could see the scenes flashing on the screen of her mind as she relived the old memories. I had more questions, but the bell above the door rang just then and a family walked into the shop.

Ginger got up two wait on the young couple and their two children, a girl and boy with blonde hair, about eight and ten. Tourists on summer vacation. I thought of the contrast of this small Minnesota town and the world of the gangsters wreaking havoc in city streets.

The spell had been broken and Granny finished her tea, pushing her chair back across the wooden floor and standing up.

"It was nice to meet you, Mr. Evans. You must come back tomorrow and tell us about your family. Ginger needs my help and we have more baking to do," Granny said as I pushed my own chair back to stand up. One did not sit when a lady was standing.

It was clear from her tone that she did not want to talk about deep matters in the presence of strangers, and again I was being asked to leave. I decided to come back tomorrow and continue the interview. Already I was writing my next book!

"I'll look forward to it, Granny," I said as she refused my money for the Cokes and rolls.

"Please, call me Fran," she said, reaching for the door. People sure were polite about opening doors out here.

"Okay, Fran. See you tomorrow. Oh, by the way, what was the name of that place?" I asked.

"Why, it's still here," she smiled. "You may want to catch some dinner there tonight, but only as a Last Resort."

I waved to Ginger who was bagging sweet rolls for the tourists and turned to step into the summer sun.

As my feet clumped along the boardwalk, I thought about these new, strange events. Here I was moving through time, from the Old West to the gangsters. My boots were gone, replaced by spit-shined shoes and my jeans had become pinstriped pants. I put my thumbs in my suspenders and opened the door of the *Merc*.

"Here's looking at you, kid," I said as I drove away.

EIGHT

I was half way to the house when I remembered the groceries. *And the furniture!* I had intended to stop at the Furniture Store ask when the Zimmerman furniture would be delivered. It was only 2 p.m. in the afternoon. I could turn around, or I could call from the house.

Granny's, I mean, Fran's, story had so preoccupied me that I forgot about my list of things to do today. When I woke up this morning I was all excited about writing a ghost story. Who was Catherine Zimmerman? What did the poem that seemed to pop up at the most convenient time mean? Had I really seen a ghost?

As if that weren't enough, why did I look like Fran's brother? Had I missed a stepping-stone in my hunt for the truth about my family? Gangsters again! Was there a connection with the ghost and me? Could the ghost story I was thinking of and the gangster story be one and the same? Were the Zimmermans' deaths connected to the mob? Who was Mr. Big, and why didn't I know about him?

"Tune in next week for the answers on Mystery Theater..." I was itching to write the story but I needed answers. I couldn't wait to talk to Fran again! In the meantime I needed to get set up. And that brought me back to my list of chores.

"Let's review; I lined up some basic furniture, especially a desk, I still needed to clean up those old curtains and call Betty Lou, finish exploring the house, eat and sleep tonight.

I could go out and eat, Fran suggested the resort... No, not tonight, I'd wait until I talked to her tomorrow, I couldn't believe I was sleeping in a haunted house and I didn't even believe in ghosts! Marianne, what would you do if you were here? God, I miss you!"

That was enough talking to myself! Thinking of Marianne was too hard. I needed to do this on my own now.

"I can get groceries tomorrow. I can call about the furniture and set up the computer tomorrow. I can eat fast food tonight." I kept talking to myself anyway. It was a habit I had gotten into after Marianne had died. Was she a ghost too?

I found myself pulling into the driveway. There was a truck in front of the house waiting; the furniture had arrived and I hadn't even called them! I pulled up behind the truck and saw the rear door open. Sitting in the old leather chair was a man I guessed to be about forty-five. Wearing jeans and an old black t-shirt, he looked like he needed a haircut. His tan and wrinkled face was overdue for a shave. An old, dirty ball cap sat on his head and a red bandana hung from his back pocket. His black leather boots had never been shined from the looks of the dry, cracked leather. The soles were worn thin. He smiled when he saw me and I noticed a lower tooth on the left side of his jaw was missing.

"Bout time! Been waitin' here for an hour. Thought you'd never show! Old Ray said to come git this stuff out of his store pronto! Said to bring it here. Can't believe anyone would want to stay here! Name's Pete, by the way."

Pete stuck out his hand as he jumped down from the box and stood facing me. I finally had a chance to talk.

"Christopher Evans. Nice to meet you, Pete. I didn't expect you so soon. Ray never told me when you'd be out."

"Well, day's wastin'. If you give me a hand I'll be gone in a shake," he said as he turned to the truck again and hoisted himself back up.

Before I even got to the truck, Pete had slid the old leather couch to the edge of the box. He waited until I walked up and said, "Grab hold."

I put my hands around the carved wooden legs and walked backwards. When Pete reached the edge he said, "Hold up." He rested his end of the couch on the edge of the box and jumped down while I held my end up. This wasn't the first time I had moved furniture.

Stepping underneath the suspended couch, Pete picked it up by the legs and we maneuvered to the steps, my end going up first. We had to set it on the porch while I opened the screen door and propped it. I unlocked the front door and swung it open, holding it a second to make sure it would stay that way. Finally we picked up the couch again and carried it into the "Family Room", which I now was sure was the study.

We placed it against the south wall, where I was sure it had originally been. Pete confirmed my hunch when he said, "Never thought I'd be putting the darn thing back! I moved this stuff out of here, you know. Right here it was, too."

One by one we carried the last of the Zimmerman furniture back into the old house. With each piece, Pete told a story. In half an hour, we were done. I hardly noticed the work, listening to Pete.

"You know, Pete, I have a couple of beers in the fridge. Haven't had a chance to grocery shop yet. Want one?" I asked.

"Well, no offense, Chris, but I'd just as soon be goin'. Place is haunted, you know. Why are you stayin' here? You could stay at the motel on the highway," he asked in a 'think you're nuts' kind of way.

"I appreciate your concern, Pete. That's a good question. Not much furniture, house is a dump, no food. A ghost. Inspiration, I guess. I have a book to write. Have to deliver on my contract. Lots of atmosphere here. History too. Since my wife died I just don't seem to care much about what happens to me anymore. This project is a sort of "last resort" for me."

"Well, I gotta be getting' back to work. On the clock you know. We can talk some other time. Maybe I can help you with your story. Been here almost all my life. C'ept for a spell in the Army after high school. Take care, Chris." And with that he climbed into the cab of the moving truck and slammed the door.

He turned the key and the motor fired up. He waved and ground it into gear. I listened to the whine of the transmission as the truck pulled away and drove out past the old stone wall.

Gilbert O'Sullivan's old song rang in my head. *'Alone again, naturally..."*

NINE

I had work to do! For the first time since Marianne had died, I felt enthusiasm! I felt an energy that had been missing for a long time. The numbness and apathy I had known so long was leaving me. I felt alive again!

The pile of old yellowed curtains was still on the porch, pushed aside from the door. I bounded up the steps and scooped them up, carrying them to the old tool shed in back of the house. I opened the old shed with the key Phil had given me and found a shovel.

Though it was a mild summer day, I soon worked up a sweat. Something I hadn't done for quite awhile. I dug deep enough, right there by the shed and buried the offending lace. With it I symbolically buried the last of my depression. It was time to get back into the world!

Returning to the house, I found my suitcase and a change of clothes. I laid them on the daybed, which we had moved to replace the desk in its original location. There were still a couple of clean towels and I stripped down for a shower. I set out my shaving kit and toothbrush and turned the old faucet handles. The water was rusty at first, but soon cleared and even though it was hard, the electric water heater was still working, and the water was warm.

Clean and shaven, I put on a clean pair of jeans, a polo shirt and clean socks. Dressed and refreshed, I set about setting up the computer. I had a laptop also, but had left it at my apartment. I preferred the monitor for big projects. I also brought the printer and scanner. If I was going to deliver a manuscript in three months, I needed all the tools.

But getting the laptop would leave me an excuse to go back to the city and my apartment. I knew when I left it that I'd be tempted to turn back, and retreat to isolation. I had not felt strong enough to break out on my own, yet.

Setting up the computer on the old desk, gave me a connection with the house. I had come here hoping for inspiration and I had found it! Now I was a detective again, determined to unlock the secrets of the house. My natural curiosity had my mind running in high gear.

I set up the new dial-up connection and pushed the start button. The familiar home page popped up and I went to check the mail. Lots of it! Junk, mostly. Credit card offers, newsletters and fan mail. All of which I devoured like a junkie, eager to re-connect with the writing side of me.

Satisfied that everything was working, I laid out the paper for the printer and the discs I had brought. There wasn't room on the desk for everything and I opened a drawer to put the paper in. As I pulled on the handle of the drawer, I heard something fall inside of it. A key.

An old skeleton key had been taped to the bottom of the drawer above it and all the moving had jostled it loose, old yellow adhesive tape and all. I didn't know what the key was for, but pocketed it for now.

It was way past six and time to eat. "Eat first, explore later." I said to myself as I grabbed the blue spring jacket from my suitcase and went in search of food.

As I walked toward the door, I looked over my shoulder. The modern computer on the old desk, in the timeworn house, was a stark contrast. It seemed to reflect the contrast in me. I became aware of the connection between the past and the present and realized I was a sum of both. So was the world.

Climbing into the Merc', my thoughts returned to food. I had been living on fast food and my waistline showed it! I decided to drive into town and find a *real* burger. I had noticed a bar in Annandale, next to the antique store and remembered seeing the sign. *Frankie's Place.* A bar and grill! Just the thing on a warm summer night! I cranked the radio and with the Beach Boys blasting *Surfin' Safari* I rolled out of the driveway onto the road as if I were driving a Corvette!

I pulled the car into the last remaining spot on the street. Crossing the street I stopped to admire the line of Harleys parked in front of the bar.

"Food must be good here," I told myself as I walked through the door into the dim light.

The noise level was amazing! And welcome. Jukebox playing, pool balls clattering, the red and blue of neon beer signs and the smell of hamburgers and onions grilling were a shot of adrenaline to my tired spirit.

I scooted past the bar, turning sideways so I would not brush up against anyone's backside. The bikers were leaning on the bar, chained wallets daring to be picked out of back pockets. Each stool occupied by their ladies.

There was one table open next to the wall by the pool table. I sat down as the one lone waitress approached, menu in hand.

"What can I get you?" She asked, setting the menu down in front of me.

Seeing the crowd around me, ordering a beer would have been a logical choice, instead I ordered a Coke. She shrugged and walked away while I tried to read the menu in the dim light. She returned with the Coke in a bar glass with a stir straw.

Looks like a drink. I thought, knowing it was supposed to. I ordered the house specialty burger and fries (the heck with my waistline!) and turned to watch the game at the pool table.

There was Pete, lining up a shot! I saw him from the back, recognizing the red bandanna in his pocket. Elbow cocked, the stick shot forward and a sharp crack echoed out. The last ball went into the pocket with a definite slam!

Setting the cue stick down, he stood up and turned around, smiling. The other man was a good loser and went to the bar to buy the beer and pay him off.

Pete looked around and saw me. "Hey Chris!" He said as he stepped over to my table.

I smiled back at him, offering the empty chair. He sat down and I said, "Nice shot."

"You play, Chris?" He asked, a challenging note in his voice.

"Not for a long time. Used to play once in a while, just for fun. You'd probably beat the pants off me." I said.

The waitress and Pete's opponent arrived at the same time, setting down the beer and food. Pool would have to wait!

"How 'bout a game after you eat?" Pete asked.

"Can't stay too late. Got to work tonight." I was anxious to get to the story.

"Well, I can understand about work. A mans gotta work! Got to eat too." Pete said, smiling. He was not offended at my decline to his challenge. "Tell you what though, next time we play!"

"Sounds good to me!" I said as I bit into the best hamburger I had in a long time.

Pete stood up to leave and I looked up, still chewing and in the process of swallowing.

He smiled again; showing his missing tooth and said, "Say hi to Catherine for me!"

I almost choked. I set down the burger and reached for the Coke to clear my throat. When I looked up again, he was gone, his words echoing in my ears.

I sat up straight as the chill traveled up my spine and my mind went around in circles.

Had he seen her, too?

TEN

The chill passed and I returned to my food. The background noise in the bar had faded while I was talking to Pete, but came back as if someone had turned up the volume. The jukebox was playing *Black Magic Woman* by Santana and I wondered if the ghost was good or bad. I still didn't know anything about Catherine Zimmerman, but apparently, Pete did.

I skipped the refill on the Coke and left the money on the table with a tip for the waitress. When I stood up to leave a plump middle-aged woman approached me.

I did not recognize her and thought she must be headed for the restrooms in back. She was wearing a flowered dress and looked like she had been enjoying the evening.

"You that writer fellow Phil called me about?" She asked as she stopped in front of me, blocking my escape.

"Could be, who wants to know?" I said defensively, aware that some people around here didn't like *Stepping Stones*.

"Wow! Hey, lighten up, Dude! I'm Betty Lou. Phil said you wanted some curtains for the old Zimmerman house. Can't believe anyone would want to stay there! Anyway, I liked your book!" She smiled and waited for me to answer.

"Sorry, I didn't mean to be so rude. I'm Christopher Evans. Nice to meet you, Betty. I'm just a little on edge." I apologized for snapping at her.

"It's Betty Lou and nice to meet you, too. Saw you talking to my brother, Pete. Was he tryin' to get you to play pool?

He's the local shark. 'Bout all he does, except work," she said with pride.

"Thanks for the warning. I knew he was good when I saw him sink that last ball. I met him earlier today when he brought the old furniture out to the house. Gotta have something to sit on," I said, which reminded me to offer her a chair at my table.

We both sat down as the waitress came back and offered us drinks. I got the refill after all; Betty Lou ordered a beer.

"Well, Christopher, I've never made curtains for a haunted house before. Phil talked to me when he bought the place five years ago and asked me if I would take it on down the road. Said he was planning on turning it into a bed and breakfast. Told him I would think about it. Thought he was crazy. Who would want to stay in a haunted house? Oh, I'm sorry," she looked at me sympathetically.

"I must be crazy, too," I said, shaking my head, only half kidding.

"Why are you there? I talked to Fran today and she told me about Ray and Martha. They were rude to you. A lot of folks here liked your book. They don't feel responsible for what their relatives have done. 'Bout time someone told the truth. *Stepping Stones* woke a lot of people up about their roots and this country's past. Something good comes out of everything," her words reassured me.

"To answer your question, I'm here to write another book. My publisher feels the house will inspire me. And it has. In some circles it's called immersion." There, I was talking like a writer again!

"Well, I can come out tomorrow afternoon, 'round 4 p.m. I'll measure the windows for you. Phil's on a budget he said, so he wants it basic. Nothing fancy." Betty Lou was talking like a seamstress.

"Can I ask you a question, Betty Lou?" I asked, one professional to another.

"Sure. Fire away!" She responded.

"Who was Catherine Zimmerman?"

"She died in that house in 1934. Whole family did. She was a writer, too. Wrote poems. She was 'engaged' to Christian, Franny's brother. But that was all before my time. Used to hear my mother talk about it. Franny can tell you more about it tomorrow," she said as she finished her beer and stood up.

I stood up also and said, "Well, I won't keep you with more questions. I'll look forward to seeing you tomorrow."

"'Round Four," she said, smiling. "You do look like him, you know." And she turned to leave. "By the way, I'll bring my copy of *Stepping Stones* and I expect an autograph!"

"You got it!" I said as she walked away, purposely bumping into the biker's butts as she passed. Several reached out to squeeze hers without turning around and she laughed all the way to the door.

I was very careful on my way out not to do the same.

ELEVEN

By the time I got back to the house it was dark. Here it was, my second day and I hadn't finished exploring the house. I would have to do it tonight.

I realized I had been putting it off. Was I scared? Maybe. I wasn't sure. There was only one way to find out!

I pulled the car right up to the porch. This time when I walked in, I didn't yell, "Honey, I'm Home!" Instead I walked in like I owned the place. Perfectly natural, right?

I knew I had to face my fears. If I had already seen the ghost then there was nothing to fear anyway. She was young and pretty, with long dark hair. Okay, so she was a little pale and had a distant look...

I pushed the button on the switch by the door and the entryway light came on. I turned on the lights as I went through the foyer into the study. There was the furniture just as I had left it.

I backed out of the study and went to the stairs, where I had stopped my search before. I looked up the stairway into the darkness and turned on the light. The old yellowed bulb in the tulip fixture lit up, revealing the wall.

There were places where the old wallpaper was pulling away at the corners and seams. I could see all the spaces where pictures had been hung, a little cleaner than the area around them. There were two spots where the wall had been patched...

What had happened here? The patches looked recent and were in 'clean spots' as if someone had been looking for something.

The silence was deafening. It was too quiet. I started up the steps listening to the old boards creak. I was used to being alone but I usually had the TV or radio on for company. I started talking to myself again.

"Okay, Christopher, so far so good. Nothing to report, but make a note of patches on the stairway wall. Coming to the top now. Long hallway. Rooms in both directions. Seven doors. Five bedrooms? A bath and a closet? Let's find out."

The lights were working so far. I hoped they all would. There was an eerie atmosphere up here. Or maybe I was just psyching myself out. It seemed almost *cemetery like*, as if it something was saying *leave us in peace*.

"Okay, contestants, let's see what's behind door number one..." I swung the first door open. A guest room, I presumed. The first room was right at the top of the steps. The doors were on either side of the hallway in both directions. They were dark like the woodwork in the rest of the house and looked as if they were polished long ago.

Oak, I guessed. The first room was empty. The floor was bare and dusty with age. The old naked window looked out at the driveway and I could see the stars through the dusty panes at the top. There were marks left by an oval rug, which must have been here a long time. The walls suffered from the same condition as the stairway. Clean spots and patches.

"Make a note of that, Chris." I moved on to the next room. Funny, the lights all worked. I would have expected burned out bulbs. This room was very much like the other. Again, patches in the walls. Phil must have been doing repairs. Maybe the plaster had cracked as the old house settled with age.

Turning around, I looked at the two doors behind me. The first one was indeed a linen closet, right next to "The Bath". The closet was bare as was the bathroom. Decorated like the downstairs bathroom, the porcelain tiles on the floor and wall were thick with dirt and age. There was a rust streak in the old white tub, flowing down from the once shiny faucet to the drain. The tub was bone dry and was not set up for a shower.

There were two rooms remaining. One in each corner of the house. These were the tower type roofs at the front. The first one was on the left of me. The door opened and revealed what must have been the master bedroom. It was quite a bit larger than the other rooms and had a large walk -in closet. Again, there was no furniture and the light worked. Again I could see the tell-tale marks on the floor where a large rug had once been. There was one large patch in the center of the east wall. I guessed that the bed had been here. A search of the floor showed marks from the bedposts. There was also a door. Another closet?

The stillness was broken by a night wind. I could feel it coming from the closed window. The caulking had cracked with time and the draft blew in around the window frame.

I looked out at the dusty sky and moved on to the last remaining room. This time the door was locked.

I stopped. My heart was pounding now. Why was this door locked? Did I really want to know? Betty Lou had said the whole family had died in this house in 1934. How had they died? And if I had the rooms labeled right, this one would have been Catherine's.

I stood in the empty hallway, undecided. I looked at the walls. Same clean spots and patches. This was a well-built house, and although it was not a mansion, it was large and expensive. It must have been lavishly decorated. The relatives must have waited a long time to take down the pictures and portraits that must have hung here. Thus the 'clean' spots. But what was with the patches? They were made with modern spackling; the kind I had used myself. And from the whiteness of them must have been recent. Had the holes they covered been there a long time? Or had someone been looking for something? A wall safe, perhaps? Was there money in this house?

"It's now or never," Elvis Presley's song played in my head as I dug the keys out of my pocket that Phil, had given me. But this door used a skeleton key, the kind I found in the desk earlier today.

I pulled the key from my pocket and wondered why Catherine's key would be in her father's desk. I placed it into the lock plate and tried to turn it. I had to jiggle it to position it correctly, and when I could feel the right placement I turned it. That is, I tried to turn it. It wouldn't budge.

"Lock must be frozen." I said to myself. "Or this isn't the right key." All skeleton keys looked alike but were not. But if not this door, then where? Maybe it wasn't even for this house. Maybe "Dad" had someone on the side?

I tried the key one more time. I could feel it connecting. I could feel it trying to open. I was sure this was the right door!

But something kept the lock from turning.

TWELVE

What kept the lock from turning? I had the feeling the answers were just beyond my reach, behind a veil that I could reach out and part...

Too much had happened these last two days. I would try again tomorrow.

It was late and I needed sleep. My mother used to say, "ask your inner mind." She believed that if we let go of a problem the answer would come to us. It would pop up at the strangest times. Sometimes it would come to us in our dreams. This was one of those times.

I needed to get beyond the physical world. I needed to open my mind to what it was trying to tell me. Like sometimes when we're hungry and don't eat. Being stubborn like children who won't listen.

I did not know the Zimmermans or the people I had met here. Yet, I felt as if I were one of them. How was it that I looked like Fran's brother? What about the gangster connection?

I had so many questions to ask Fran! But right now it was time to sleep. I turned off the lights as I went down the stairs, the once fine wood creaking under my feet. Reaching the bottom I turned left and walked into the study. I sat down on the edge of the daybed and took off my shoes and shirt. I needed to brush my teeth. Mechanically, I went into the bathroom and finished getting ready for bed, deliberately shutting down my mind so I could sleep. It was a discipline

I had learned from many years of working nights so I could sleep in the daytime.

I returned to the bed and instantly fell asleep.

Something woke me up. I felt the need to relieve my bladder and still half asleep I went into the bathroom to answer the call. Turning off the bathroom light, I walked past the kitchen table. One of the old wooden chairs slid backwards, almost knocking me over. I danced around it, heart beating in my chest and a wave of panic running through me. I ran into the study and dove onto the daybed and covered my head like a child.

This must be a dream I thought, *I am the only one here!* I convinced myself that the power of suggestion was working on me and decided to escape into sleep. With discipline I shut down my mind and tried to return to the sleep I had been in.

Just before I dropped off I heard a whisper.

Christopher...

Christopher...

THIRTEEN

The chirping of birds woke me. A beautiful summer morning! I was a little surprised to find I was still here. The events of the night played in my mind and I sat up with a chill.

An old Sixties song played in my head, *It was just my imagination, running away with me...* I think it was the Four Tops. Looking at my watch I saw it was 9 a.m.. The oldies were still playing in my head and I heard Chuck Berry singing, *I looked at my watch-it was half past ten..."reeling and a'rockin"*

I was reeling and rockin'. I walked past the kitchen table into the bathroom. The chairs were tucked in, as they should be. *Just my imagination...*

I showered, shaved and brushed my teeth. The routine restored my confidence. I stretched and did my morning exercises. I was hungry and anxious to get to Granny's for some breakfast and some answers. I also needed to be here at Four O'clock for Betty Lou.

There were butterflies in my stomach, a kind of excitement I hadn't felt in a long time.

I threw on my last pair of clean jeans and a clean polo shirt making a note that I would have to find the Laundromat. When I was finally ready I looked around the old house.

Something was different. The house seemed brighter today. Almost as if someone had come in and painted during the night. The kitchen cupboards were whiter and the table was no longer cracked. The chairs were polished and had a new look to them.

I shook my head and turned to the study. Someone had shined up the leather while I had been asleep. The duct tape was gone from the couch and it was no longer cracked! Behind the desk was a chair. A matching desk chair that had not been there before!

Was someone here last night? I had slept longer than usual and who was whispering my name?

I stood quiet, listening to the house. It had changed somehow. It felt more peaceful now and the silence was not so empty. The house seemed more alive! I had not noticed the birds chirping yesterday and now they were just outside the window behind the desk.

I walked over to the desk. My computer sat just as I had left it. I touched the chair. It was real. A fine polished wood. I sat in it and was surprised at its comfort. I spun around first to the left, then to the right, then straight ahead again.

That's when I noticed the poem. It was laying on the desktop, old and yellowed. I picked it up and read:

CATHERINE'S DOOR

In the room
Where pillows wept
Through lonely summers
As I slept
The window to the placid lake
Where my lover
Chance did take-

Left me standing
At my door
Heart upon
The polished floor

Between my breasts
The weathered wood
Touched me
As no lover could...

Catherine Zimmerman
1934

That did it! I went back up the stairs under the protection of daylight. I put the key in the lock and tried it again. This time it opened!

Here was a room untouched by time. I heard the *Twilight Zone* theme playing in my mind as I stood in the door and looked at the past. There was a brass bed, polished headboard and white hand made quilt of roses and lace. Matching pillowcase and a small round table next to the bed in front of the window, covered also in the matching embroidered linen. A small lamp sat on the table alongside a tablet and pencil. Not a tablet but a diary! A leather case with Catherine Zimmerman embossed in gold.

I turned and looked at the dresser next to the closet. It held a large mirror and all the things a young girl needed;

brushes combs and jewelry, on a table runner with the same embroidered pattern of roses and lace. No doubt done by Catherine's mother.

Next to the door was a desk with an old Underwood typewriter on it. The carriage held a clean sheet of white paper; not like the yellowed one I was holding.

I looked down at the poem I had found downstairs. The old yellowed paper was now white...as white as I must have been at the moment it had been written!

The walls were covered in fine flowered wallpaper and the lace curtains were white also. I expected Catherine to walk through the door any minute and ask, "What are you doing in my room!"

What was I doing here? How was it that this room was untouched by time? What was happening? Had I gone back in time? I looked out the window at the Merc. It was just as I had left it.

I was about to explore the closet when I heard the phone ring. Backing out of the *Twilight Zone* I almost hit the wall behind me. I turned and ran downstairs, feet flying on the carpet that had not been here last night!

I hit the front door and kept going, jumping into the Merc and turning the key.

Tires spraying rocks I roared out to the road, hardly noticing the young girl working in the garden!

I looked in the rearview mirror and saw her standing in the driveway, an odd smile on her ghostly face.

FOURTEEN

I had always expected spooky things to happen at night. On this bright summer morning I realized that they were even spookier when they happened in the daylight!

Here I was in the *Twilight Zone,* running from the *Twilight Zone*! How far did I think I would get?

I turned on the radio partly for comfort and partly for a time check. What year was it? It seemed that the house was traveling back in time; or was it me?

The oldies station was on and I received another chill when I heard Chuck Berry singing *Reeling and a rockin'*... At least I knew it wasn't 1934.

I hadn't even thought of where I was going. I had just run, scared. Well, I was going to see Granny Franny this morning anyway. I needed answers!

By the time I got to Franny's, I had calmed down some. I was sure the color had come back into my face. I wasn't reeling quite as much as I parked the car, but I couldn't help but wonder if Granny hadn't gotten younger too.

I reached up and took the gold locket off the rearview mirror clutching it in my hand as I drove. I kept it with me for luck and to remember my mother by. She had given it to me as she was dying in the hospital. "It was handed down to me and now I hand it down to you."

I still had to choke back the tears even after fifteen years.

The familiar bell rang as I opened the door of the shop and walked in, the locket still in my hand. I was stroking the carved golden face with my thumb. Funny, it never contained a picture or an inscription, just tradition.

Ginger looked up from behind the cash register and smiled.

"Well hello again, Christopher!" She smiled as the cash drawer dinged shut. "How are you this fine summer morning?" she said, sounding Irish.

"Top O' the mornin' to you, Ginger. And yes, 'tis a fine mornin' indeed," I replied, mocking her. "I didn't realize you were Irish," I said, grateful for the light humor. I was still fidgeting with the locket, a habit I had whenever I was nervous. I was anxious for the morning's events to fade.

"I'm not, though people say I look Irish. My husband Mike is though. Mike Murphy. About as Irish as it gets. He used to be a policeman in St. Paul, but now we own the shop. We bought it from Granny and Mike is the butcher."

"Well, I'll have to meet him. Is he here?" I asked.

"No, he's gone to Minneapolis. He'll be back this afternoon," she replied.

"I suppose you have children, too," I said, feigning disappointment.

"Yes two. We have one of each, a Girl ten, boy eight. Sorry, Mister. I'm out of circulation," she laughed.

"I have a confession to make; I really came to see your Grandmother," I continued the game.

"Well now, I won't be denyin' ya. Sit down at the table and I'll get her for you. And what'll you be havin' in the meantime, Mr. Evans?" She asked, still using her mock accent.

"Well, the usual will be fine, Miss. A sweet roll and butter if you please and a Coke will do nicely," I was impressed with my phony accent, but Ginger was more honest.

"Your accent is terrible!" She laughed. "You sound Swedish and that's a stretch!"

"Can't have everything," I said. "Guess that's why I write. But it was fun while it lasted!" I continued, feeling almost calm again.

I went to the same table we sat at yesterday and waited while Ginger went to get her grandmother.

FIFTEEN

I sat in the same chair I had before. The bright summer morning made the morning's events even more frightening. It was hard to keep from replaying them in my mind.

As Ginger and Fran approached the table, I was still rubbing my mother's locket absentmindedly. Fran noticed it as she sat down. She asked Ginger to bring her some green tea and then looked at me.

"What's that you have there, Christopher?" She asked, skipping the "Good Morning", I had expected.

"My mother's locket. I keep it with me," I replied, glad she hadn't said "Good Morning." It was a strange morning and I was not anxious to tell anyone about it.

"May I see it?" She asked.

"Of course," I replied, scooping up the fine, dangling chain and handing it to her.

She took it and held it up in the air, examining the gold heart, then let the chain hang as she opened it. There was nothing inside.

"There is no picture here," she said, matter-of-factly.

"No, there has never been a picture in it. There wasn't one when my mother got it either. She said it was handed down. She passed it on just the same way she had received it from her mother and with the same words. No history, no pictures, just the words 'It was handed down.' My mother received it when she got married, and having no daughter, I received it when I got married. My mother died when I was fifteen and I've kept it with me ever since, for luck and to remember her by," I said, anxious to ask questions of my own.

Ginger returned as Granny handed the locket back to me. I put it in my pocket as she set down the sweet roll and Coke and Granny's green tea. I expected her to join us but she said she had work to do and went back into the kitchen.

Granny sipped her tea, taking her time. Finally, she set the cup down on its' matching saucer and looked into my eyes.

"You look a little pale this morning, Christopher. Are you not feeling well? It can't be the weather. It has been exceptionally mild for June." She smiled at me took another sip of tea.

"I'm fine, just stayed up too late last night," I was avoiding more questions.

"Well, tell me about your mother. What was her name?" She asked.

"Dorothy Ann. Everyone called her Dorothy, but she would correct them. "It's Dorothy *Ann!*" She would say. Eventually she gave up and just accepted Dorothy as a nickname," I replied, taking the locket back out of my pocket and rubbing it absentmindedly.

I always smiled when I talked about my mother and Fran, encouraged, asked another question.

"You say your mother died when you were fifteen, did you live with your father then?" It was a natural question.

"You must not have read my book," I replied.

"Well, you did say *Stepping Stones* was a work of fiction. I suspected there was more truth in it than you let on," Fran parried.

"After mother died, I lived with my grandfather, Franklin White. He was married to my mother's mother, Anna. The

'Ann' in her name. I am the last in the family. After high school I joined the Navy, and Grandpa Franklin died while I was in San Diego at boot camp."

I always got emotional when I thought about my family. It seemed like everyone I had ever loved had died.

"I know what it's like to lose family," Fran replied sympathetically. "Tell me about Anna."

"She was the daughter of Judith and Robert Carlson." I continued. "They owned a small grocery in St. Paul. They died long ago and Anna was their only child. My mother knew them and talked about them a lot. They helped a lot of people during the Depression. Seems they were the only ones not involved with gangsters. Judith's two sisters were both involved with gangsters and if Anna had not met Robert Carlson, she may have gone that way too. But, they extended credit to a lot of people who were down on their luck."

"I can see the pride showing Christopher. You have a good heart. You have had a sad life, losing everyone as you have. Did Anna own that locket?" Fran asked, her eyes darting to it again.

"Yes. Mother would reach up and stroke it whenever she was nervous. Said it calmed her down and brought her luck. I guess I picked up the same habit. It's always been a mystery to me. Mother would always talk about Anna whenever she did that. Said she asked Grandma Judith about it once, why there was no picture in it. Judith replied that it was tradition that it had been handed down that way. I used to wonder if that was the reason there weren't more children..."

"Superstitions," Fran said. "Some families are blessed with a lot of children, some are not. But I do believe there is a reason why each of us is here."

I sensed sadness in her voice. Her eyes took on a distant look and I saw the opportunity to turn the conversation to a different track.

"Fran, tell me about Catherine Zimmerman. Did you know her?"

SIXTEEN

Ginger had come over to the table and refilled Granny's tea. She brought me a new Coke and said, "Well you two certainly look deep in conversation!"

I smiled at her as she took the plate from in front of me. I hadn't even remembered eating the sweet roll. I heard Pat Boone singing *April Love* on the jukebox and wondered how long it had been on.

There was that same sense of "time warp" I had felt at the house! Must be the atmosphere and all the memories. I looked at Fran and noticed the same distant look. Ginger just shook her head and walked away. When she was gone, Fran spoke;

"Did I know Catherine? Yes, I knew Catherine. She was my best friend, though she was two years younger than me. She found out I was an artist and began to encourage me. She said she was a writer and always wished she could paint...she fell in love with my younger brother, Christian. I hated her for that! For years, I blamed her for his death!"

"What happened?" I prodded.

"It's a long story," she answered.

"I have time. I don't have to be anywhere for a while," I was not going to let this opportunity go by.

Fran sipped her tea and looked around the shop. We were the only ones there.

"When did you meet her?" I asked.

"Watched her grow up through school." Fran said, taking another sip of tea. "Our generation was to be the first around here expected to finish high school. 1923, I believe. I had made it to the second grade. It was a one-room school so we knew everyone. We went to school together until her father moved them to Florida to open another bank. Catherine was fifteen and I envied her for getting out of this one-horse town. I cried when she left, though. She was going to come back for the summers. Said her mother's health was the real reason they were moving. Better climate. But I knew better!" Fran sounded bitter and sipped some more tea.

"What was the real reason?" I kept prodding, wanting to keep the story going.

"Mr. Big. He had been laundering money at her father's bank. Wanted Albert to help him build a resort where his cronies could lay low. "Vacations" he called them. He wanted to call it The Last Resort. At first, Albert was innocent. Mr. Big posed as a businessman in Minneapolis who didn't trust the banks, what with all the gangsters and bank robberies and the stock market. He told Albert he wanted to keep his money in our little bank. In those days, Annandale was a favorite vacation spot for Hollywood celebrities. The Annandale Hotel was very popular in the summers. People would come here for the hunting and fishing. Martha's brother was the 'runner'. Every week he would drive into Minneapolis and pick up a large package from one of Mr. Big's 'Associates'. Eventually, after the plans had been drawn up for the resort, Albert got suspicious."

She stopped, sipping more tea and biting into a cookie.

"What tipped him off?" I asked.

"Mr. Big didn't want his name on any papers. His real name was Bigelow. And he wasn't very big. About five ten and a hundred and fifty pounds soaking wet. He liked being called 'Mr. Big' by his cronies.

"Anyway, Albert found out who he really was and where the money was coming from. Mr. Big was skimming from the Mob. He upped the prices on his protection rackets and gave false reports to his bosses in Chicago. He felt he was powerful enough to get away with it. The only thing was, he couldn't put his name on the money or anything he did with it. When Albert found out, he got cold feet and Mr. Big sent one of his floozies to the bank to warm him up and change his mind. She had just sat on Albert's lap when Catherine's mother walked in..." Her voiced trailed off.

I could see the scene in my mind. Fran told the story as if she were watching it happen.

"She snapped! Rose was so in love with Albert! She thought he was the White Knight! His attempts to explain could not erase the picture from her mind. She had a nervous breakdown and Albert didn't want to alarm the investors in The Resort. He had an opportunity to take over a small bank in Florida, so he cited her need for a climate change, saying they would return here for the summers. Construction got underway and two years later they held the Grand Opening of The Last Resort."

"So, Albert knew where the money came from?" Again, I jump-started the story.

"He knew. But Mr. Big made him nervous. He threatened his business and his family. Albert had created a phony account at the bank to hide Mr. Big's identity and rumors still exist that he was skimming money from Mr. Big in case he and his family had to suddenly leave. Catherine knew he was stuffing money somewhere in the walls of that house."

"That explains the patches on the walls. People have been looking for the money!" My heart was pounding with excitement now. "Tell me more. How much money?" I asked.

"No one knows. It's never been found. They audited the books at both banks when the Zimmermans died but never could find any evidence. Their personal holdings were quite a lot of money and they were distributed in the will. Albert's father had owned all the land around the lake and Rose was heiress to a tidy family fortune." Fran was brushing cookie crumbs from her dress and pushed her chair back to stand up.

"What about the house?" I asked, having a personal interest in it.

Ginger had come over to assist Granny. "The house was willed to Albert's family." Fran said as Ginger helped her up. " No one wanted it though. They had their own and after the tragedy Rose's parents wanted nothing to do with it. Eventually it was let go for back taxes. Oh, people came for the summers and there was some remodeling, but the ghost stories and the history drove them away. The younger generations wanted out of this one-horse town also. Phil can tell you more. I'm tired now, Christopher."

"Of course, Fran. Forgive me for taking so much of your time. You must tell me the rest of the story…"

"Must I?" She said, looking up at the portrait of her brother, "Yes, I suppose I must. There is a price, though," she said, looking at the locket I was holding again.

"And what is the price?" I asked, blankly.

"The locket, may I keep it overnight?"

"Why, yes. But why?" I was puzzled. I had noticed her constant attention to it, but thought it reminded her of one she had or someone she knew. Ginger hid a knowing smile and looked up at the wall of photos from the past.

There was Fran, Christian and a girl who must have been Catherine. The picture was taken at the opening of The Last Resort.

Around Fran's neck was the locket that Catherine had given to her when they had moved to Florida.

The same one I was holding now!

SEVENTEEN

I felt a little vulnerable when I got back into the *Merc*. The locket was my good luck charm and now it was in someone else's hands. I felt butterflies in my stomach as I thought of the picture of Fran, Catherine and Christian at The Last Resort.

How could my mother have the same locket? Of course! There was more than one! Silly of me to think there was a connection between my mother, Fran and Catherine Zimmerman! Why, I had researched my family's history all the way back to my great-great grandparents! The whole novel *Stepping Stones* was based on it! I had even found the birth certificates for my mother and grandmother!

Still, there were too many odd things to ignore. Earlier I had the feeling that there may have been a stepping-stone I had overlooked and as I drove back to the Zimmerman house I ran through the list.

First of all, how was it that I resembled Fran's brother? Coincidence? Nationality? And talking to Fran was like talking to my own grandmother. Was it just that *all* grandmothers have things in common?

Then there was Catherine! A writer, like me. I did not want to even think about the ghostly aspects. The piano music, her appearance at the door, the poems appearing at the right times as if she were trying to tell me something, leading me along from stepping stone to stepping stone as I tried to cross an unknown river.

And the house itself! The strange feeling of time shifting. The house appearing newer as if it were traveling back in time. I had the distinct feeling that the answers lay in the past. I knew that I had to find out the whole story. What would the next stepping-stone be?

"Tune in next week for the answers on Mystery Theater!" I said out loud as I pulled back into the driveway. Though I was scared, I was determined to see this through!

Betty Lou would be here soon to measure for the curtains. I would have to ask her more questions. I had to start writing soon!

The morning's events had faded now and as I unlocked the front door I noticed that the porch looked as if it had been freshly painted! The glass on the door windows was now shiny and clean, the brass plate gleaming in the warm summer sun.

"They're Baaa-ck!" I said as the memory of the morning came rushing into my mind. I pushed the door open, resisting the temptation to turn and run!

I wasn't sure what to expect as I stepped in, but my mind was prepared for anything. I reminded myself that the only thing to fear was fear itself and closed the door behind me. It shut soft and sure on well-oiled hinges, unlike the dry creaking door I had left.

I remembered the first time I had stepped in and had been assaulted by the dry stale air. This time the air was pleasant, smelling of cooking and wood polish. There was a warmth to the woodwork. The wainscoting looked rich and the wallpaper was bright and cheerful. The frosted globe of the light fixture above me was clean, cobwebs gone from the chain that suspended it.

Heart pounding in my chest, I walked to the kitchen following the cooking smells. The appliances gleamed as if new and I bent down to peer into the oven. Nothing there. I was disappointed. It had smelled like a roast.

Shaking my head, I opened the refrigerator and reached for a Coke. The rusted racks were gleaming now and the motor ran quietly.

My mind raced for logical explanations. My publisher was behind all of this...trying to drive me crazy...trying to give me ideas...Phil was arranging all of this while I was gone...someone was trying to drive me away. Why? Was it the money old man Zimmerman had hidden in the walls?

Logic got me nowhere. The things I had seen and experienced did not fit in the natural world. No one could have done all of this in the short time I had been gone! I had to follow my gut.

"Seek and ye shall find," the Bible quote rolled onto my tongue and I quickly followed it with, "the Lord is my Shepherd..."

I walked back into the study and looked at the desk. The computer was there, just as I had left it, waiting expectantly for me to bring it to life. Many were the hours I had spent with it, writing and sharing my innermost thoughts with its circuits, giving it purpose and usefulness; a fair exchange.

How strange it looked, a modern, high-tech typewriter in this antique setting. How fitting to the crazy world I was now becoming accustomed to.

I looked at the polished desktop and noticed the sheet of paper. My stomach tightened into knots as I picked it up, both excited and afraid. I looked at my watch before reading it; three-thirty. Betty Lou would be here soon. But I still had time to read it.

It was another poem.

JOHN E. CARSON

SLEEPWALK

Though I sleep
I am not still
My spirit won't be kept

Though they try
My love to kill
It has only slept.

My lonely hearts'
The one who walks
In silence through these walls

Disturbing not
The peace within
The empty waiting halls.

Catherine Zimmerman

I stood frozen. Over and over I read the poem. It had been written on the same old typewriter as the others had. The paper wasn't mine, but rather an old paper with a watermark I couldn't make out. Yet it wasn't yellowed with age...

Along with the computer, I had brought a box of writing supplies. I took out a paper folder and placed the poem in the pocket, then I took out the other poems I had placed in the right hand drawer of the desk and also put them in the folder. I attached a white sticker to the cover and wrote Catherine Zimmerman on it.

I looked at my watch and noticed it was almost Four O'clock. I hadn't realized how long I had been standing there! I shook my head again and picked up the now warm Coke.

I walked back to the kitchen and exchanged it for a cold one. As I snapped the tab open I heard the doorbell.

"Funny, I didn't even know we had one!" I said as if I were not alone. Walking to the front door I noted that somehow I had taken possession of the house. Or had it taken possession of *me*?

EIGHTEEN

Betty Lou was pushing the doorbell for the second time as I opened the door. Holding a large sample book and a leather satchel, she looked nervous and puzzled.

"Hello," I said, smiling, "Come on in."

She smiled back and followed as I turned around. "Can I get you anything? Coke? A beer?"

Juggling her load, she followed me into the kitchen. She reached the kitchen table just as they escaped from her grip. As the book and bag fell she followed and landed in one of the chairs just as I turned from the refrigerator holding a Coke and a beer. I put them both down, planning to take whichever she didn't want.

I sat down in the opposite chair and smiled at her again. She looked even more dazed and confused.

"Christopher, what have you done to this place?" She asked, incredulous.

"Oh, just a little cleaning." I replied. "A little T.L.C. goes a long way, don't you think?"

"This is more than a little T.L.C! Why, the last time I saw this place it was so dusty you couldn't even breathe! Have you been cooking?" She asked, picking up the still lingering odor of a pot roast.

"No, it's too hot to use the oven. Must be just the atmosphere. When were you here last?" I asked

She avoided my eyes, not wanting to answer. "When we were kids, Pete used to bring me out here on Halloween and scare me. We would climb in one of the basement windows and walk through the house holding candles. More than once we were convinced that there was a ghost in this house." She shuddered at the memory.

"It sounded like you were here more recent than that," I said, taking the Coke.

"My husband and I used to ride out here on his Harley with his biker buddies on summer nights. We partied until the wee hours," she was smiling now and took a long pull on the beer.

"Where is your husband now?" I asked, thinking of Marianne.

"Ran off and left me for a young biker chick. Let's get to work," she didn't want to talk about it.

"Yes, we're here to talk about curtains," I replied, holding back my questions. I was anxious to find out more about the history of this house.

"Now, Phil said to keep the price down, so I've taken the liberty of choosing some inexpensive materials and styles..." she sounded professional now. Funny how an ex-biker chick could slam a beer and sell custom decorating at the same time.

She started to page through the big book to the earmarked styles. I stopped her and said, "Whoa! Phil might not care what kind of curtains, I mean, draperies go into this house, but *I* do!"

The edge on my voice surprised her and she stopped in mid-stride, holding the next page at the ready. She looked at me and said, "Look, Christopher Evans, I'm doing Phil a favor here! If it were up to *me* I'd never see the inside of this place again! In fact, on the way here I considered turning around."

"I'm sorry, Betty Lou. I did not mean to be so sharp with you. I don't know what's happened to me. Before today, I didn't really care about curtains either. I guess the house must be getting to me. What I meant to say was that I'd pay the difference. If we're going to do it, let's do it right! I think the house deserves better, don't you?"

Shaking her head, she continued, "Okay, let's take a look at the good stuff."

Betty Lou opened the catalog to a different section and removed it from the book. Pushing her chair back she stood up explaining that we would get a better feel for the style by looking at the windows and rooms.

I followed her back into the dining room as she talked, wondering where she had gotten her training. This was not the same Betty Lou I had met in the bar.

"Now, you know," she said, "These will be custom draperies. If you wanted the less-expensive ready-mades Phil talked about, Pete and I could put them up. But since you want better, we should get installation, too. Are you sure Phil won't mind? I thought you were just renting this place for the summer."

"Oh, I'm sure he won't object if I pay the difference. As a matter of fact, I'm thinking of making him an offer." I couldn't believe what I was hearing myself say.

"How do you know he wants to sell?" She asked.

"I don't," I said. "Let's get to the windows. I'll take care of Phil."

We walked from room to room and I saw a side of Betty Lou that I knew few people had. She warmed up to the house and for the first time in her life was not afraid of it.

She suggested a white lace similar to the ones I had buried, pointing out the masculine tone of the house, the dark heavily ornamented woodwork and how the lighter feminine touch would offset it, creating a balance and harmony. In the process she became excited about the possibilities of the Zimmerman House.

"No wonder Phil thought of the bed and breakfast. Why, this house has a charm I've never seen before. There is something about it..." she couldn't quite grasp it.

I smiled as we walked from room to room. A common style would unite the rooms, she said. She measured each window, making notes of the location and size until the entire downstairs was done.

"Okay. Sheers, draperies and valances. And in the study I would suggest blinds instead of sheers, to leave you with that masculine touch while you work. Also, you would be less likely to get them dirty."

She understood men.

"What about the upstairs?" She asked.

"No, that's a different story..." I said, waiting for her to get the joke. "What I mean is that we're not ready for that yet."

"We?" She repeated.

"Yes, Phil and I." I explained.

"Oh. I see. Well, lets go to the table and figure this up." She was much more confident than when she had arrived.

I watched as she took an order form out of the catalog and figured the price on her calculator. By the time she had finished it was eight o'clock. It would be getting dark soon, and we had both missed dinner.

I had wanted to ask her some more questions and had planned on writing tonight. I became aware that time was slipping away.

"Wow!" She said as she looked at her watch. "I didn't realize how late it was getting! I've got to get going," she started getting nervous again.

I looked at the estimate and calculated my bank account. It was a lot but I could handle it. Betty Lou would get a nice commission.

"How about getting something to eat?" I asked, settling for the research I could do. My stomach was growling and she laughed.

"Tell you what," she said, "there's a chicken shack down the road where they serve good broasted chicken. It's called Mooney's and they serve it fast. I'll have some chicken with you and then I have to get home."

"Sounds good to me!" I said, remembering Marianne. It was one of our favorite things to eat. "I'll follow you."

I turned off the lights as Betty Lou gathered her book and bag and we closed the front door.

I was surprised to see her climb into a restored, maroon painted, '78 Trans Am.

"Is that *your* car?" I asked.

"It's Pete's. My Corvette is in the shop."

This lady was full of surprises! I climbed into my little Mercury feeling very humbled.

Turning on the radio I heard Jan and Dean singing, *"It's the little old lady from Pasadena..."* Even though she was far from a granny, the song fit my surprise.

As Betty Lou turned onto the road ahead of me, I looked back at the house in my rear view mirror. I smiled as the lights came back on.

"Go, Granny, Go, Granny go..."

NINETEEN

Mooney's was just a few minutes down Highway 55. The yellow bug lights strung like Christmas lights all around the edge of the roof. You couldn't miss it!

Betty Lou pulled the Trans Am right up to the sidewalk and I parked next to her. She opened the door and waited for me to catch up. I held the door for her and followed her in.

The smell was fabulous! I didn't realize how hungry I was until I smelled the chicken in the broaster. I could have eaten just on that aroma!

"Hi, Mooney!" Betty Lou said as we approached the counter. He waved from behind the window while a young girl stepped up to the register to take our order.

"Hi, Allison!" Betty Lou greeted the girl, who looked about fifteen. "Like you to meet a friend of mine, Christopher Evans." She turned toward me and explained that this was Mr. Mooney's daughter.

The young girl smiled, brushing a lock of blonde hair from her forehead. "*The* Christopher Evans? The one who wrote *Stepping Stones*? Wow! I loved that story!"

I blushed from the praise. "Thanks for the compliment. Say, I hear the chicken is really good here." I smiled back at her, wanting to change the subject.

"We got a fresh batch in, you just missed the dinner rush. What would you like?" She asked.

"The three-piece dinner with jo- jo potatoes, and a Coke," Betty Lou was quick to reply.

Allison looked at me. "Sounds good to me," I said.

While we filled the Coke cups at the dispenser, Allison went back to help her dad. She was eager to tell him about the "celebrity." We settled in a booth along the wall and waited for the food.

Looking around the "chicken shack", I noted the "cruising" theme. There were posters of vintage cars, 57 Chevy's, Roadrunners, Fords, even a Mercury or two.

"Big cruising place in the summer. They even have competitions on Friday nights for the best cars," Betty Lou explained. "Mr. Mooney owns a customized 51' Merc."

I looked around some more and noticed the trophies on the shelf above the counter.

I liked cars but was anxious to question Betty Lou.

"Have you and Pete ever won any trophies?" I asked, wanting to warm her up to other questions.

"Nah, we just like to have fun with cars. Keeps us young, you know."

Allison arrived with the food. There were four pieces on each plate and an extra large order of jo-jos.

"On the house," Allison said, smiling.

"Did we look that hungry?" I asked, reaching for the ketchup.

"Not every day we get an *author* in here! Dad wants to take your picture. Would that be okay? Good publicity, he says," she was still smiling.

"Sure," I knew Betty Lou and I were not going to have much privacy in here. I decided to save my questions for Fran.

Mr. Mooney came out with his Polaroid and took posed pictures of us eating his "famous" broasted chicken. Allison managed to get in a couple of pictures, serving us and sitting next to me in the booth. I kept smiling and eating. I was not going to let this chicken get cold!

Betty Lou had no trouble eating hers! I hoped I didn't have chicken stuck between my teeth in any of the pictures.

Some time after 10 p.m. we finally said goodbye. I watched Betty Lou start the Trans Am and climbed into my little *Merc.*

Betty Lou squealed the tires as she hit the highway and I patted my little car on the dashboard. "It's okay, girl. You're still a hot car to me." I reassured it as I turned the wheels the other way and drove back to the Zimmerman House.

Turning on the radio, I heard Jan and Dean, still singing the same song as I looked into the rearview mirror and watched Betty Lou's taillights disappear.

"Go, Granny, Go, Granny, Go!"

TWENTY

Full of Mooney's broasted chicken, all I could think of was sleep. In a few minutes I was back at the house and walking in the door almost automatically. I was tired; tired of thinking, tired of being scared. and tired of being the only one in my little world.

I turned on the lights, not caring what this weird house was doing now. I hardly noticed how new everything looked. Whatever was happening here would have to wait!

I found the daybed. Funny, I didn't remember making it up; must have done it because Betty Lou was coming over. For a while after Marianne died, I kept the house spotless, as if she were still here. But eventually I realized that she wasn't coming back and slipped into a depression. I no longer cared as much what the house looked like and only the book signings kept me from becoming a total slob.

I crashed on the daybed, too tired to undress and brush my teeth. I felt drugged and immediately fell into an exhausted sleep.

Something woke me. I stood up and walked to the front door. Someone was on the porch. I looked out the window and thought I saw Marianne!

When I opened the door, the woman turned around before I could see her face and walked away.

I followed, calling her name but she didn't hear. I remember thinking that my mouth was working but no sound was coming out!

I heard the sound of a car on the road as we reached the end of the driveway. There was a 1934 Lincoln convertible driving away as I approached. The woman I thought was Marianne was in the passenger seat, an older man driving the ghostly Lincoln that seemed to vanish, leaving me alone on the other side of the road.

As I stood there watching, I heard the almost silent approach of an animal, claws clicking on the pavement. The sound came closer and I watched as a large dark brown German Shepard came running from town.

The dog ignored me and ran down to the dock. I followed in a trance-like state, my footsteps silent on the old boards.

When I caught up with the dog he laid down, hanging his head over the side of the dock, and began whimpering.

"What's' wrong, boy?" I started to say, but again could not hear my words. The dog looked up, but not at me, and seemed to respond to some kind of call. He stood up as if he were with someone and walked right past me; head hung low, a lifeless look in his eyes.

I felt an incredible sadness for this beautiful animal. It was a magnificent looking police dog. I wondered why he had come down here and cried. It was as if he were waiting for someone - someone who would not return.

I don't remember going back to the house, but that's where I found myself in the morning. I must have been dreaming, I thought, as I recalled the events of the night so vividly.

I shook my head and yawned, noticing that I needed to brush my teeth and take a shower.

I swung my legs over the side of the daybed and sat up. A chill ran down my spine as I saw the wet footprints of my bare feet on the floor. *It wasn't a dream!*

I must have been sleepwalking!

"But I've never sleepwalked in my life!" I said to no one there. And no one answered.

Walking into the bathroom I tried to understand the significance of the "dream".

Who was the woman at the door? Whose dog was that? What about the car? How did I know it was a 1934 model?

The warm summer morning and the hot water of the shower could not take away the chill in my spine!

While I was shaving I thought I heard a noise in the other room. I stopped shaving and listened but only heard the drip of the faucet in the shaving water as I held the razor in mid-stroke.

Should I call out? I hadn't heard the door but someone could have come in while I was in the shower! Heart thumping, I dried my face and wrapped a towel around myself, deciding to take a look first.

I stepped out of the bathroom quietly, not wanting to scare the intruder off. Stealthily, I went from room to room and found no one. "Upstairs?" I thought and went back into the study headed for the stairs.

I stood at the bottom of the stairway, listening. Then I heard the whisper.

"Christopher…Christopher…" as if someone were right next to me.

My back was an ice cube now! I stood motionless not knowing what to do.

I don't know how long I stood there, but suddenly the chill was gone. And so was the fear. Everything seemed perfectly normal now and I turned back toward the study.

I walked to the desk and looked at the computer. That's when I found the next poem.

It was titled "*Scout.*"

SCOUT

Noble friend don't go away
Don't take your heart so true
Walk with me to the lake
To the water blue.

Remember how we played and ran
Remember how we grew
Remember how we shared his love
This I ask of you!

Where were you that fateful night?
Who locked you in his room?
Who kept you from his side?
While he met his doom?

Noble friend don't go away
Don't take your heart from me
Walk with me to the lake
Set my lover free.

Catherine Zimmerman

I was not alone! It was clear to me now that Catherine Zimmerman was trying to tell me something! Reaching out from the grave the only way she knew how. Writing.

"Brilliant deduction, Holmes!" Dr. Watson's line from an old Sherlock Holmes movie ran through my mind. It was time for me to stop acting like a victim and start acting like a detective!

Until now, I had been behaving like a scared tourist. Now it was time to take charge! I couldn't help Marianne in the accident; I even blamed myself for her death. But maybe I could help Catherine!

Something had kept her spirit here all these years! I still did not know the details of her death, or her family's. I would have to find out what really happened.

I also had to assess the facts. Somehow the house seemed to be moving backward in time. As if my being here was waking it up. Or waking Catherine's spirit...

Was it possible that her spirit had been asleep, that her ghost was sleepwalking, waiting for the right person to wake it up? Did I know the Lincoln I had seen in my sleep walk dream was a 1934 because that was the year she died?

The poems were stepping-stones! Written by Catherine so long ago and brought out for me to read by the writer's soul, leading me to the truth of her death, just as I had found the truth about my family in my first book.

Was it a coincidence that I was here? Why did I look so much like Fran's brother, Christian? What about the locket? Catherine had given it to her best friend, Fran. It had belonged to my mother, having been "handed down".

Was I somehow related to Catherine, or Fran? And that Catherine was a writer...

All these things had occurred to me along the way, but now I was linking them together. Everything that had happened so far was related. What about Mooney's? What was the connection there?

So many questions! Could Catherine answer them? If only I could talk to her...

Just then the eerie silence of the house was broken by the sound of the piano. Startled, I jumped and felt the icy cold return to my spine. It was the same song I had heard when I first arrived, though I did not recognize it.

I walked through the study into the entryway and through the living room. Looking into the dining room I expected to see the same dinner scene I had seen before and a young girl playing the piano.

But there was nothing there. Like a cat playing hide and seek, I knew that Catherine was just around a corner, waiting to pounce. I could feel her presence. Yet, I knew that there was nothing to fear from her.

The music had stopped when I walked in; and though the house looked newer there was still no piano, and no curtains.

I decided to take a shower, get dressed and make another visit to Fran. This time, however, I would stop and do some research first.

The local library was a small, one room building with an elderly lady who volunteered as a librarian. I parked on the street in front of it and climbed the white painted schoolhouse steps. This had been the original school at one time.

I walked up to the old school teacher's desk and read the name on the placard. Henrietta Jones.

The old, white-haired lady looked close to ninety and I saw she was asleep. Her chin was resting on her chest, almost crushing the flower pinned on the beige dress she wore.

"Excuse me," I said. "Could you help me?"

She looked up as if caught and quickly took up her "fancy work". She had been crocheting and as she sat up I saw the half finished doily.

She placed it on the desk and looked up at me again, more awake now.

"Yes, can I help you?" She said.

I introduced myself and asked to see the newspaper archives for 1934. Did they have any?

"Yes, we do have a book. I update it every week when the paper comes out. There are several books. You'll find them in the corner," she answered.

I went to the table in the corner. There was the complete history of Annandale! They took up most of the library itself! What space was left for bookracks held a modest selection, mostly donated by residents.

As I searched for 1934, I wondered how the old woman could handle these heavy, oversize, archives.

There was no microfilm here or computers. Just the old newspapers themselves, carefully placed in order into large black covers. I set the volume for 1934 on the table and chuckled when I looked up and saw the sign that said *SHHH!*

TWENTY-ONE

It was the quietest library I had ever been in. Henrietta seemed to have fallen asleep again, hands in her lap, the j-hook suspended in mid-stroke. I took the archive to the one table by the window and opened it to 1934.

As I scanned the old pages, I had a real history lesson. The paper I had found in the cupboard was dated June of '34. Whatever had happened to the Zimmerman's must have happened after that. I carefully turned the brittle pages, picking up information along the way.

National Housing Act passed. Securities and Exchange Act passed. "Last Resort" Set To open...

(June 30, 1934)

The new resort on Zimmerman Lake in Annandale is set to open on The Fourth of July. The Resort, Owned by Albert and Rose Zimmerman and a silent partner from Minneapolis will be host to a gala celebration on our Nation's Birthday. Attending the affair will be Albert and Rose Zimmerman, His Honor the Mayor of Annandale (and local Ford dealer, Virgil Mooney) as well as Jake and Ann Marie Peterson (owners of Peterson's Meat Market) and their daughter Fran, long time friend of Catherine Zimmerman. Their son, Christian will be in attendance as an employee of The Resort. Several other business owners and city officials will also be attending. Duke Ellington and his big band will provide entertainment in the new ballroom overlooking the lake. The festivities will start at six with fireworks at dusk. Attendance is by invitation only but the fireworks are free to all.

(July 6, 1934)
TRADGEDY MARS GRAND OPENING
Annandale's leading citizens, Albert and Rose Zimmerman and their daughter, Catherine were found dead in an apparent murder- suicide in their home on the west end of Zimmerman Lake early this morning.

The County Sheriff's Office is withholding details of the tragedy pending further investigation.

Also of note is the possible disappearance of Christian Peterson, son of Jake and Ann Marie Peterson. Christian was last seen escorting the Zimmermans to their home across the lake from the new resort. He was piloting the launch owned by The Resort. The Sheriff's Office is investigating.

The article said that not only was this a great loss for Annandale and the Zimmerman family, but also marred the gala celebration held at The Resort on the Fourth of July, which had been a splendid affair.

I flipped through the book some more. Baby Face Nelson, shoot out at Little Bohemia Lodge in Northern Wisconsin... July 20, 1934-Teamsters's strike...Franklin D. Roosevelt named Man of The Year...Pretty Boy Floyd killed by F.B.I... Floyd B. Olson elected governor...Zimmerman deaths ruled murder suicide, Rose Zimmerman kills family...

(December 17, 1934)

After a long investigation and much speculation, the mysterious deaths of The Zimmerman family have been ruled murder-suicide by Rose. Mrs. Zimmerman had been suffering from health problems for two years that had forced the family to move to Florida where Albert had opened a second bank. The family returned to Minnesota in the summers where Albert oversaw the construction of The Last Resort.

Rose apparently killed their daughter Catherine by pushing her down the stairway into the entryway of the house. She allegedly then ran to the shed where she found an axe and pursued her husband back into the house where she killed him with it. She then apparently took an unknown substance and died of a heart attack. She may have also been responsible for the death of Christian Peterson, whose body was found under the Zimmerman's dock two days after his disappearance.

No reason was found for Rose's actions, but speculation was her health problems had been mental rather than physical. The families have declined to comment on the tragedy.

I read the article again. No wonder the house was haunted! Catherine's poems ran through my mind. The song her mother "forced" her to play on the piano, the dinner scene...who were those people? The guest who had been flirting with Rose, until Catherine walked in and sat at the piano...

It certainly looked as if Rose had gone crazy! But if this were true, why would Catherine be contacting me? Was there more to the story?

I reviewed my notes. Virgil Mooney had owned the Ford dealership. Mr. Mooney's grandfather! Had he sold the

Lincoln to Albert? Was this the connection to the sleepwalk dream I had?

I closed the book, looking at my watch, remembering I was going to see Granny this morning. Henrietta was still asleep and I replaced the volume in the rack, trying not to wake her.

Tiptoeing past her desk, I reached for the door.

"Ahem! Thought I was asleep did you? Are you checking anything out?" She was awake and on guard

"No, I found what I was looking for," I replied, as if I *had* been caught with something.

"And what was it you were looking for?" She asked, a suspicious tone in her voice.

"I think that's personal..." I began to say, but then thought better of it. "Why do you ask?" I said.

"Well, I could have probably saved you a lot of work. Been in this town most of my life. We don't get many strangers in here. Don't get much of anybody for that matter," she replied, sitting up a little straighter and leaning forward slightly.

Her eyes were a mix of curiosity and suspicion and I found myself compelled to ask her what she knew about the Zimmermans.

"Got what they deserved, if you ask me. Thinking they owned this town. Rose with all her money from back East. Their stuck-up daughter thinking she was going to be a famous writer! And grabbing the only good-looking boy around! And Albert; running with the gangsters!" She was bitter.

I was glad I hadn't asked her first, and her bitterness drove me away. I reached for the door again, thanking her for her help and telling her I had an appointment. I didn't think anyone could live so long with an attitude like that!

"These boots are made for walkin'..." Nancy Sinatra's song accompanied me down the schoolhouse stairs and to the street. I was happy to see my little car and sat down with a sigh on the bucket seat. It was still morning and the sun was not too hot. Leaving the air conditioning off, I rolled down the window and started the motor, pulling the car into the driving lane. I reached into the door pocket for my sunglasses, taking my eyes off the road for a brief second. When I looked back up, I slammed on the brakes!

There was a dog in the middle of the road! A big German Shepard like I had seen in my "sleepwalk". The ABS brakes held and the car lurched to a stop, just inches from the dog! I expected him to flinch but he sat motionless as if nothing had happened.

I opened the door to get out and see if he was all right and he turned around and ran up the road. I jumped back in and followed.

For some reason I could not keep up with him. The faster I drove, the farther he got ahead of me. Just as I thought I was catching up, he vanished.

TWENTY-TWO

The news article I had found in the library flashed into my mind. Christian's body had been found in the lake, apparently caught on the dock but still submerged.

In my "sleepwalk" I had seen the same dog, a dark brown, purebred German Shepard with large standup ears. He had been lying on his paws looking over the edge and whimpering. Was this Christian's dog, Scout? Had he found the body? Where was he leading me to now?

I was no longer surprised at seeing ghosts, four-legged or otherwise! Something wanted me here! I was operating in a state of expanded reality, aware that this place had its own rules.

There were so many questions on my mind as I drove on, anxious to talk to Fran.

Yet, even as I hurried I knew I was being led and a strange calmness came over me. It was a confidence that the answers *would* come and my haste was unnecessary.

Except, I had a book to deliver in less than three months! And I knew what to write about! First Catherine, now the dog, both seemed to be leading me to the truth about the Zimmermans!

But, why me? And after all these years

It was only when I pulled the car into my 'usual' spot that I remembered the locket. I had reached up to touch it and it wasn't there!

Of course! Granny had asked to keep it overnight. I was supposed to pick it up today!

And that brought me full circle once again. What was my connection to all of this?

Was I somehow related to Granny, or Catherine?

I stepped out of the car in a daze, walking across the old street on an eerily quiet summer day, jumping across the cracks in the pavement as if I were crossing a river, catching my balance after each little hop from stepping stone to stepping stone...

TWENTY-THREE

The little bell woke me from my daze, almost. Looking around the little store, I felt that somehow time had been suspended. Everything looked the same...

"Hello, Christopher! How are you today?" Ginger's voice floated to me, still bright and chipper, but not as sharp and crisp as it usually was. She was behind the cash register and as I looked over at her, she gestured for me to come closer.

I smiled, mentally shaking off the fog I had come in with and walked to the counter.

"I want you to meet someone," she said, staying behind the counter and walking towards the adjoining meat department.

A large man stood behind the counter. He looked about 35, dressed in the white apron of a meat cutter, holding a cleaver and bringing it down on the butcher block he was facing. With a decisive, *WHACK!* He neatly sliced the beefsteak in two. Turning around to face me he smiled, wiping the blade of the cleaver with a towel and then setting it into the sink next to the butcher block.

"This is my husband, Mike. Mike, this is Christopher Evans, the writer." Ginger introduced us.

"Pleased to meet you Christopher; I've heard a lot about you from Ginger. How do you like our little town?" Mike asked.

"Well, it's growing on me. Nice to finally meet you, too," I smiled and reached my hand over the counter, thinking what a matched set they made. Mike had red hair too and freckles, but was definitely Irish.

His hand was wet and I tried to ignore the little bits of meat that clung to it as he shook mine. Catching the look on my face, he laughed and handed me a clean towel.

"Sorry about that. Not every day I meet a celebrity," he said.

"Never thought of myself as one," I replied, "Not every day I meet a butcher, either." I smiled back.

"I suppose you're in town to write another book?" Mike asked with a suspicious tone.

"Well, call it a 'working vacation'. I came out here to get away for a while so I could concentrate on my next book." I was curious about his suspicious tone and waited for him to say more.

"Well, what's it about? Not much happens out here. Lot of fishing hunting, and swimming, the usual summer stuff..." *He* was fishing now.

I waited for Ginger to break in and end the inquisition. As if she hadn't told him about my conversations with Granny! But she stood silent, smile frozen on her face.

"It's about America," I said, suddenly on unsure footing. "Annandale has been promoting itself, like a lot of small towns these days. The Fourth of July is big here. I thought I'd write about its roots."

"What you ought to write about are the gangsters," Mike surprised me. "My grandpa was on the St. Paul Police force. He was there when they got Baby Face Nelson. Told us lots of stories. My dad was a policeman too. If you need to know anything you can ask me."

Relieved, I smiled, letting my shoulders relax. I wondered why he wasn't a policeman also. So I asked.

"Bad shoulders. Same thing that kept me out of the service. Probably a good thing. Never would have met Ginger..." His voice trailed as he smiled at her, telling me all the unsaid things about his life, his family and his peace of mind.

Realizing he had said so much, he reached over the counter again and we shook hands, signaling the end of the interview.

"Gotta get back to work. I've got deadlines, too. Gotta get this order done."

"Every customer is important! I know. I used to work in a supermarket," I said.

"This is for our biggest customer!" He said as he ripped a long sheet of white paper and wrapped the steaks, marking them and placing them into the white plastic tubs on the cart sitting next to him.

"Oh, who's it for?" I asked.

"Why, The Resort of course," he said, picking up his cleaver and wiping the blade.

"Which resort?" I asked.

"The same one you came to write about," he said, knowingly.

A chill ran down my spine. I arched my back, not knowing why anything should surprise me.

"The Last Resort," he said, bringing the cleaver down on another slab of meat.

TWENTY-FOUR

W*HACK!* The sound woke me from my sleep. I rolled over on the daybed, sitting up and holding my head. It was still dark, moonlight shining on the polished floor of the study from the kitchen window.

I looked at the digital clock on the desk and realized I had been dreaming. 2 A.M.! The whole day I had just lived had been a dream! Or had it been real and I skipped the rest of it?

That would explain the foggy feeling, a dream, that is. I had to know. I went to the computer, waking it from *sleep* mode. But all it showed me was the time. I clicked on the Internet for my home page. There was the date! It had been a dream!

Nature was calling and I pushed the sleep button again. I stumbled to the bathroom and found the light. Niagara Falls! I thought as the noise echoed on the tiled walls.

"Well, at least I can go back to sleep. I'll start over in the morning," I said out loud as I turned off the light.

Walking back to the bed, I heard the quiet hum of the computer as it slept. There was a comfort in that sound. I checked the alarm clock and gratefully fell back into bed, enjoying the soft darkness.

The room was suddenly lit with a familiar light. Something had awakened the computer.

"Probably scheduled maintenance," I said, resisting the urge to look.

But I couldn't ignore it. I thought of turning the monitor off and letting the darn thing run.

I rolled over and got up again. *I* wanted to go into sleep mode! I'll show it who's boss!

When I sat down in the chair and looked at the screen, I was suddenly awake!

There was a document on the screen. The *Word* program had been started and someone had been writing.

"I'll never get used to those chills!" I said, as one went through me again. I knew I was about to find out more of the story. There was another poem!

"Catherine must be catching up with the times," I said, looking at the title.

THE BRIDGE

There is a bridge that we can cross
Have you not already seen?
For the boat is never lost
That travels down the stream.

We can call across
The water of the night
Two ships upon the surface
Floating by moonlight.

Hailing from a common port
Two riders on the sail
We can find an Inn
And share a common tale.

There is a bridge that we can cross
It's found in common bonds
Like stepping stones across the stream
That ties the garden ponds.

Last Resort

Let us meet on the bridge
At the appointed time
We'll tell stories of the sea-
The Ancient Mariner's Rhyme.

Catherine Zimmerman
1934

I read the poem again, expecting at any moment to see Catherine's ghost materialize...

Again my back felt like a block of ice! My heart started to pound. I was sure I was awake this time!

The other poems I had "found" could have been explained logically. Even this one could have been done by someone else. I started to feel like Charlie Chan's "No. 1" son. I wished I felt more like Charlie Chan. Or Sherlock Holmes instead of Dr. Watson!

"Okay, Christopher! Relax! And that's an order!" I told myself. I needed to think. There had been a lot of goings on in the few days I had been here. Some things I hadn't wanted to see!

I looked around the room. Somehow the house seemed to be restoring itself, as if it were traveling back in time. The walls were brightly papered and intact, the floors were polished, missing furniture had appeared, all except the curtains.

If the house was traveling back in time then I must be too! Was Catherine drawing me to her time? Was her spirit locked in 1934? Was this The Bridge she mentioned in the poem?

Her reference to stepping-stones really chilled me! I could not help but feel that I was somehow related to these people. But I had researched my book so well, I thought! Yet her mention of "common bonds" was hard to miss. And how had she used the computer? Was it there on this desk in her world, too?

Twice I had "sleepwalked", seeing things that must have happened in the past, and in this last dream actually interacting with people in the "present"! Was Catherine sleepwalking also?

"The *Ancient Mariner's Rhyme...*" I said out loud, "What did she mean by that?" I had only read it once, years ago when I was in high school. I was not sure how it applied here. Maybe she was referring to the story of the tragedy.

Of course! She wanted to meet and talk to me! To tell me the truth about what had happened here! At the appointed time...when was that?

The thought of interviewing a ghost was both exciting and scary! I remembered *Interview With a Vampire* by Anne Rice. That was a chilling tale! But to do it in real life! Now that was sheer ice.

Would she look like I had seen her at the door that first night? Or would she look alive?

I thought more about *when*. "The Appointed Time". I did not know when that was! I was to meet Granny again this morning and Phil was going to call at the end of the week. I wondered what he would think of the place now? Would he see the changes?

I looked up at the clock. Two hours had passed and I had not even realized it! The clock said 4 a.m. The hum of the computer was beginning to annoy me now and I was suddenly very tired. I decided to sleep until eight and start the day over.

"If nothing weird happens!" I said out loud, hoping that the spirits would hear me!

I pushed the sleep button again and the computer clicked down. I reached up and switched the monitor off also.

Stumbling to the daybed, I thought of Marianne. How I missed her! I felt incredibly lonely! The daybed looked too big now and I hugged my pillow and fell asleep.

TWENTY-FIVE

This time when I walked into Granny's, I was awake.
There was no fog in my head when Ginger greeted me from
behind the cash register.

I looked beyond her to the meat counter but did not see
Mike anywhere. Ginger finished her task and closed the
cash drawer.

"Back for more?" She asked, smiling.

"More what?" I asked, warily.

"More rolls, of course!" She laughed.

"Best rolls this side of the Mississippi!" I said.

"Have a seat, I'll tell Granny you're here," she said,
turning towards the kitchen.

I sat at the "usual" table and looked around at Fran's
paintings. Christian was looking down at me from over the
door. Only eighteen, how sad! Next to him was a dog. A big
brown and black German Shepard, the one I had seen in my
"sleepwalk"! The one Catherine had written about! Funny I
had not noticed the painting before...

I heard the metal chair slide on the old wooden floor and
turned around to see Fran, smiling, wiping flour from her
hands on her apron.

"Hello, Christopher! Nice to see you again! Rolls for
breakfast again? You really should eat better, you know!"
She said, just like a grandmother would.

"Morning, Fran! Yes, I know I should eat better. But, who could resist the best rolls this side of the Mississippi?" I said, as I stood.

"Such a gentleman! Sit down and tell me what's been happening," she said as Ginger helped her into the chair.

"I don't know if you would believe me," I said, looking into her eyes. She looked back as if watching a movie.

"I think it would surprise you if I said I already knew," she replied, drawing the chain out of her apron pocket and handing me the locket.

"Noticed you looking at my paintings again," she prodded.

"Fran, you are a great artist! How come you didn't pursue it?" I asked

"Oh, but I did!" She replied.

"Tell me about it," I said.

"It's a sad story, Christopher. Such a beautiful summer morning, I would hate to spoil it," she said, not wanting to remember.

"Fran, I saw Henrietta. Well, sort of," I wanted to lead her into the story.

"What do you mean, 'sort of'?" She asked.

"I went to the library, only I wasn't awake. I thought I was, but I must have dreamed it. She was knitting behind the desk and I looked up the tragedy of the Zimmermans'." I said, and then continued with, "I saw Scout, too."

"You must have been dreaming, Christopher. Both of them have been dead for years," she looked right into my eyes.

"Tell me the whole story, Fran. I've got to know."

"Okay, I'll tell you," she resigned herself to it.

As Ginger set down the tea and rolls, Fran's eyes went to the locket, which was lying in front of me on the table.

"Where to start! I am not a writer like you! It was 1932, no, it started way before that. Back when we all went to the one-room school, no, even before that. Back when our parents went to the one-room school…"

Biting into the sweet roll and sipping on the Coke, I fell into a trance-like state as I listened to Fran, traveling back in time with her to the turn of the century, seeing the events as if I were there.

TWENTY-SIX

The summer day faded away as Fran began her story. Looking into her eyes I could see the scene emerging as the shop faded with it.

Gone were the painted windows and the cash register, replaced by a field and a dirt road. We approached the little red schoolhouse together, riding on a farmer's flatbed wagon.

"Old man Zimmerman drove his sons to school almost every day, picking up the other kids along his "route". There were three of them, Albert (the oldest), Ray and Jerome. Henrietta and Gertrude were the only girls. Henrietta had a crush on Albert all through school, and they had several scraps about it. Both were the same age as Albert and his brothers teased them constantly with the old childhood rhymes, "Gertrude and Albert sitting in a tree, k-i-s-s-i-n-g'." Fran repeated the old rhyme as if she could hear their chant.

"The other Zimmerman boys were too young for them and there were other girls in the class who had similar crushes on them. Gertrude soon outgrew her crush on Albert and Henrietta claimed full ownership of him. Of course, she never talked to him about it and through the years they all went skinny dipping in the lake. Albert never led Henrietta on, telling her that one-day he was going to college at the University and time would tell. But Henrietta never gave up and insisted he play with her. She loved to come to school telling the other girls about her and Albert's escapades at the lake. Albert just shook his head and made swirling signs with his fingers pointed at his ears and rolled his eyes. The class would laugh at this, and the teacher, Henrietta's mother, would bang her pointer on the desk for silence. She was aware of what her daughter was going through and was quite pained at how she was treated."

I could see it as if I was there; the old wooden desks, new then probably but etched with initials and impossible to remove, "dirty" words. Henrietta in pigtails and a flowered dress that hung as straight as the yard stick brought out for occasional discipline, Albert in his overalls and glasses, already looking different than his brothers who were destined to remain farmers. The frustrations of one teacher having to deal with all ages and grades.

"There were others there you should know. "Mooney, who grew up from the round little boy into the local Ford dealer, the Sheriff, who even then played cops and robbers at recess, and Ray and Martha's parents were both there also. Phil's grandfather was there as well, and like Albert was very smart and destined for the University.

"These were all stories I heard through the years from Catherine and others around town. By the time I was born the one-room school was just elementary and Annandale had a high school. Eventually, a grade school was built and the one-room school was turned into a library."

Fran stopped to sip some tea. I was still in a trance when she continued.

"In 1916, Albert graduated and went to the University. That's where he met Rose. It was at a piano recital. The famous Leo Friedman had come to the University and they fell in love listening to one of his songs, *Rose of My Heart*, which Rose would have Catherine play incessantly when she was old enough. Rose was from Chicago, the daughter of a successful railroad man who used to bring his family to Minnesota to vacation. He often came to Annandale to hunt and fish. So when they met in college, Albert and Rose had something in common. They married in 1917 and Rose became pregnant soon after. Albert brought her home to Annandale and Henrietta never got over it. They lived in his father's farmhouse while Albert started his bank and in 1920 the new house was built. The one you are staying in now."

Fran stopped, sipped some more tea, and then continued.

"But I was going to tell you about me. I was born in 1915 and had been in the one-room school about two years when I met Catherine. I knew she was different the first time I saw her. She had dark hair, blue eyes and was very quiet. Everyone thought she was shy but when we got around each other she talked a blue steak! I never hit it off with the boys, even at that young age I wanted to travel. Catherine would tell me about her mother's trips and my longing grew. The boys could see I was somewhere else and they left me alone. Of course, as I started to mature it was a different story!"

A smile crossed her face and she drank her tea more zestfully now. We were racing through time, having jumped a whole generation! She put down the cup and continued.

"Catherine always wanted to be a writer. She didn't get to go on the annual trips with her mother, but would listen to the stories and write about them in her journal. Soon she started to write poems and her talent became apparent.

"I wanted to be an artist! Some of my early paintings were good enough that the teacher wanted to hang them in the old school house and when we got to high school, I excelled in art. I dreamed of going to Paris! By the time I graduated I knew somehow I would get there."

"My parents owned the butcher shop, now supplied by Albert's brothers. Though they were successful in Annandale, they could not afford to send me to college, let alone Paris! They still had to think of Christian, my younger brother, they said. By the time Catherine and Christian were graduating, I was ready for a "Last Resort"."

Fran's voice seemed harder now and her eyes blazed as she remembered.

"Last Resort?" I asked, catching the reference.

"Yes, everything goes back to The Resort. That's where I met "Mr. Big". The night that picture was taken; I made a "deal with the devil" that I've never forgiven myself for! That night changed my life forever! And the lives of everyone in this town! Of course, I, like Christian and the Zimmermans, was just another victim. Their deaths were not my fault. The events had been set in motion two years before when Mr. Big came to town with his cronies, looking for Albert."

She stopped again and poured another cup of tea.

"It was 1932," Fran continued. "Mr. Big's car pulled up in front of Albert's bank. When the three "businessmen" walked in, people on the street expected a holdup. They were surprised when Albert escorted them into his office. And that's when The Resort was born."

Ginger had refilled my Coke without me noticing and I was suspended in time, watching the black car with the suicide doors pulling into town and stopping in front of the bank.

"Fran, I think we've come full circle on Mr. Big and The Resort. What did you mean when you said you'd made a "deal with the devil"?" I asked, pulling myself back into the present.

"The night of the Grand Opening, so much happened! Everyone was excited and drinking. I was so determined to get out of town! Catherine was leaving and I wanted to.

Mr. Big had brought the world to us. Money, fine cars and big bands! For two years the people of this town had had their heads turned one way or another! They either ignored the facts or were in favor of them. Mr. Big and his gang never mistreated anyone here. They made legitimate deals and kept them. They paid well and good people deceived themselves into ignoring the crime behind it all, happy to take their money. It became politics and some people even supported the gangsters, calling them "rebels" and talking about their "American Spirit". I, too, put my selfish desires ahead of everything else."

"What do you mean?" I asked, sensing her reluctance to elaborate.

"Mr. Big had a proposition for me. He wanted a baby."

The Coke glass slipped through my fingers and I grabbed it just before it hit the table, narrowly avoiding a spill. I was shocked!

"A baby? With you? I mean..." I was stammering.

Now Fran recovered, chuckling at my shock. "Oh, come on, Christopher! I thought you knew something about life! Yes, with me. I was not unattractive you know! And I have not always been this age!"

"Yes, I know you were attractive, still are..." I was already stepping in it! "But, was Mr. Big married?" I asked, hastily.

"Yes, he was married! His wife could not have another child. They had lost their first one, a girl. Robert wanted a boy to pass on "the business" to. They had agreed that if they could find a surrogate mother they would adopt the child. Of course, Mr. Big did not want his name on any papers, much like Al Capone and for obvious reasons. He'd had eyes on me for some time and that night made me an offer I couldn't refuse." She stopped and stared into her teacup, stirring it absentmindedly.

"Why couldn't you refuse?" I prodded.

"Once the offer was made, he could not take the chance that I might make it public. He did not want his "associates" to know he could not have a child. Nor did he want the Mob to know anything about his dealings in Annandale. His wife stayed at their home in St. Paul and never came here. She was "P.R."; entertaining society and smoothing relations -- staying behind the scenes, as a crime bosses' wife should. He assured her there was nothing between us. She knew he played around anyway and decided not to fight it. After all, he could have left her. Anyway, this was the deal..."

Fran described "the arrangement". If she became pregnant, she would receive a six-month stay in Paris with $5,000 to boot. There, she could study art. He had done his homework on Fran! The baby was to be delivered in New York and when it was born an "adoption" would be arranged. If it was a boy, he would live with them in St. Paul, to be raised as theirs. If it was a girl, another adoption would be arranged. Mr. Big did not want a daughter growing up around 'the business'. She would be cared for by a loving couple and her every need would be provided, after all, she would still be his blood.

"I would get my trip to Paris to study art and opportunities would come my way in the art world. I didn't want to go there pregnant, but I was afraid I wouldn't get there at all! I'd had too much to drink and in the atmosphere of the Grand Opening I impulsively agreed." Fran stopped, as I sat frozen. The look on my face brought a flash to her eyes!

"I am not telling you this so you can judge me, Christopher! But facts are facts! God and I will be the judges." She softened a little with this last sentence.

"I'm sorry, Fran. I did not mean to judge you. What happened then?" I asked.

"I'm tired now, Christopher. We'll talk another time," she said, pushing her chair back and motioning for Ginger to help her.

I stood up, feeling awkward.

"Of course, Fran. We'll talk some other time," I said.

Ginger looked at me over Fran's head as she helped her away from the table. There was a question mark on her brow as she caught my eyes.

I shrugged, looking blank. I had no idea if Ginger knew this story or not.

When I climbed back into the Merc, I hung the locket back on the mirror. I had missed seeing it there.

But something was different now. The comfort it had always given me was gone. Now it felt like a stranger to me. There was a queasy feeling in my stomach and the seed of a thought I wanted to squelch.

Was Fran's story leading me to a stepping-stone I didn't want to know about?

I turned on the radio and heard Jan and Dean again, only this time the words in my head were *No Granny, No Granny, NO!*

TWENTY-SEVEN

It was eighty degrees and chilly. There was something especially chilling about Granny's story. Here it was, 1 O'clock on a summer day and I felt cold. These were the kind of things you usually do at night, telling tales around the kitchen or a campfire, not in a bakery/malt shop/dairy store/ meat market.

The unusual setting added to Granny's hypnotic stare and the strange quality of her voice. The chill I felt was not caused by a fever. It wasn't the temperature but rather a dread.

The last few days had changed my whole perception of reality. But I hadn't let it sink in. I viewed everything with the detachment of watching a horror movie. "It's only a movie..."

I had been around the past too long. Too long thinking of Marianne. Reliving our life together that had been cut short just as we were about to realize our dream. Reliving the accident over and over in nightmares and waking moments when my mind was not totally occupied. Becoming numb to life and quoting lines from movies that kept me at a safe distance from what was happening to me.

Now, Granny threw a stone into my pond. A stepping-stone. I watched the ripples on the water reaching out for my foothold.

I drove to the beach where it was warm and there was life. I wasn't dressed for it but there was a folding chair in the trunk and I had my shades. I found a place to park and bought a Coke from the machine and found a place in the sand.

Socks and shoes came off and I wondered at the order; shouldn't shoes come off first? Shrugging at the thought I rolled up my jeans and popped the pull-tab as I sat down to watch the sunbathers, safely hidden behind my Ray-Bans.

There was life! The noise of the jet-skis and motorboats, children cannon-balling off the dock into the water with a *whoosh!* Dogs were barking, and chasing Frisbees. The mingled sounds of people on vacation, cooking hot dogs and burgers.

I sat soaking it all up with the sun, letting my mind roam. Somewhere along the way I decided to join the human race again. I smiled.

A beach ball rolled to my feet and I bent down to pick it up. Holding it in both hands I looked up to see a young girl with blonde hair in a still-dry one-piece swimsuit.

"Can I have the ball back, Mr. Evans?" Allison Mooney smiled at me.

"Allison? Of course. Dad give you the day off?" I asked, surprised to see someone I recognized.

"It is summer vacation. Can't work all the time!" She replied. "Looks like you're taking some time off yourself. Must get pretty boring sitting at the keyboard all of the time."

"You'd be surprised," I said, and then continued with, "actually I haven't even begun typing. I'm still doing research."

"Oh, I see." she said, looking around at the bikini-clad women on the beach.

"That's not the kind of research I meant," I said, catching her look.

"Safely hidden behind your Ray-Bans, eh?" She chided.

"Isn't someone waiting for the ball?" I asked, suddenly hoping she would go away.

"Just my niece. She's six and I am "working". Baby sitting. She's building the sand castle over there." She pointed to a little sundress now covered in sand.

"Must be pretty boring, working all the time..." Now it was my turn to chide her.

"Nah, brought my Ray-Bans too." She smiled, nodding in the direction of the lifeguard.

"Looks like were even, and I'm out of Coke. Better be getting back. Tell your dad I'll be by for more of that chicken again; say how did the pictures turn out?" I asked.

"Dad says something was wrong with the camera. You came out fuzzy in all of the shots. Betty Lou looks okay, though. Must have been where you were sitting. Oh, looks like I better go, before Marianne hits the water."

"Marianne?" I asked, suddenly chilled.

"My niece, that's her name. See ya'!" And she ran off to rescue the little girl.

"Bye," I said as she ran away. But she didn't hear me.

"Eighty degrees and chilly." I said to myself.

Darn! There I was just about feeling normal and now I felt 'fuzzy'. What was wrong with Mooney's camera? What was wrong with me?

"Marianne! You get back here right now!" I could hear Allison yelling as she stood by the water's edge.

I picked up the lawn chair and folded it. I knew I had a choice. I could let it all get to me again or I could stay detached. Everyone in my life had died. I was the last of my family and my hopes of having children looked dim. Depression and being unwilling to let go of Marianne kept me single. It was still too soon. Whatever was waiting for me would just have to keep waiting.

As it was, this was my life. I could cringe or I could embrace it. People had all sorts of 'things' in their life, yet they managed to enjoy it. So what if mine was strange? There were far stranger and far worse lives I could live.

Brushing the sand from my shoes and socks I took one last look at the beach and headed back to the *Merc*.

Billy Joel's song played in my head; *I don't care what you say, this is my life...*

As I turned the key the radio came on again and I expected to hear the same song that was in my head. Not this time.

This time it was a commercial.

TWENTY-EIGHT

It was time to get to work. I had enough material and a rough idea in my head for the story. I was anxious to get started.

I stopped at the drive-through at Mooney's and picked up an order of broasted chicken. Mooney had taken the day off and I didn't have a chance to talk to him about the fuzzy pictures. I had an idea of what had caused the effect but like the suspicion I felt about Granny's story and the missing stepping stone in my life, I was not ready to deal with that yet.

Writing was my way of dealing with life. It put me in control and I could approach it at my own pace.

I knew that soon I would have to hear the rest of the story from Granny and see the Last Resort. I knew also that Catherine would have something else to say. I was not ready to deal with the 'bridge' yet, either.

For now, I was focused on writing.

When I arrived at the house it was still light. The sun would not set for a few hours yet. I preferred to write at night, but this was close enough.

Grabbing a Coke from the fridge, I sat down at the kitchen table with my notebook and chicken and began to write down key words while I ate. I ignored the fact that the house had changed again, looking even cleaner and brighter than when I had left.

I reveled in the silence as I worked. This was how I had worked with Marianne. First I would write down key words and phrases and then we would talk about it, framing it in my mind and emotionalizing it. Then I would sit down at the computer and write one chapter at a time. I rarely needed a rough draft and would have Marianne proof read each one as we went.

This time I would have to do it myself.

The chicken disappeared as I worked, leaving only telltale crumbs on the scraps of paper and the copies of Catherine's poems. Excitement growing, I scooped them up and walked into the study.

I looked at nothing but the computer, determined to strike while the iron was hot and sat down and booted up the Word program.

My fingers flew on the keyboard as I worked and time flew with them. When I looked up again it was dark and I had the first three chapters written. True, they were not long but that was my style.

I surveyed the desk as I stood up and stretched. Funny, I had not even remembered getting up and getting two more Cokes.

I began to come down from the adrenaline high I had been on and felt suddenly drained and tired. I decided to get ready for bed and print out the chapters I had written.

The old brass desk lamp with a dark green shade of heavy glass lighted the room with an eerie glow and I tried to remember if it had been there before.

Turning toward the bookshelf wall, I was surprised to see it was gone!

There was now a fireplace where the shelves had been!

"Oh, oh, Toto, I don't think we're in Kansas anymore!" I said out loud.

I felt the now-familiar chill in my spine traveling up to my shoulders and refrigerating my back and while still in the 'Popsicle' state I heard piano music again.

Drawn to the sound, I opened the double doors of the study — funny; those weren't here before — and walked into the living room expecting to see Catherine sitting at a piano in the dining room.

The music stopped, and so did I.

But there was a piano!

I walked up to it and ran my hand along the smooth wood. The keyboard was covered and I wondered where the music had come from. Catherine must not be ready to be seen yet.

I walked back into the living room and turned around hoping to catch a glimpse of her...

Instead I saw the bookcases next to the arch that formed a divider between the two rooms. The glass doors were clean now and each shelf was filled with old volumes that looked new...

And sitting on top of each one were pictures. On one side a picture in a silver eight-by-five frame of Albert and Rose Zimmerman, on the other a picture in a matching frame of Catherine!

As in a trance I walked up to the picture of Albert and Rose. It was only when I picked it up I realized that someone had turned on the lights.

Albert was a handsome man of about six feet with broad shoulders and big hands. His dark hair was combed back in the style of the times and he was wearing a dark pinstripe suit with a carnation. Rose had long flowing red hair and was wearing a high-necked dress.

It was not a wedding picture but must have been taken about the same time as the one of Catherine. She was about seventeen - 1934.

A beautiful cross between the handsome Albert and the fiery Rose, Catherine had dark hair and a fine nose. Her blue eyes looked deep and full of life as a young girl would. Her dress was not as formal as her mother's and revealed her neckline and the now familiar locket...

Heart thumping, I replaced the picture and looked at the piano again.

There was the sheet music. I walked over and picked it up, noticing the title, *Rose of My Heart*-words by Milton Weil, music by Leo Friedman. Along one side of the cover was an illustration of three roses on a vine.

This was the song I had heard playing that first night. It must have been the song Albert and Rose had fallen in love with at the recital in 1917. This must have been the song Catherine had written about in her poem. The one her mother insisted she play.

The chill left me and my heartbeat returned to normal. I stood for a few minutes and pondered the events. Apparently, the house was still waking up, drawing on my energy and moving back in time. Catherine's spirit was waking up also. Locked here with a sense of purpose, she had been sleepwalking all these years, waiting for me to arrive. There must be some link between us. Something deeper than the writing. The locket! How could it have belonged to my mother and Catherine? What was the connection? Catherine's last poem contained a clue when she wrote about *Stepping Stones*.

That brought me full circle to where the day had started. Soon I would have to deal with the link, and The Bridge.But was I ready to cross it?

TWENTY-NINE

I felt like I was standing on that bridge right now. As I stood there looking at the photographs, the phone rang.

I walked over to the polished oak phone table and wondered where it had come from. Sitting on a white lace doily the old black handset jiggled on its cradle.

"Hello..." I said nervously.

"That you Chris?" It was Phil.

"Yeah, hi Phil, what's up?" I tried to sound normal.

"Are you okay, Christopher? You sound different."

"Yeah, I'm okay Phil. Just adjusting to the house..." my voice trailed off.

"Well, I told you I'd call at the end of the week. How's the writing coming?"

"Haven't got too much done yet. Been working on research and cleaning up the place," I was regaining my composure.

"Hey, what are you up to this weekend? Are you staying in town or headed back to the city?" Phil asked.

"Staying in town, Phil. Got a little more research to do and some more work on the house," I replied. "Why do you ask?"

"Thought we'd drop in, June and I. See what you've done with the old place."

"Don't expect too much. I was just supposed to clean the place up a bit, remember?" I was worried about what they might see. Would they see the house restoring itself, too?

"Oh, don't worry about the house, Chris. How about Saturday at noon? We'll bring the food and a grill."

"Sounds good to me. I could use a little life around here," I said.

"Okay, Chris. We'll see you then." Phil said and hung up the phone.

I looked at my watch. Ten O'clock. Early by night shift standards. I was glad I was off nights. Matter of fact, I was glad I was out of a job. I much preferred working for myself. But I had let myself go since Marianne died. It was time to get back in shape. I didn't know what the future held, but I knew that I couldn't stay like this. It had felt good to be writing again.

I went to the computer and set up the printer for the three chapters I had written. I watched the first page appear and thought that this was a little unusual. Normally I start with a title but this time I just opened the story. I read the first page with a sense of detachment. Had I really written that? Where had the words come from? I didn't even need to polish it.

"Christopher, old boy, you still have it!" I patted myself on the back and then remembered that if it hadn't been for Marianne I would never have gotten this far...

I let the printer run while I cleaned up the desk and got ready for bed. The fact that the house had changed and there was now a fireplace and doors on the study were lost on me. It seemed that they had always been there.

I had been living out of my suitcase since I arrived and now I took the clothes to the entryway closet and hung them up. The closet was clean and there were hangers. Hangers that I had not brought.

But nothing was unusual here.

I was so excited about the writing I had done that I found myself looking forward to getting up early tomorrow. Friday.

My fifth day here! I had to get back and see Granny! I needed to hear the rest of her story and find out what the connection was between the locket and me.

I also needed to get to The Last Resort. Maybe I could talk Betty Lou into going there with me tomorrow night.

I wondered how the draperies were coming. I looked at the windows in the house as I turned out the lights. They looked clean and even more naked now. I wondered too, why the former draperies hadn't appeared back on the windows. Was it because I had buried them? There were other things in the house that had appeared that had not been there before.

I shrugged. *"And that's the way it is."* I recalled Walter Cronkite's voice from when I was a child and got to stay up until 10 p.m. watching the news with my mother.

I needed to hear some music and put a CD in the computer's disk player. It was a collection of oldies and I heard one of my mother's favorite songs *Stranger on The Shore* from 1962. Somehow the gentle saxophone fit the house. It was one stepping stone back in time.

Chubby Checker's *Limbo Rock* picked me up again as I turned on the bathroom light to shave.

Listening to the music I had heard my mother play so many times as I grew up took away some of the loneliness I felt for Marianne. I remembered running out to show her what I had written every time I had an inspiration.

Now there was no one.

The computer was set on repeat and I clicked off the bathroom light and flopped on the daybed listening to Mary Wells singing *Two Lovers* as I drifted off to sleep.

Sometime deep in the night I awoke to silence.

And someone staring down at me as I slept!

THIRTY

There was only moonlight in the room as I looked up, heart thumping and my sleepy brain wondering what had happened to the music.

"Marianne?" I said groggily to the shadowy figure of a woman silhouetted by the lunar light.

I started to sit up as the figure backed up from my voice, rubbing the sleep out of my eyes and squinting in the darkness.

"Is that you, Marianne?" I asked, hopefully.

There was no reply, only the impression of long flowing hair and a white nightgown.

The shadow was still backing away as I stood up, my heart still beating wildly.

Once on my feet, I felt like running! But there was no place to go! I still couldn't see the ghostly face but there was something in her hands that caught on the moonlight.

My manuscript fell to the floor as she vanished, scattering like leaves in the wind.

I sat down on the daybed and leaned forward, picking up the pages closest to me.

Who had been reading my story?

The last few pages were closer to the desk and I followed their trail to the computer. Why had the music stopped? I had set it on repeat. It should have played all night.

I could hear the hum of the processor as I approached, and I saw the light from the monitor.

I looked at the screen and found the answer.

Catherine! Of course, she would have read the manuscript!

On the screen was another poem.

NIGHT LIGHT

Tell me a story-
Tuck me in...
Read to me 'till
I feel safe again.

Cover me with armor-
Blankets soft and warm...
The sound of your voice
To keep me from harm!

Let me drift off-
On Pegasus wing
While guardian angels
Softly sing.

Tell me a story-
Keep the goblins at bay...
Help me on the journey
To the next day

Tell me a story-
Make it your best...
Chase away the monsters
And put old ghosts to rest!

Catherine Zimmerman

"Put old ghosts to rest..." I said out loud, Catherine's poem was full of double meanings. Why did she write like that? Why didn't she come right out and say what she wanted? But that wasn't her style. She was a poet and liked to make you think. She liked to lead you to a conclusion and then let you discover it yourself. I recognized the technique. It was not unlike my own.

But how had she learned to use the computer? And when? I felt like Sherlock Holmes again.

"Elementary, Watson. Obviously the house is traveling backward in time. The computer is in the house and exists in Catherine's time also. It has a keyboard and Catherine is intelligent. The house is the 'bridge'. Catherine died with so many unfinished dreams. Her lover was dead and her dreams of marrying him were dead too. Her dreams of becoming a famous writer were also gone. And, her family was dead. Were all those things together keeping her spirit trapped here? Who were the old ghosts to put to rest? Who were the goblins? The "appointed time" must be drawing near; would I see her face to face? Would she be alive or a ghost? Would we finally be able to talk?"

Watson didn't reply. I had started out giving answers and then fell into questions. I reviewed my notes from the library; Rose Zimmerman had been accused of the murders. That may have explained Albert and Catherine, but what about Christian? Was that an accident or had he witnessed the murders and ran, pursued by Rose?

A chill ran through me. I had thought enough tonight. I did not want the scene in my mind when I went to sleep. It was enough that Catherine had been standing over me holding my manuscript!

I put the computer into sleep mode and stacked the printed pages neatly on the desk.

I stood up and stretched. 2 a.m. "Past my bed time," I said, talking to myself again.

I resisted the urge to open another Coke. The last thing I needed was more caffeine.

Walking back to the daybed I began to think of Catherine. I felt safe enough even if she was a ghost. So far she hadn't tried to harm me and through her writing I had gotten to know her. She was almost like a sister.

Now that was fitting, I thought. My life had been strange to be sure, but I had never had a sister. But then I had never met a ghost either.

I plumped up my pillow, getting it just right then carefully arranged myself in the now well formed depression on the bed, placing my head on the one flat corner of the fluffed pillow.

As I drifted off, I told Marianne that she had nothing to worry about; Catherine was only my sister.

THIRTY-ONE

At Nine A.M. Friday morning I pulled the Merc into "my" spot and walked across the street to Granny Franny's. It was a cool summer morning with clear skies and a slight breeze. The radio had said there was a chance of rain tonight, but would be clear tomorrow.

I hoped so. This was going to be a big weekend! Tonight I was going to visit The Last Resort, taking Betty Lou to dinner for helping me with the drapes, which she would put up tomorrow. Tomorrow! Phil and June were coming over for a bar-b-que! I hoped we would have them up!

I was also curious to see if anyone else could see the changes in the house that I did! I wondered what would happen with Catherine with all that activity about!

But now, as I walked through the door I was anxious to talk to Fran. Today I hoped she would tell me the rest of her story!

I spotted Ginger behind the register and waved. She just smiled and pointed to the table where Fran was already waiting, sipping her tea.

Fran looked up at me as I turned and waved me over, a look of resignation on her face.

"Good morning, Fran!" I said cheerfully.

"Good morning, Christopher. I suppose you are here to do more "research". Well, sit down." She acted impatient and I wondered if she was annoyed or just anxious to finally tell the rest of the story.

Suddenly, I was not as anxious to hear it. There was something ominous in the air. I had a feeling that my life was about to change again.

Ginger brought a sweet roll and Granny repeated her admonition.

"You really should eat better than that, Christopher. Ginger, bring him some bacon and eggs and orange juice!" Granny commanded.

I started to protest but she snapped a look at me and said, "The rest of the story comes with a price, Christopher. And this is it!"

"I certainly don't mind paying by eating good food!" I said, smiling. I knew it was not wise to argue. And I was hungry.

"Fran," I started to say but she interrupted me.

"Hush! I'm giving the orders this morning, young man! You want to hear about my life as an artist, eh? Well, I'll tell you a story you may not be ready to hear."

Ginger had left the sweet roll and Coke and I started in while I waited for breakfast and Fran started in on her story. "It was the Fourth of July and the Grand Opening of The Last Resort. Prohibition had ended and it was good timing all around. The Zimmermans had come across the lake on the boat and I spotted Catherine as I walked in with my parents. Christian was already there in his white uniform. The ballroom was full and the band was already playing. The guests were dressed to the "nines". It was the biggest thing that had ever happened around here. Everyone was excited, including me. I was dressed in a blue evening gown a little low cut for the times. I can't tell you what an argument I had gotten from my father! But my mother had softened him, reminding him that I was a grown-up woman of nineteen – and it was about time I thought of finding a man. Father looked around at some of the other ladies and was pleased with what he saw. Mother would punch him in the shoulder every so often when his eyes lingered too long on a particular gown. She herself had dressed conservatively as had Catherine and Rose."

She stopped and sipped her tea as Ginger brought breakfast.

"Mr. Big and his party were there also. Carlisle, Mr. Big's crony, was in charge of the "ladies" of the evening. He was quite a dancer for a big man. The 'ladies" were scandalously dressed and in "the mood" as they used to say.

We were seated at neighboring tables, the Zimmermans and Mr. Big at one table; my parents and I were at the next. It did not take us long to get the adults all at one table and Catherine and I by ourselves. Mr. Mooney and the other "dignitaries" were seated on the other side of the Zimmermans. All the young men eyed Catherine and myself — and for the first time in our lives we did not feel like small-town girls. Mr. Big couldn't keep his eyes from us either, to the consternation of our fathers. But they were reluctant to say anything to him."

Fran stopped again sipping her tea and I could see the scene in my mind

"Catherine had brought a going-away gift for me. A locket. She said now that The Resort was open; she would be leaving with her parents for Florida, returning in the summers. I knew that I might not see her again."

The scene in my mind shifted and now I heard their dialogue as if I were there.

"Oh, Catherine! You shouldn't have! That looks so expensive! And I have nothing to give you!" Fran said, tears beginning to well up and run her mascara.

"It wasn't, Fran. You deserve it for all the encouragement you've given my writing, you being a real artist and all. If not for you I may not have written to Johns Hopkins about their new poetry program! And someday I will write a novel!" Catherine was so excited.

"Hey, you two! What's all the crying about?" Christian said as he approached with the food. "Why you ought to be dancing and having some fun!"

"Oh, Christian, you know I wouldn't dance with anyone but you!" Catherine said, hiding their secret plan to elope tomorrow.

"I have to work, and I'm not allowed to dance with the guests," he said over the music.

"But you can dance with your father," he added, noticing Albert's watchful eyes.

"Well, Mr. Big himself has been staring at us all evening," Fran said.

"Who wouldn't?" Christian replied, causing them both to blush.

"Just don't dance with Carlisle or the hoods," he added as he walked away with a wink.

"Only as a last resort!" Fran said as Mr. Mooney stopped the band and stood nervously on the stage calling for attention.

"Ladies and Gentlemen! Welcome to the Grand Opening of The Last Resort! This is a historic night for Annandale! We welcome Duke Ellington and his band..."

Here he stopped for applause. Mr. Mooney was not an emcee — but he was a car salesman and so he was chosen to be the Master of Ceremonies.

He continued over the applause as the Duke and the band took their bows. "We also welcome the man responsible for all of this..." looking over to the table at Mr. Big as the band's drummer quietly tapped the cymbals building to a crescendo; but Mr. Big shook his head "no" and nodded to Albert...

"Albert Zimmerman and his lovely family!" The cymbals crashed and Mr. Big prodded Albert and Rose to stand up. Rose looked nervously at Catherine and motioned her to stand also. Fran threatened to pick her up if she didn't. Catherine stood and the room applauded all three.

Mr. Mooney looked at Mr. Big who smiled and ran his finger across his throat, giving Mooney the "cut" sign.

"Enjoy the evening folks! The staff has prepared a fine dinner and fireworks will be at dusk! Let's celebrate!"

Then he turned to the band and motioned them to play as the lights dimmed.

The room grew quiet as the band played a low- key song for the dinner hour and Mr. Mooney made a grateful exit from the stage, crumpling his carefully prepared speech and stuffing it into his pocket in a huff.

THIRTY-TWO

Fran stopped as Ginger brought the bacon and eggs and set them on the table. I was brought back to the present for a moment.

I smiled at Ginger as Granny sipped at her tea. She could see that I was still in the middle of her grandmother's story. With no customers in the store to attend to, she pulled up a chair to listen also as I absent-mindedly started on breakfast.

Fran was nervous. She seemed reluctant to continue.

"Go on, Grandma, finish the story," Ginger said.

I stopped eating and looked up. Granny was clearly not anxious to talk with Ginger here.

"Now, Ginger, you've heard about the Grand Opening before. Don't let me keep you from your work," Fran said.

"I'd rather listen to you than work, Grandma!" Ginger said.

Fran was trapped. This must be a part of her past she had not told anyone about before. She needed some time to think.

"Ginger, this is the best breakfast I've ever had!" I said, hoping to distract her.

"Thank you, Christopher. But you are not fooling me! What is it you don't want me to hear?" Ginger said, somewhat annoyed.

"A burden," Granny said. "One I've been carrying too long and one I don't wish upon you, or the rest of our family.

But if you insist, you must promise never to tell anyone. This may be the last chance I will ever have to tell this. I'd rather you didn't listen. This is something that Christopher must know..."

Ginger was looking up at the picture of Christian. Then she looked at me. Then at the picture again. Her eyes grew wide with the realization. My stomach was tightening. I too, knew that Granny was about to reveal a secret connection between Christian and myself. Fran sighed and started again.

"I suppose I did have a choice. I could have turned Mr. Big down. But I was young and foolish and desperate to leave this town. There was Catherine about to go to Florida and my parents who could never send me to Paris. I had too much to drink and was afraid of the consequences of refusing Mr. Big's offer. I've already told Christopher about the proposition he made me."

"I overheard that the other day, Grandma. You don't have to worry. I would love you no matter what! I have children of my own, you know. I'm not a little girl."

There were tears in Fran's eyes as she continued her story, holding Ginger's hand across the table. Ginger's eyes welled up also, and I was too choked up to eat, my fork suspended in mid-air.

"When dinner was over the dancing began again. Catherine's mother and father were the first on the floor. Soon everyone was up and a line had formed for all the single ladies. Catherine's father danced with her first and Christian looked on jealously, busy waiting on the guests. I sat at the table alone and watched, shaking my head at the gentlemen waiting to dance with me. I was not ready yet," Fran sipped some more tea before continuing, the tears dry now.

"I looked around the room at the tables. Mr. Big was gone and I did not see Christian anywhere. Then I spotted them in the hall near the rest rooms. Christian was pulling himself away from Mr. Big, who had a grip on his sleeve. He was shaking his head "No".

"Catherine's father was returning to his table and saw them talking also. He did not see Christian pulling away as he sat down but he was frowning. He knew his daughter was in love with Christian and did not want to see him involved with the gangsters.

"Mr. Big had offered Christian a place in his organization. Christian refused. I should have, too. Eventually, I did get up and dance. I don't know how many young men I had danced with while avoiding the dreaded Carlisle. Somehow I found myself in the middle of the floor with Mr. Big. That's when he made his offer."

I was drawn back in time again, seeing the events that Fran had described. Ginger was under the spell too, hearing things about her Grandmother she never knew before.

"As dusk drew near, Christian finally danced with Catherine."

"Oh, Christian! I can hardly wait until tomorrow!" Catherine was holding him tightly as they danced.

"Shh! Not too loud. People are listening! What would your parents say?"

"Let's not talk about my parents! Sometimes I think I'll never get away from them!"

"Okay. Look, the fireworks are starting! Where is Fran? I thought she wanted to watch them with us?" Christian was frowning as he searched the room.

"Probably off with some suitor." Catherine replied. "Let's pretend it's just you and me."

As they made their way to the deck overlooking the lake they did not see Fran and Mr. Big coming out of the restrooms and going up the stairs to the guest rooms. They disappeared un-noticed while the fireworks held everyone's attention.

THIRTY-THREE

Upstairs in the Honeymoon Suite, Fran was anxious and scared.

"Let's get started before I change my mind," the full impact of the agreement began to sink in.

"It's too late to change your mind, Fran," Mr. Big said as he took off his collar and began to unbutton his shirt.

"But," he continued, "I don't want any child of mine to say I raped his mother."

"I thought the child would never know," Fran's voice was quavering.

"Of course he won't know. But this isn't a perfect world, is it? Besides, we'll know."

"Yes, we'll know," Fran said, as she worked out of the evening dress.

The room had been prepared with champagne on ice and the lights were down low. Both of them stood for a moment in their underwear and sipped the champagne Mr. Big had poured. The fireworks lit the room with color as they watched from the window above the deck.

Fran would remember later that Mr. Big had been a gentle and respectful lover, making the arrangement a sweeter pill to swallow.

Below, on the deck, the guests stood and cheered at each new burst of celebration.

Christian put his arm around Catherine and she leaned into him. Her parents were watching but they smiled, holding each other the same way. There was something romantic in all the noise and smoke.

When the display drew to a close Fran appeared beside Catherine and her brother, smiling as if she had been there all the while.

Granny left us there!

"No more today, Christopher. The memories are too painful. That was the last time I saw Catherine or Christian or the Zimmermans. I would like to hold that picture just where it is."

I returned to the present with a chill. Ginger was crying softly. I could not get over the feeling that somehow I had been there, watching the events as they had happened.

"Sure, Fran. I think I need some time too." I was tiptoeing to the edge of the truth. Maybe it would have been easier to just jump in. But, like the cold water of the lake we wade in slowly, gradually adjusting to the truth. I knew I wasn't Granny's son but I could have been her grandson! That would explain my resemblance to Christian. That would mean I was Mr. Big's grandson! My whole life had been a lie!

But what about the research I had done into my family history? How could I have written *Stepping Stones*? I had to know what happened next! Did Fran have the baby? Was it Mr. Big's? How did I come to be a part of a different family? I knew my mother was...*adopted!* She must have been adopted! My grandparents were her adoptive parents...

Of course! My aunts had been involved with gangsters! There were three sisters. One who had married a dentist... one who would have raised a child away from the world of crime. One who would have adopted my mother!

Now I knew what the locket meant! It *was* the same locket that Catherine had given to Fran that night! That was the link between Catherine and myself. And Christian's blood, rather Fran's blood, ran in me also!

This is why I was drawn here!

"Christopher, are you all right? You look pale," Ginger was trying to snap me out of my thoughts.

"Yeah, I'm alright," I said as I stood up and turned toward the door.

Like a man in a trance I pushed open the screen door and walked into the summer sun without saying good-bye.

THIRTY-FOUR

I had been in a trance all week. Like a protective shell, a sort of hypnosis that said "Nothing can happen to you here. You'll wake up and everything will be fine."

I had come here to get back to work and recover from the shock of Marianne's death. Instead I had found more! Ghosts, tragedy and now the realization that the life I was so sure of and even had written a book about was not entirely true.

My own disclaimer ran through my mind. "This is a work of fiction...any resemblance to actual persons is entirely coincidental..."

But there was a resemblance! Christian! Fran's brother. Catherine Zimmerman's lover; now my great uncle!

Whether Fran told me or not, it was too obvious not to see that Mr. Big was my grandfather. My mother was his daughter! I came along late in her life, she was thirty-five when she had me. The math worked! She would have been born when Fran was twenty!

Again, I wanted to run away! But how do you run from the truth? It would follow me everywhere like Marianne's death, until I dealt with it.

I retreated to the present, looking at my watch and climbing back into the familiar comfort of the *Merc*. I left the radio off, determined to focus on the tasks at hand.

Tonight I was taking Betty Lou to The Resort. The dinner served two purposes, a way to thank her for the curtains that would be put up tomorrow and a chance to see the now-famous ballroom in person.

I had a deadline to reach also. I had a novel to deliver. I recalled the first three chapters and smiled. Not bad for a beginner!

Then I shook off the chill as I remembered the ghostly reader that had awakened me.

I started the car and turned towards the house. I could get a couple hours of work in this afternoon. I would turn my shock into energy and weave this new information into the story.

Writing was my therapy. It was my toes in the water. Gradually I would become used to the chill.

The crunching of rocks under the tires woke me from my trance and wide-awake I pulled the car up to the house, almost hitting an old pickup truck.

The front door was open and I walked in to see Pete standing on a short folding ladder, struggling the long white panel of drapery he was holding.

"Need a hand?" I asked, startling him almost off the ladder.

"Jeez! Scare a man to death why don't you?" He said, regaining his balance.

"Sorry, I didn't mean to sneak up on you. Looks like you're about done," I said.

"Got here this morning. No time to do it tomorrow. What with the bar-b-que and Phil and June coming."

"Where's Betty Lou?" I asked. "Didn't she come to help you?"

"She left just before you got here. Helped me hang the other panels. Said she had to get ready for her big date tonight. I've hung lots of jobs for her." Pete climbed down from the ladder the last panel finally hung."Looks great!" I said as I surveyed the windows. "Want a cold beer?"

"Sounds good. Need a break before I start on the yard."

"The yard?" I asked.

"Yeah, brought the rider. Mow it this afternoon for you. Tomorrow I'll bring the grill and table and Betty Lou will help with the fixin's."

"Pete, it's really good of you and Betty Lou to do all of this. What do I owe you?"

"Free food and a game of pool," he said as he followed me into the kitchen.

I reached into the fridge and took out a beer, realizing that I would have to go into town and buy supplies for the picnic.

"Well, I was going to do some writing today. Guess that can wait," I said, a little forlorn.

"Why? Betty Lou and June have done the shopping. And all the ladies are bringing something…" Pete's voice trailed off.

"*All* the ladies?" I asked suspiciously.

"Wasn't supposed to tell you. Supposed to be a surprise. Ginger, Fran, Martha, the girl scouts and Mr. Mooney's daughter…"

"What?" Now I was in shock again.

"Well, you *are* a celebrity. Big event around here. They wanted to throw a surprise party for you. A 'welcome' celebration. Guess I blew the surprise!"

"No you didn't. I'm definitely surprised! But what about the free food I owe you?" I asked.

"It is free. I didn't say you had to buy it. But I will hold you to the game of pool."

Pete emptied the can of beer and crushed it, handing it to me, as I stood there dazed.

Then he walked outside and down the steps to the mower waiting by the shed.

THIRTY-FIVE

I followed Betty Lou's directions to The Resort. It wasn't that far away. Many times in the past week I had seen its lights at night, shining across the lake from the Zimmerman House.

This was a Friday night and there were a lot of cars in the lot. The sign at the entrance proclaimed Steak n' Shrimp Night and live entertainment by The Fishermen, a local band.

I parked the car and Betty Lou waited while I got out and opened the door for her.I still had no idea how formal or informal The Resort was, but Betty Lou was not going to pass up being treated like a lady.

We walked up the half dozen steps to the double doors and I opened the door for my "date". She smiled and said "thank you" as we stepped inside.

A young man in a white waiter's uniform and a young woman behind the desk inside the entrance greeted us as we approached.

"Mr. Evans?" The young man said.

"Yes," I replied. "We have reservations…"

"Yes, I know. A pleasure to meet you, sir and a pleasure to see you again, Betty Lou. This is Gloria Rogers, our hostess and I am Robert."

"Well, it's nice to meet you both. Are you always so formal with your guests?" I asked.

"You are somewhat of a celebrity, Mr. Evans. I have read your book *Stepping Stones*, and recognize you from your picture. When I saw your name on the reservation list I was excited to meet you. Our manager asked me to call him when you arrived."

"Please, Robert, no publicity. We would just like a quiet dinner tonight," I explained.

"Of course, sir. Perhaps he could stop by your table?" Robert inquired.

"Sure, but no pictures, please," I was still wondering about the pictures from Mooney's.

"Oh, don't be such a stick in the mud, Christopher!" Betty Lou broke in. "Wouldn't you like to have your picture on the Wall of Celebrities? I would!"

"Let's find our table first. It was a pleasure meeting you, Gloria. Robert?" I prompted.

"Of, course. Follow me please," he replied and turned toward the dining room.

At least he hadn't said, "Walk this way."

We followed Robert as he led us to a front row table at the edge of the dance floor. The round tables were set up at the edge of the ballroom floor and on a raised balcony on two sides so that every table could view the stage and the large glass windows overlooking the deck and the lake. Ours was the center table and the only one empty. The "Reserved" sign was done in a style reminiscent of the Thirties.

Most of the tables were occupied and I was relieved to see people in semi-formal dress.

Opposite of the windows was a bar and several other tables. Here the people were in more casual dress and seated without reservations. The lake could be seen in the mirrors behind the bar as well as across the floor. Along the top of the mirror and on both sides was the Wall of Celebrities. The picture I had seen at Fran's was there as well as many others from Opening Night. There were pictures of the rich and famous, the rich and powerful and many notorious gangsters who had visited The Resort over the years. It was hard to imagine myself there.

I knew Betty Lou wouldn't mind her picture up there and I resigned myself to it as Robert seated us at the white linen table.

"This was supposed to be a quiet dinner with a little privacy," I said, grinning.

"Why, Christopher! Are you being romantic?" Betty Lou asked in a mock Southern accent.

"Well," I said, "You are a lady. It's just that I never have gotten used to celebrity-hood, and here we are front and center. What I really wanted was to thank you for helping me."

"Well! Should I take that as a rejection, Mr. Butler?" She said, assuming the role of Scarlet O'Hara.

She wasn't going to let me off the hook! I was glad to see the waiter arrive with the salads.

As we ate I decided to change tack.

"Would you like your picture taken?" I asked.

"Before you put your foot in your mouth I would have loved it! Now I'm not so sure." She was making me pay.

"I can understand them wanting your picture, Betty, but why they want mine I'll never know. I'm certainly not rich…"

"Charm won't get you off the hook, Christopher! When you ask a lady out for dinner she naturally assumes you have other things in mind."

"Forgive me. I guess I'm still avoiding relationships. I was hoping that out here I could finally put the past behind me. Diving into this new project was a sort of 'last resort' for me."

"Who said anything about a relationship? I was talking about *sex*," Betty Lou shocked me and then smiled. "I understand about Marianne, and I'm letting you off the hook. I should not have teased you that way. Of course I would like to have my picture taken with you! You are *somewhat* of a celebrity, anyway. And I like your book. You really are a great writer you know. I can't wait to read the next one!"

"Whew! And I thought I was in trouble!" I said, relieved that Betty Lou wasn't really upset.

"Oh, I didn't say you weren't in trouble, Buster! You better watch your step or I will just have to..."

She didn't get the chance to finish her sentence as the waiter returned with the food and the Manager.

"Good evening, Mr. Evans! And Betty Lou, you look splendid tonight!" He said. "Forgive me for interrupting your dinner, is everything satisfactory?"

I smiled and nodded.

"Allow me to introduce myself. I am Raymond Claiborne, manager of The Last Resort, and grandson of the original manager. I would like to ask you for a few minutes of your time after dinner. I need your help."

"It's a pleasure to meet you Raymond. I'm intrigued. If Betty Lou agrees we will see you after dinner," I said.

"Oh really, you two! Don't be so formal. Sure, Ray, we'll see you on the way out. Now we better eat before it gets cold." And she dug right in.

"Thank you, Betty. I'm sorry I interrupted," Ray said as he turned and quietly walked away, somewhat embarrassed.

"So much for an intimate dinner," Betty Lou said.

THIRTY-SIX

But it was an intimate dinner. There was only the sound of quiet conversations in the dining room and the tinkle of silverware occasionally striking a glass or plate. "The Fishermen" played quiet music through the dinner hour, promising to kick it up at ten o'clock.

We ate in silence for a while, embarrassed by the romantic setting and feeling awkward. By the time we had finished dessert, dusk was turning to dark and the moon rose over the lake, creating a shining pathway across the water to the deck of The Resort.

Fran's story of the Grand Opening replayed in my mind. Looking around at the other tables I did not see the people who were presently there but the people from Fran's story. Mr. Big and Albert and his wife would be sitting where we were now. Next to us would have been Catherine and Fran. Our waiter became Christian. Mr. Mooney was talking on the microphone and across the room near the windows sat Carlisle and the ladies of the evening.

I felt a chill running up my spine and I shook my head, feeling woozy and out of touch. The combination of the music and the conversation of two different times clashed in my ears.

"Betty Lou..." I started to say but was stopped by her upraised hand.

"Shh! Don't spoil it, Christopher! Most of the guys I've been here with take me to the bar. I know you're not looking right now, neither am I. But it isn't often I get taken to dinner by a celebrity and have a "Photo Op" too!"

"Would you like to stay for livelier music? Maybe dance?" I asked, determined to return fully to the present. Sure, I had wanted to see The Resort but in the safety of the here and now.

"No, I would rather have one slow dance with you and have Raymond take our picture. I would like to remember the occasion that way. Why don't you call him over?"

I looked around. It was dark outside now and the stars were bright. It was a perfect summer evening. A few couples were dancing to the slow music and Robert was standing at the edge of the dining room. Was it Robert or Christian? I still felt the presence of another time and nervously signaled the waiter.

Who would it be?

"Yes, Mr. Evans?" Robert said as he approached the table.

"Robert, we would like to have our picture taken on the dance floor. Please ask the manager to come to our table." I was relieved to see the present was back. I looked at Betty Lou and winked.

"Very impressive, Mr. Evans!" Betty Lou smiled back. "You know how to turn on the charm."

"Years of practice," I lied. "Actually it was watching lots of old movies."

Betty Lou laughed again as Raymond approached our table.

"How was your dinner?" He asked.

"Excellent! The steak was just right, and the wine was delicious. Ray, can I call you Ray? We would like our picture taken on the dance floor, and you are welcome to stop at the Zimmerman house tomorrow and join the picnic. What was it you needed my help with?" I asked.

"Well sir, we are planning a 4th of July celebration, an anniversary of the Grand Opening and closing out the old century. The year 2000 is not the new millennium but it does signal the end of an era. Your presence as an author and a guest at the Zimmerman house would be good publicity for the event," he said, hopefully.

Somehow it felt like I was meant to be a part of this.

"Well, why don't you join us tomorrow and we'll talk some more," I replied.

"Of course, Mr. Evans. It would be a pleasure to join you tomorrow. Meanwhile I will talk to the band and have the photographer ready."

"One more thing Ray, I would like to make this a special night for my friend Betty Lou," I said.

"I'll see to it, sir," he said, rising from the table.

We watched as he walked across the dance floor to the stage. A few couples were still dancing and he was careful not to interfere. He skirted the floor and approached the stage from the side, talking quietly to the piano player.

As the song ended, he walked up the steps and talked to the lead singer. Then Ray took the mike.

"Ladies and gentlemen how about a round of applause for The Fishermen!"

There was a round of applause and hoots from the bar also. I was glad Betty Lou hadn't wanted to stay for the livelier music. I did not want to find myself dancing with a ghost.

"Now, before we kick it up a bit, we have a special selection. A spotlight dance for our honored guests, the author Christopher Evans and his lovely companion, Betty Lou Brown!"

The noise quieted down as the band began to play *Strangers On the Shore* with a classic saxophone and the lights dimmed, revealing the moon and stars reflecting on the water outside.

Betty and I had the floor to ourselves for the spotlight dance as the photographer moved around us, shooting from different angels as we waltzed.

About halfway through the song, Raymond took the microphone again.

"How about joining our lovely couple, folks?"

The floor began to fill and we were suddenly in the middle of a dozen couples while the sax continued to play.

As the song ended, the dancers broke into applause again.

The lights came up and we made our way back to the table.

Sitting down, I motioned for the check.

Robert came to the table, smiling and applauding.

"You looked great out there!" He said.

"Thanks, Robert. It's been a great evening. Could we have the check please?" I said.

"Compliments of The Last Resort, sir. Enjoy your evening. A pleasure to see you again, Betty Lou." And making a slight bow he turned and walked away.

Betty Lou rose from her chair.

"I must get home before the coach turns into a pumpkin, Chris."

"Yes," I said, standing also, "Tomorrow will be a busy day."

"I'm still on tonight, tomorrow can wait," she replied.

I turned for one more look at the lake and felt a chill run down my spine.

Standing on the deck was a young woman dressed in white, one hand reaching toward her neck and clutching the gold chain of a locket.

THIRTY-SEVEN

I did my best on the way to Betty Lou's not to break her glass slipper. Although she rode in the passenger seat next to me I felt someone else's presence in the car. My eyes were drawn to the rearview mirror again and again. Would I see Catherine's ghost in the back seat?

I reached for the radio to break the tension but Betty Lou's hand intercepted mine.

"I'm still hearing *Strangers On The Shore*, Christopher. I want to hold that a little longer. It's not midnight yet and I want to be Cinderella."

"Okay," I said, returning to silence and shielding my thoughts from her. The ride was maddening! No one had ridden there since Marianne and when I looked over at Betty Lou, I saw Marianne instead.

How many women was I riding with?

If Betty Lou had noticed my state of mind she didn't say. I walked her to her door and said I would see her tomorrow.

The coach had turned into a pumpkin again and I did not kiss her goodnight.

She smiled anyway and thanked me for the lovely evening.

I turned towards the Merc' and smiled at Marianne, the only woman in my heart.

Turning on the oldies station I heard the familiar sounds of a saxophone playing *Strangers On The Shore...*

The notes still haunted me as I crashed on the daybed of The Zimmerman House hugging the pillow that had become Marianne...

It was a strange dream. There was Marianne on the dance floor of The Last Resort, alone under the spinning ball, turning gracefully under the glittering lights and looking out at the darkened faces at the tables.

I saw myself in a white tuxedo joining her for the spotlight dance. The faceless crowd stood and applauded as we bowed and left the floor, Marianne's gown of white and glitter flowing out behind her.

Like Fred Astair and Ginger Rogers we left them in their standing ovation.

Not such a strange dream at all, really.

I was awake now, or so I thought. I laid there for a few minutes listening to the forlorn sound of a far off train. The light of the full moon through the windows gave the house a ghostly look.

My eyes struggled to make out the dim-lit shadows that seemed to move in the darkness. I waited for them to adjust and reassure me that the shapes were solid after all.

I avoided looking at the clock, knowing I had to be up early for the picnic. I would be glad when it was over and I could finally get down to writing.

There! Wait! Something did move! White gown...no, it was nothing.

"Come on Christopher!" I said out loud, "Remember where you are! This house is haunted. I am not afraid of you! Come out, Catherine! Enough of this cat and mouse game! You said we should meet on The Bridge. Is this the appointed time?" I was sitting on the edge of the bed now, my heart beating faster by the second. I struggled to slow it down, determined to stay in control. Catherine was a peaceful ghost, I told myself. She had not harmed me, always staying one step away and leaving poems.

I had already theorized that the house was The Bridge and the river was time. In her time she was still alive and I would be the ghost. In my time, she was the ghost. At some point as the house moved backward in time, seeming to restore itself along the way, we would meet and talk face to face.

"Catherine! Come out! Please let me see you..."

I was interrupted by the sound of wood crashing and splintering. It was a violent sound accompanied by desperate heavy breathing and the sound of a snarl beneath it. I held my ears as the sounds grew louder and the faint shapes of chairs in the room began falling over and thudding on the floor.

The blinds clashed with the windows one by one and objects hurled themselves from their shelves flying through the darkness.

I covered my head to protect myself and dove for the light. This was a side of Catherine I had not seen before! What had I done to make her so angry?

"Catherine! Stop, please! What have I done to you? Why would you do this to me?"

The light switched on and the room was quiet. Once again I had to adjust my eyes. I looked around the room for the signs of carnage.

There was none. Now my heart was really pounding. I stood still and quiet for a moment, willing it to slow down. I couldn't even think of a snappy line to help me out.

Now I knew fear again! I still could not understand Catherine's outburst. Was she a schizophrenic? Had *she* murdered her family? Or was this a young girl's tantrum?

I called out again.

"Catherine? Is that you? Are you still there?"

I moved to the desk and switched on the computer. Perhaps she left a message.

"Catherine? Marianne?" Of course! Marianne was here and angry with me for taking Mary Lou to dinner...

The monitor lit up as the sound of desperate pounding came from upstairs. Catherine's door! As if she was locked in!

The pounding went on and was joined by a wailing sound. My skin crawled as I listened and turned to the two words on the monitor...

NOT CATHERINE!

My shoulders hunched in a sudden chill as I looked down at the desktop, now covered in dust.

Some unseen movement drew my eyes there as the pounding continued.

"Not Catherine? Then who?" I asked.

I froze like a Popsicle in the winter as I watched an invisible finger draw letters in the dust.

R...O...S...E!

It was suddenly quiet.

THIRTY-EIGHT

I must have passed out. I woke up in the morning to the sound of banging on the door. The sun was just beginning to rise. I must have slept a few hours at the most.

The pounding on the door coincided with the pounding in my head.

"Okay! Okay! I'm coming!" I shouted as I sat up and tried to straighten my hair and the pants I had slept in. I could not figure out who was knocking so early. I made it to the door and turned the polished knob.

"Hey Chris!" It was Pete.

"Hey, Pete!" I mimicked.

"Man, what happened to you? Must have been some date you had with my sister last night," he chided.

"Despite my appearance, I was a perfect gentleman!" I defended myself from his brotherly wrath.

"Yeah, I know. She complained about it for two hours," he laughed, and then continued, "you'll get another shot at it in a couple of hours."

"Another shot? Couple of hours?" I was confused.

"Yeah, man it's Saturday! Big picnic, remember? Half the town will be here!

"The picnic! Now I remember!" The events after last night were pushed to the back of my sleepy mind as alarms went off in my head. I had to play celebrity today!

"That's why I'm here so early! To help you set up!" Pete explained.

I looked beyond him at the sun rising over the lake. I was fully awake now.

"What time did you say they were coming?" I asked.

"Betty Lou will be here at nine with the Girl Scouts. I'm going to start unloading the picnic tables. Can you give me a hand?"

"Sure," I said.

I went back to the daybed and slipped on my shoes. So Betty Lou was disappointed, eh? I was flattered.

The sockless shoes made sticky sounds on my feet as they crunched over the small rocks on the dirt driveway.

Hefting the first of three picnic tables stacked in the bed of Pete's pickup I heard the Everly Brothers singing *Hello Mary [Betty] Lou-Goodbye Heart.* I smiled as we set the table in place and went back for another. This was going to be an interesting day!

THIRTY-NINE

A shave and a shower later I was ready to face the world. I didn't want to admit it but I had missed being in the spotlight. Maybe being here was a good thing for me, I thought as I slid on clean socks and clean black slacks. I did not want to dress up for a picnic but I still wanted to look sharp.

I chose a two-toned pullover sport shirt with short sleeves and a pair of black loafers. There! The writer at play!

Pete had been working while I was getting dressed. The picnic tables were in place and there was a large mound of charcoal on the grill.

I stepped out onto the porch. It was seven-thirty and the dew was still on the summer grass. I looked at the sky for signs of rain.

"Weatherman says it will be in the eighties today," Pete said. "No sign of rain."

"That's good to know!" I said as I walked down the steps.

I looked around. It was amazing how different the place looked! Everything looked new and full of life. Was it the house or was it me?

"Yard looks great, Pete! Hey thanks for coming by early and getting me up! You eaten yet?" I asked as my stomach growled.

"Nope. You offerin?"

"Well, it's a long time to the burgers. You want some eggs? I can't make 'em like Marianne did but they're edible."

"Maybe I should cook them," Pete said, smiling.

"I hate to have a guest do the cooking," I said.

"Okay, I'll take my chances. I'll be cookin' burgers and hot dogs later though."

"Won't argue with you there, Pete. Come on in."

Walking back up the porch steps I noticed how natural it felt to be here. It had hardly been a week and yet I felt as if I had lived here all of my life. The house had changed in this short time also. Though I hadn't really done anything it was bright and shiny. The wood had new life in it, as did the paint. The brass was gleaming and rich and the swing on the porch no longer squeaked on rusty chains.

It all seemed perfectly natural to me.

Inside the kitchen I opened the fridge and found a carton of eggs. There was a pound of bacon also. I could not remember if I had bought them or not. I found a cast iron skillet waiting in the oven and lit the burner under it. Soon the bacon was sizzling and the sweet smell of a country breakfast filled the air.

The cupboard held a set of dishes that I hadn't seen before and there was silverware in the drawer. I shrugged and set the table as Pete found an old percolator and a can of Folgers on the counter. Soon the aroma of coffee mingled with the bacon.

Perfectly natural, I said to myself. Seek and ye shall find, ask and receive...

I began to chuckle at my thoughts. *If this were a ghostly breakfast would it be fattening?*

Pete looked at me with a puzzled look on his face.

"Mind tellin' me what's so funny?" He said, a little defensively.

"Nothing, really." I said as I cracked the eggs in the pan. They sizzled, spit and looked quite real. "It's just that none of these things were here yesterday," I continued dramatically and laughed again.

Now Pete began to laugh! Soon we were both laughing like a couple of kids. As we sat down to eat the bacon and eggs there were tears streaming down our faces. The food was getting cold as we tried to eat between the laughing fits.

I finally willed myself to settle down enough to ask Pete what *he* was laughing about.

"Nothing," he said as he munched on the bacon, "I brought the groceries and pan in while you were in the shower!"

The laughter erupted again and though I don't remember how the food tasted it was one of the best breakfasts I had ever had.

I think we were still chuckling when the cars pulled in precisely at 9 a.m. We were certainly in the mood for a fun day. I hadn't felt this good in a long time and I hoped that nothing would happen to spoil it.

FORTY

They wouldn't let me do anything! Betty Lou, Pete and half a dozen Girl Scouts took over! Folding chairs and table covers appeared out of nowhere as well as coolers with pop and beverages, pitchers with lemonade and beer for the "adults".

Mr. Mooney and his daughter arrived in a vintage '49 Merc, chopped and customized with flames running along the black fenders. It was his prized possession. The car was loaded with his famous broasted chicken!

Fran and Ginger arrived with ice cream from the shop towed in a special trailer behind Mike's pickup. The kids rode with Dad in the car.

Mike had brought the hamburgers and hot dogs, and soon Pete set the huge mound of charcoal on fire.

I sat down on the porch swing, overwhelmed. It was all like a circus. How I wished Marianne were here with me!

I looked around through misty eyes. This was so much like a family picnic. Like the ones I remembered and the ones I spent with Marianne and her family so long ago.

I had been alone for so long! Someone had brought a "boom box" and soon the oldies station was playing through the happy noise as everyone went about their assigned tasks turning the yard into picnic grounds.

More cars pulled in, arranging themselves diagonally alongside the driveway out of the way.

Here was Phil, June, and Raymond from The Last Resort, who I had met last night. There was a mini pickup with a reporter from The Annandale *Times*, camera slung across her shoulder and making her way through the crowd asking questions. Someone pointed me out and she smiled, waved and headed my way.

I sensed she wanted an invitation and a story.

Ray had found Pete and was busy setting up an amplifier and a microphone.

Soon the young reporter with dark shoulder length hair was at the top of the porch and I stood to introduce myself.

I didn't get the chance! Raymond vaulted the steps three at a time, arriving just in time to take over the introductions.

"Julie Ackerman! How nice to see you! Allow me to introduce the famous author Christopher Evans."

"Hello, Ray," she said, rolling her eyes. "Can't resist a little free publicity can you?"

Ray smiled and shrugged as she turned to me.

"Mr. Evans, it's a pleasure to meet you! I have to tell you I loved *Stepping Stones*. I apologize for not contacting you earlier, but I heard about the "surprise" event today. Would you mind if I stayed?"

"Of course not. You are welcome, Julie. It's a pleasure to meet you." I said, wondering what to say next.

"Of course, I would love the chance to interview you also, for the paper and I brought my copy of your book..." she prompted.

"You know," I said as I looked out at all the people and activity in the yard, "I would like to make an announcement."

I walked down the steps leaving Julie and Ray staring at each other and made my way through the crowd. Nodding at people and saying "Hi", I walked through the smoke of the grill and the smells of the food to the microphone, which had been set up in front of Catherine's garden.

I tapped on the mike a few times and adjusted the volume on the amplifier. Someone turned off the boom box cutting the Beach Boys off in the middle of Daddy taking the T-Bird away.

Eventually I had everyone's attention.

"Good morning! Thank you all for coming. I would like to take this opportunity to introduce Raymond from The Last Resort. Come on up here Ray…

There was a scattering of applause as Raymond, looking surprised and eager strode up to the microphone.

Raymond reached for the microphone, but I pulled it away.

"There is another event coming up that Ray would like to tell you about," I said as I finally handed him the mike.

"Well, hi everyone," Ray's voiced boomed out as the amp squealed. "I would like to invite you all to the Re-Grand Opening of The Last Resort. It's a kick-off celebration of the end of an era and the end of the Millennium. July 4th marks the 66th year of operation of Annandale's oldest and most famous resort. At that time we will place the noted author Christopher Evans' picture on our Wall of Fame with all of the other celebrities who have graced The Resort since its opening. With your permission, Mr. Evans," he added, turning to me.

"Of course, I'd be honored." I said, as he handed me back the microphone. Julie walked up, taking pictures and wearing a tape recorder. We smiled for the camera, shaking hands.

"Now," I continued. "I know that other people have planned this day so I am going to turn the event over to Betty Lou, but first I want to take this opportunity to give something in return. I cannot accept all of this fuss just for me. I propose we take a collection up for the hard-working Girl Scouts who are here today. I am sure their troop could use some extra funds. How about kicking it off, Raymond?"

"As the manager of The Last Resort, I hereby donate $100." There was a round of applause and soon people had their checkbooks out.

"I'll match it!" I said. "Betty Lou, come on up and take over."

I handed off the microphone to Betty Lou and looked around for a place to sit.

Ginger smiled and held up a Coke and I joined her and Granny at a table in the shade.

"Nice going, Mr. Evans, that was a neat way to get yourself off the hook!" Ginger said as she handed me the Coke.

"I like to start things." I said.

"Better get yourself some food, Christopher," Granny said as I sat down, "before Phil and June descend on you."

I looked up to see the awed look on Phil's face as he stared at the house and grounds. Shaking his head he looked like a victim of *The Twilight Zone*. I could read his thoughts.

When had all of this happened?

They caught me by the grill as Pete put a dog and burger on my plate.

"Chris!" Phil said. "I would like you to meet my wife June."

"A pleasure. I think there is room at our table. Won't you join us? Right now I'm going to load my plate," I said, eyeing the corn on the cob.

"Sure. We'll meet you over there," Phil said as June smiled.

I looked over at the table. Ginger, Fran, and Mr. Mooney were already eating. Mike was still grilling with Pete and the kids had all banded together by the edge of the garden away from the adults. Betty Lou had left the microphone after turning over the activities to the Girl Scout Troop Leader and was talking to Julie the reporter.

The weather was holding out and the radio was back in play. I sat at the table across from Fran next to Mr. Mooney who looked to see if I had some broasted chicken on my plate.

"Of course I do!" I said. "And I'll be going back for more!"

His mock frown turned into a smile and he slapped me on the back with a laugh. It all felt so natural.

FORTY-ONE

What felt natural, I finally realized, was the feeling of being detached. Of watching from the outside. Part of me was always the writer, always observing other people who seemed totally immersed in their lives.

In a strange way, this was how I coped with new things. How I could deal with all the strange events that had taken place this last week and still hear myself say how natural it all felt.

Even as Granny was talking and telling stories of the house and Catherine, I heard Gilbert O'Sullivan singing *Alone again, naturally*.

"Christopher! You haven't heard a word I've said!" Granny was scolding me.

"I'm sorry, Fran. What were you saying?" I asked, dazed.

"I was just saying how much Catherine loved that garden. I used to stand and watch her at work in it. She used to get her hands in the dirt and talk about being a writer someday. She would have been a good one, too!"

I felt a chill in the air. The sky was clouding up and a breeze from the north brought a rush of cold air. It was getting toward noon and the warm summer morning looked as though it would turn stormy.

I felt another chill as Granny talked about Catherine's writing. I had seen some of it but could not tell the others. Catherine was still writing.

The others at the table felt the cold too. They hunched a little closer to their food and began to look nervous. The whole tone of the picnic had changed.

Ginger spoke up. "Granny, I think we should change the subject."

Just then there was a scream from one of the Girl Scouts near the garden!

Everyone froze. "A head! It's a head!" The girl screamed out.

Clumsily, I climbed out of the picnic table and ran to the semi-circle of scouts huddled near the edge of the garden.

Pete dropped his spatula and ran over too.

We all looked down at the object of horror.

It was a skull. A dog's skull. Lying near it was a weathered strip of leather. Obscured by a bush at the edge of the garden, it had gone un-noticed all these years. I picked up the strip of leather. The remains of a collar, it was embossed with the name Scout.

Ginger and Granny had walked over and I could see tears in the old woman's eyes.

"Scout. Dear Scout. So that's where you've been all this time! Waiting for Catherine and Christian to return." Granny said, forlornly.

"You see," she continued, "They would meet over the wall — and if Albert wasn't home, Christian would come into the garden and sit with Catherine. They would hide by the bush and Scout would lie alongside, keeping watch. After their deaths he ran through the streets back and forth to the cemetery and the garden. Searching and waiting with his broken heart."

The story touched everyone. The clouds broke up and the warm summer day returned. Slowly everyone returned to the picnic and the girls ran off to talk about their adventure and tell the story of the two lovers.

Pete had gotten a shovel and dug a grave for Scout, burying what he could find of him with his collar.

Granny, Ginger and I stood in attendance and said one last goodbye to the faithful dog.

Gilbert O's song was still playing in my head as Pete placed a hastily made cross on the makeshift grave.

Alone again, naturally.

FORTY-TWO

I stood by the garden lost in thought as Granny and Ginger made their way back to the table.

"Are you coming, Christopher?" Ginger asked, looking over her shoulder as she held Granny's arm.

"In a minute." I smiled weakly, wanting to be alone.

An only child whose mother had died, I was used to being by myself. Gilbert's song had a special significance for me. I hadn't known my father, either.

I laughed at my earlier smugness about staying detached. I hadn't stayed "detached" when Marianne died.

That's why I spent the last two years in depression and was now facing a deadline on my contract. That's what had led me here.

My mood turned dark again and so did the sky. It looked like we'd get that storm after all.

As the first drops of summer rain began to splash on the tables, people began to groan and pack up. Cars were already pulling out of the yard as I walked back to the table, waving back at the fleeing picnickers.

Pete held out at the grill as long as he could, finally closing the lid as I reached the table. Cold splashes of rain pinged loudly on the metal surface and the wind began to pick up.

Mr. Mooney and his daughter had packed the car and said goodbye, leaving only Granny, Ginger, Phil and June at the table, with several buckets of broasted chicken destined for the fridge.

Mike and the kids had left with the Girl Scouts. Betty Lou was approaching the table, holding a notebook over her head.

"Hey," she said, "we raised $350 for the Girl Scouts!"

"That's great!" I said, looking around for any stragglers. Raymond had monopolized the reporter and both had left the party.

"Well, looks like we'll have to move inside," I said, sensing that these guests were not ready to leave. I knew Phil and June were anxious to see the inside of the house.

"Yes, let's see those curtains you bought from Betty Lou," Phil said, looking at June.

"Oh, yes, let's do!" She replied on cue.

I smiled and shrugged. This would be a surprise I would enjoy!

The rain was falling hard now and any thoughts of leaving were gone. The closest shelter was the house and the others waited as Pete and I helped Fran up the steps of the porch.

Opening the front door we stepped inside the once derelict haunted house.

Fran nearly fainted and Pete and I helped her to a chair in the living room.

Ginger rushed to her side. "Grandma, are you alright?" She asked.

"Yes, I'm alright, but the house, it looks just like it did when I was a girl!"

Phil and June were standing in shock also. "How did you do all this, Christopher? WHEN did you do all this? I hope you don't expect me to pay for it?" Phil said, worriedly.

"Yes, Christopher. How *did* you do it? It didn't look like this when Pete and I hung the curtains! Sure, it looked pretty good, but this…" Betty's voice trailed off.

Pete just shrugged.

"I told you curtains would do wonders for this place!" I said, smiling.

Everyone complimented Betty Lou on the craftsmanship of the draperies and how she had captured the "feel" of the house. She blushed, basking in the praise.

The sound of the wind and rain increased and we lapsed into silence.

Pete wandered into the kitchen and put on a pot of coffee. Ginger followed with a packet of tea from Granny's purse. June and Betty Lou joined them.

Pete returned to the living room. "They kicked me out," he explained.

The familiar sound of dishes rattling took some of the strangeness away and we all began to relax.

"I'd like to see the rest of the house." Phil spoke up, breaking the lull.

"Sure, Phil. It is your house. And don't worry, you won't get a bill." I said leading the way to the study.

Pete stayed behind with Fran while they waited for the coffee and tea.

"I can't believe you did all of this in such a short time," Phil said as he ran his hand over the polished wood desk that had once belonged to Albert Zimmerman.

"And you still had time to write?" He continued, eyeing the manuscript stacked neatly by the computer.

"I had help." I replied with no further explanation.

He poked his head into the bathroom noting the polished tiles and the shining fixtures. Even the wallpaper looked new.

Leaving the bathroom he popped his head into the bright shiny kitchen and shot a bewildered look to Ginger and June and Betty Lou as the teapot began to whistle.

The coffee was bubbling in the percolator and there were cookies on a platter and sandwiches from the washed-out picnic.

"Let's finish the tour later," I said. "Looks like we have refreshments."

"Okay, but I want to see the rest of the house," Phil replied.

"Of course. You *are* the owner," I smiled, wondering what I was apologizing for. The house looked totally restored.

Following Ginger and June, we returned to the living room with the coffee and tea.

Fran was composed again and took the cup Ginger was offering. Sipping at her tea, she noticed the pictures of Albert and Rose and Catherine.

"Just like they were the last time I saw them," she marveled.

I knew we were in for another story.

FORTY-THREE

The summer rain outside came with a chill, as the dark clouds hid the afternoon sun.

We felt it as Granny sipped her tea and began to talk about the past.

"You know," she said between sips, "they say Rose killed her family. I never believed it. I never believed she killed Christian, either. I think it had something to do with the money Albert was skimming from Mr. Big. The money everyone came looking for and no one ever found."

The thunder of the afternoon storm seemed to punctuate her words. I looked at Phil and June who had both looked up at the mention of money. They were listening now!

Granny looked at them, then me, as she continued.

"I think Mr. Big had found out and he came after it. That was the reason Albert was hiding money in this house. So they could escape if Mr. Big ever turned on them. You see, he was the silent partner in The Resort. Now that it was open he had what he wanted and did not need Albert anymore."

The pieces fell into place in my mind and I knew Granny would not reveal the other reason Mr. Big wanted The Resort. Ginger and I kept quiet about Fran's part. About the baby she had for him who would one day own The Resort. Only, it was a girl. She would not inherit it. Instead it would fall to her first male child or grandchild.

Granny looked at the pictures again.

"Those pictures were taken on Catherine's graduation day. They were planning to leave for their other home in Florida after The Resort opened. I was there when that was taken." Her eyes glazed over with tears and her voice trailed off. Her teacup held suspended between her mouth and the plate on her lap.

Phil broke the trance. "What about the money, Fran?"

Fran's eyes flashed. "Yes Phil, *what about* the money? You never found it, did you? If you had, you and June would have been long gone! I heard how you punched the holes in the walls looking for the loot! I know June has never been happy here and you bought this house in hopes of owning the treasure! My brother and my friend died for that money! Now you want to ruin this fine old house too!"

Ginger stood up and came to Granny's side. "Hush, Grandma. Don't get so excited. It's not good for your heart."

"Don't worry child. I'm not going anywhere. I won't leave until the story is over. And it's not over yet!"

Betty Lou looked at Pete. "Say, why don't we take a look at what Christopher has done with the house?"

Her cheerful tone of voice broke the tension in the room as the storm lightened to a refreshing rain.

We walked into the study, Ginger holding Fran's arm. As they passed the desk, Fran looked down at a sheet of paper, which I had not seen there before.

She picked it up and read, tears welling up again. She handed it to me and said. "Did you write this, Christopher?"

I took it from her and shook my head. No, I had not written it. The tears welled up in my eyes too as I read Catherine's latest poem.

FORTY-FOUR

WORLDS APART

Do not cry for me my friend
Though we may be worlds apart
The picture in your locket
Keeps me close to your heart.

I must leave
You must stay
We cannot hold
Time at bay.

Do not cry for me my friend
As I won't cry for you
We will always be together
No matter what we do.

You will seek your dream
As I am seeking mine
May your path be pleasant
As we leave our works behind.

Do not cry for me my friend
Though we may be worlds apart
Part of you is with me
Locked within my heart.

Catherine

I passed the page to Ginger amid the wondering looks of the others. She seemed to understand it was written for Fran and without reading it she folded it and put it in her purse.

"Hey, what about the rest of us?" Phil said, obviously curious about the monetary value.

"Oh Phil! Can't you see it's private?" Betty Lou spoke up. "Come on, let's take a look at the rest of the house... Christopher, where did you get that screen?"

I turned to see what Betty Lou was talking about. There in front of the daybed was a six-foot tall oriental screen. It was in three hinged sections on black painted wood. Each panel was done in beautifully painted seashell and depicted geishas in front of a temple with carved dragons on the pillars.

We walked over for a closer look. Behind it was a fireplace where an empty bookcase had been before. The daybed was gone!

Even Pete was surprised at this. Phil almost fainted and June was in shock.

"One week is not enough time to have done all of this! Christopher, what is going on?" Phil asked, shaking off another chill.

"You wouldn't believe me if I told you, Phil," I replied.

"I know that screen!" Fran spoke up. "Rose loved going to the Orient. Each year she would take a trip there and return home with a new treasure. On that trip she took Catherine. She had let Catherine pick it out and when they returned she couldn't wait to show it to me."

"It is beautiful!" June said, reaching out to touch it, running her fingers along the gowns of the geishas. "Funny I've never seen it before. It must be worth a fortune. I thought the looters had gotten everything."

"Let's go upstairs. Maybe there are more treasures!" Phil had gotten over his fear.

"I don't think this is a good time, Phil." Pete spoke up. Christopher has a lot of work to do and a short time to do it. Why don't we let him finish it? The house is obviously in good hands."

"You're keeping something from me, Pete. What is it you don't want me to see?" Phil sounded threatening.

"If you're worried about the money Phil, don't. I don't need it," I said, breaking in. "I just need to write. Don't you trust me?" I asked.

"Sure, I trust you. You can't blame me for wondering though. Something strange is happening here."

"Ginger, please take me home," Fran spoke up. "I need to rest now."

"Sure, Grandma. June, Betty Lou, please help me take her to the car."

June seemed relieved and anxious to get outside. This was all too strange for her.

The rain had stopped and the moisture in the air magnified the warm afternoon sun. The day had turned humid.

The spell had been broken and Phil returned to his more congenial state.

"I guess I should be going, too. House looks great, Christopher! We'll see you at the Grand Opening of The Resort, eh?"

"Sure Phil. I'll be there." I smiled warmly and he smiled back, all traces of tension gone.

"Betty Lou and I will be there too!" Pete said, sticking out his hand.

"Well, we'll see you there too, then," Phil said, shaking Pete's outstretched hand.

I followed them down the porch steps and stopped to say good-bye to Fran and Ginger.

"Come for breakfast tomorrow, Christopher!" Granny ordered, squeezing my hand.

"I will," I said, catching the hidden meaning.

Phil and June had started their car and waved as they drove off. I wondered what they were thinking, or planning.

Betty Lou and Pete stayed as the two cars drove off. Pete looked at the devastation from the picnic.

"Guess we got some cleanup to do," he said, looking at the wet plates and papers strewn about by the storm.

"I'll get it. You've worked enough today," I said.

"Tell you what," Pete said, looking at Betty Lou, "If you got a couple of beers we'll stay and help. You've got work to do."

"Yes," Betty Lou said, "We won't take no for an answer. You get the beers and I'll crank the tunes!"

I couldn't argue with both of them so I went to the fridge to get the beer. Outside Betty Lou had found the radio and I heard Glenn Miller's *In The Mood* playing in the yard.

"Hey, " I said, as I stepped out onto the porch holding the beer, "what happened to the oldies station? I was hoping for some Beach Boys at least."

"Funny thing, this is all I could find," Betty Lou said, taking the bottle. "Must be swing day."

We got into the "swing" and soon the cleanup was done. But I had not gotten any writing done, though.

It was getting dark when Pete and Betty Lou drove off. I stood and watched their taillights as they pulled onto the road. I made a note to myself to talk to Pete about today. It almost seemed like he knew more about the house and Catherine than he was telling me.

It wasn't the first time this week that I'd felt terribly alone.

FORTY-FIVE

Another Saturday Night and I ain't got nobody... I recited the words from an old Sam Cooke song as I walked up the porch steps. I had to admit to myself that I was a little disappointed that Betty Lou had not stayed. For so long now I had spent Saturday nights alone, reliving memories of Marianne.

"Ain't got no body..." I smiled at the ghostly reference. I really wasn't alone. I was surrounded by ghosts!

It was hard enough to write in the summer. All around there were people on vacation or going fishing or camping or boating. Being across from The Resort did not help either. I could see the lights shimmering in the lake and hear strains of music floating across the water.

With a sigh I turned and opened the front door, stepping into my strange new world.

I was determined to write.

The computer was still sitting on the desk. Nothing had changed in the last few hours. The "swing" music from the radio was still playing in my head, helping to get me *In The Mood*.

The hum of the processor soon lulled me into a trance-like state and my fingers began to fly across the keys. The story poured out onto the paper almost by itself. When I looked up again two hours had gone by and another chapter was complete.

I sat proofreading what I had just written. Not too bad, some minor errors that spell check could fix.

As I read in the silence of the green shaded desk lamp I heard a creak in the floorboards upstairs! I froze!

Was someone in here with me? The ghosts I had been pushing to the back of my mind came rushing forward now and my heart was pounding like a drum!

I sat very still and listened.

There it was again!

Gathering my courage, I reminded myself that nothing had hurt me so far. I pushed my chair back and stood up slowly, quietly.

The sound seemed to come from Catherine's room. I felt myself pulled to the stairway.

I stood at the bottom looking up. The upstairs hall light was on and cast long shadows of the banister onto the moonlit floor next to me. Who had turned it on?

Clutched by fear I climbed the steps one by one and found myself outside of Catherine's door.

Heart pounding in my ears, I turned the knob and the door swung open!

There in front of me was a wild-eyed Rose! Her hair flying over her shoulders she looked at me with bloodshot eyes holding an axe over her head, poised to strike!

Terror flung me back and I struggled to keep my balance as I backed away and turned to the stairway. My hand missed the railing and I tripped on the top step, falling clumsily down the rest.

My head hit the hardwood floor as I landed and I was sure that this was the end. Everything was dark now.

FORTY-SIX

"Christopher! Christopher! Wake up!" A lovely voice was pulling me back to life.

"Marianne?" I asked, eyes still closed.

"No." A saddened voice replied.

I opened my eyes. I was still lying on the hard wood floor. Bent over me was a lovely young girl in a white dress. She looked familiar.

"Catherine?" I sat up in shock. "Am I dead?"

"No. You are on The Bridge between life and death. This is the appointed time."

I rose to my feet surprised that I was not stiff and sore from the fall.

"How can this be?" I asked as my head cleared.

"This is the place where I died. This is the way I died. But my spirit was not ready to leave this world. Your sprit is not ready to leave. You have not died. Your energy has moved this house back in time drawn to my energy locked in 1934. As long as we are on The Bridge we can see and talk to each other. Through my mind and my memories you can live in my time," she explained.

"You mean I can walk around in 1934?"

"Yes. But not the way you think. Here, you are the ghost. Since you don't exist yet, no one can see you or hear you."

"Why am I here?"

"To learn the truth."

"About what?"

"What you already know. Who you really are and what really happened here. Only by telling the story can Rose and I rest. Only then will I be released and join Christian."

"Then it was you guiding my writing. You who drew me to this house."

"Really Christopher! The universe must balance. Everything will be perfected. Do you really think that we have that kind of power?"

I started to answer as she pulled the locket from the front of her dress. Holding it before me she began to swing it back and forth in a hypnotic fashion.

"Look at the locket, Christopher. Let your mind go. It is 1934. When you awake I will be real and you will be the ghost. Until you awake the second time you will remain here."

I watched the locket swing back and forth like the pendulum of a clock. Soon I was under its spell. Everything went dark, again.

FORTY-SEVEN

I felt the sunlight in my eyes and woke up. I was lying on the floor at the bottom of the stairs.

"Boy, what a dream!" I said out loud as I came to.

I stood up.

"Did I really fall down the steps?"

I checked myself for bumps and bruises.

"Guess not. I don't feel stiff or sore."

I walked back to the study and looked at the desk. My computer was gone!

"Whoa! What's going on here?" I asked myself.

Before I could answer I heard a woman's voice.

"Catherine! Get up! Breakfast is almost ready!"

It was coming from the kitchen.

I could smell the coffee bubbling in the old percolator and I followed the aroma.

The woman in front of the stove was not Mrs. Olson from the old Folgers Coffee commercials. It was Rose. Not the apparition I had seen upstairs but a young Rose as she appeared in 1934.

She wore a white ruffled apron over a print summer dress and held a spatula instead of an axe. Melting a chunk of real butter in a cast iron fry pan, she called out again.

"Catherine! Are you up? Breakfast is almost ready!"

"Yes, Mother! I'm up!" Catherine walked up behind her from the study.

Startled, Rose jumped. The butter was hissing in the pan and smoke was streaming upward.

"I didn't hear you come in, dear." she said, waving the spatula to clear the air.

Catherine walked up to her mother and kissed her on the cheek. She was wearing white pajamas with a blue stripe on the sleeves. Her hair was pulled back into a quick ponytail. I wondered if she could see me or knew I was there.

"I'll be out in a minute," she said as she entered the bathroom.

Rose turned back to the stove, cracking two eggs into the pan. I felt hunger as I heard them sizzle.

This was too real. If I was the ghost here why was I hungry? Ghosts don't eat or do they?

There was bacon already cooking in another pan and Rose was busy keeping up with the stove as she opened a loaf of bread and put two slices into the side-door toaster.

Catherine came out and sat at the table.

"Where's Dad?" She asked.

"Oh, he went to The Resort. Said he had to meet Mr. Bigelow and get ready for the Grand Opening next week."

Rose flipped the eggs and turned the toast, poured a cup of coffee for herself and a glass of juice for Catherine.

"I can't wait for the 4th!" Catherine said. "Now that I've graduated, I feel like an adult!"

"You mean you can't wait to dance with Christian, don't you?" Rose replied as she drained the bacon and placed it on the table. Turning off the burners she finally sat down to eat.

"Oh, Mom! I know how you and Dad feel about him. Don't my feelings count?"

"Of course, dear. Your father and I just want what's best for you."

"Why can't I be the judge of that?" Catherine asked with a shot of temper.

"Young people don't always know what's best. That's why they have parents." Rose smiled.

"Then why do parents have children? So they can have a second chance?" Catherine said sarcastically.

That stopped Rose in her tracks. For a moment I could see the wheels turning. Should she escalate the debate or laugh it off? In the end she just sighed and concentrated on her breakfast. No use arguing.

"I'm sorry, Mom. I know you and Dad mean well, and I appreciate you looking out for me. But, I feel so frustrated sometimes. Like everyone has my life planned out for me. Like I don't have any choices."

"Well, you are a beautiful young woman with responsibilities." Rose answered.

Catherine rolled her eyes. "I should have been a boy. Men have all the choices!"

"What about your writing, dear? You are a lovely writer! I do wish you'd spend more time on the piano though."

"Thanks for the compliment, Mother. I want to write to Johns Hopkins. They are starting a Poetry Department! They are having a competition and I want to enter. I know I can win!"

"That would be wonderful, Catherine!" Rose smiled. All the tension was gone now.

"And someday I will write a novel!" Catherine smiled, her eyes traveling to another time.

"Well, anyway, this will be an exciting week for all of us! Thank God The Resort is finished! I'll be glad when this is over. That Mr. Bigelow bothers me. I wish he had never come here!"

Just then the old phone rang and Rose got up to answer it. There was a barking outside and Catherine jumped up also.

"That's Scout! Christian is here!" Catherine ran to the door.

"Just a minute young lady! You are not going anywhere until the dishes are done! And certainly not in your pajamas!"

The phone continued to jangle and Rose finally picked it up.

"Why, hello Henrietta..."

Catherine opened the back screen door and stepped out. Seeing Christian and Scout she waved them in as Rose continued her conversation.

"Maybe I'll get some help with the dishes!" Catherine said, with a sly smile.

Christian opened the screen door, telling Scout to "stay". He stepped in as Scout whimpered and sat on the top step nose pressed against the screen.

I was shocked at the resemblance of Christian and myself, even though I had seen his picture at Fran's. There was no denying the relationship. By now I knew that no one could see or hear me, except Scout. He cocked his head and seemed to look right at me through the screen as I moved into the kitchen and sat at the table in one of the unoccupied chairs.

I felt like a spy watching Christian and Catherine steal an embrace while Rose was on the phone.

"You can help me with the dishes!" She said to Christian.

"But you're still in your pajamas! Your mother..."

"Shhh! She's on the phone. She won't notice. Here, you dry."

Tossing a towel to Christian she asked him about the upcoming dance.

"Well, I'll be working that night. Your father will be there and I know he doesn't like me. I don't know if we will get to dance."

"My father likes you. He just thinks I should marry into society."

"We'll just have to elope, then." Christian said in a whisper.

"SHHH! Don't let Mother hear you!" She whispered back.

Just then Rose came back in the kitchen, wiping a tear from the corner of her eye.

"Catherine, go upstairs and get dressed. A young man should not see a lady in her pajamas! Christian, thank you for helping but you'll have to wait outside. I have to drive into town."

"What's wrong, Mother? Are you crying? Is everything okay?" Catherine asked worriedly.

"Everything is fine. I just need to talk to your father," Rose replied, more composed now.

"Can I get the car for you?" Christian asked.

"Yes, that would be fine. I'd appreciate it," Rose said going to her purse on the counter and fishing out the keys.

Catherine and Christian exchanged worried looks as he took the keys and went out the back door, Scout running ahead down the porch steps.

When he was outside Catherine turned to her Mother again.

"What is it, Mom?"

"Like I said, dear, I just need to talk to your father."

"Is he okay? Did something happen to him?"

"Oh, that Henrietta! I don't know if I can believe her or not! She always had a crush on your father. She always resented me marrying him away. I was against your Dad hiring her for a secretary but apparently she has some pull with Mr. Big. Anyway, she says I should come right down. I'm sure everything is fine."

Christian pulled the car into the driveway and tooted the horn.

"I'll be back later. You kids be good!" Rose said as she walked to the front door and climbed into the '32 Ford.

I decided to follow Rose. I did not want to spy on "the kids".

FORTY-EIGHT

I rode in the car with Rose. She did not talk to herself but put the car through the gears with a determined look on her face. Clouds of dust flew out behind us as she sped down the road, arriving at the bank in a matter of minutes.

The Annandale Bank was next to the Hotel. There was a 1934 Lincoln parked in front. Rose parked behind it and got out of the car. I followed as she plowed through the front door like the owners wife.

Ignoring the teller she walked into her husband's office at the back of the bank. Henrietta did not try to stop her as she headed for the inner office.

Swinging the door open she was shocked to see Mr. Big and his "associates" standing off to the side of her husband's desk leaving her a clear view of a young woman sitting on Albert's lap, arms around his neck.

Albert looked up and saw Rose, pushing the young woman off his lap and onto the desk as he scrambled to get up.

"Rose! What a surprise!" Was all he could say.

"I'll bet you're surprised, mister!"

"It's not what you think!" Albert said.

Mr. Big cocked his head, motioning the young woman and his associates to leave.

"We'll see you at the Grand Opening, Al," he said as they left closing the door behind them.

Rose leveled her gaze at Albert.

"So, this is what you do at work! This is why you agreed to work with Mr. Bigelow!"

"Now, Rose, don't think like that. Mr. Big thought I was getting cold feet. I told him I was unhappy with the rumors around town about his "business" in the cities. Some of our investors wanted out of the project. He threatened me if I pulled the financing."

"Some threat! I saw that floozy on your lap! What was she doing? Warming your toes?"

"He threatened you and Catherine. He brought that girl into the office with his bodyguards. He told her to sit on my lap! He said he could destroy my marriage and talked about how attractive you and our young daughter would be to his "friends". I wasn't doing anything!" Albert vigorously defended himself.

I had to give him credit. It looked like an impossible situation to explain and he was pretty convincing.

"I knew that man was trouble! Half the people in this town think he's Al Capone and half of them think he's a saint! The way he spends money and talks so nice to people! But I remember how he leered at our daughter and me when he first came to dinner at the house! I never did trust him and I'm still mad at you for agreeing to this project! For the last two years we've put up with him and his cronies! And if you are lying to me I swear I'll cut you to pieces!" Rose's anger had cooled a bit but was still very much alive.

"I swear, nothing went on. Those men have guns and they mean business. Next week The Resort will be open and this business will be over!" Albert was mopping his brow. The old wire fenced fan was not enough to ward of the early summer heat.

"You're a fool. It will never be over. Why do you think he wanted The Resort? Who do you think will be staying there?

People are going to accuse you of bringing crime to Annandale! They do already." Rose admonished him.

"Don't worry, we still have our house in Florida and the bank there. We only spend the summers here as it is."

"Then why is my inheritance still in this bank?" Rose asked. "Why not transfer it to the Florida bank? Is my money still safe? I don't want it tied to this project!"

"Of course your money is safe! Do you think I would risk anything we have?" Albert said approaching Rose with his arms out to hug her.

"Then whose money are you putting in? We are supposed to have a half interest in The Resort."

"I re-mortgaged the house."

"What! Your father's house! You tied it to The Resort!" Rose was incredulous at this new information.

"I had to. I couldn't use your money and the investors in town wanted to take the other half. I had to put in on it too. But don't worry. We'll get it all back!"

"How? What if The Resort fails or Mr. Big wants to take over? He could just take it by force." Rose *was* worried.

"I've been using his own money. Ours is safe at home," Albert said slyly.

"What? What do you mean 'safe at home?' You just said he threatened Catherine and me! What makes you think you can take his money and be safe?"

"He doesn't know. He thinks his money is going into The Resort but he himself said he doesn't want a paper trail. He only wants the contract, which is kept between the attorney and us. The investors' half is protected and we can buy them out later. I set up a dummy account and moved some figures around. The weekly deposits he sends are going to go straight to the house."

"Where do you keep it? In your desk?" Rose asked.

"For now, but I'm having a special safe installed. It's better you don't know."

"Oh, thanks! Now if they torture me I can only give them half the information! And what's going to happen when Mr. Big wants to claim his ownership of The Resort? Are you going to tell him he's out?"

"No, we can't cut him out. The papers are already drawn and signed. It's just costing him more than he thinks it is."

"You're skimming from him!" Rose was incredulous that Albert would take such a chance.

"The same way he's been skimming from the Mob! If he's found out...anyway it's all money from protection rackets. Think of me as a modern day Robin Hood." Albert was pleased with himself.

"Oh, please! Spare me! My husband the crook! I wish we had never heard of Mr. Big!"

"It's not like we had a choice! He's the Mob! He chose *us,* remember? Are *you* going to tell him no?"

"Okay, okay! So we didn't have a choice! I just hope you know what you're doing!" Rose's shoulders drooped in resignation.

"Honey, I promise nothing will happen to us!" Albert said, drawing her into an embrace.

I shuddered, invisible and powerless, I wanted to shout "NO! It won't be okay! Something will happen to you!"

But they wouldn't have heard me if I did.

FORTY-NINE

There was a break in the conversation. In that break I heard another sound. A slight rustle on the wood of the door. It was as if someone had been listening with their ear pressed against it, and was now moving away.

Henrietta! Was she a spy for Mr. Big? Probably. Before I could wonder too long, Albert spoke up.

"Rose, why don't you do some shopping? I'll be along later. I have other business to attend to."

"You can't buy me off, Albert! I'll be at home. Just make sure your "other business" doesn't involve any women or I'll tell Mr. Big all about your plan!"

"Now, Rose, you know I'd never do anything to hurt you!" Albert looked wounded.

"Yeah, right. Don't be too late."

Rose opened the door, ignoring Henrietta and knowing she had heard everything; she marched out and went straight to the car.

Albert sat behind his desk and mopped his brow. The sweat wasn't just from the heat.

I stood like the ghost I was, not knowing what to do next. Here I was in 1934. It was irresistible and I decided to take a walk.

I didn't notice the heat as my feet stepped silently on the boardwalk. Usually clunky, they didn't make a sound. I realized I was thinking physical but was not. Still, somehow I was here.

I looked for Granny's shop. I found it across the street but it wasn't called Franny's. It was Peterson's.

Reaching for the handle, I expected to hear the bell as the door opened. But I never reached the handle. Instead I found myself inside.

The shop hadn't changed too much over time. There were no records on the wall though. The meat counter was in the same place though this one was wooden instead of white metal. There were still windows in the front of it and inside were white trays of fresh ground meat.

Behind the counter stood a handsome man with a cleaver and behind him a window to the kitchen where an old black and white oven was baking the familiar sweet rolls.

A brown-haired woman in a gingham dress was rolling out dough while her teenage daughter helped.

"I just don't know, Fran. Paris is so far away. Expensive too! I don't know where we'll get the money. Can't you study art here?"

"I know, Mother. Maybe when The Resort opens there will be enough..."

"Oh, that Resort! It's bringing the gangsters to this town! I wish Albert had never started it!"

"But you and Daddy have the contract for all their meat. We need the business!"

"We got along fine before. Still, we haven't much choice..."

"And Christian has a job there, too!" Fran reminded her mother.

"There's plenty of work here for him! He just wants to be closer to the Zimmerman girl! Your Dad is upset with him too!"

"Well, you can't blame him. She is pretty," Fran said as they placed another tray in the oven and removed the previous one.

"That Resort will ruin this family!" Her mother said as she took a hot roll and put it on a plate.

"Well, it's going to happen whether we like it or not. I can't wait for the Grand Opening next week!"

"Take this roll to your father and no more talk about Paris! I don't want him upset tonight. He feels bad enough about money."

"Okay, Mom." Fran sighed as she took the plate and turned to the door.

I stepped aside, still thinking they could see me.

The talk about Catherine made me wonder what was happening back at the Zimmerman house and before I could wonder how I was going to get there the bell above the door tinkled.

In walked Christian, followed closely by Scout.

"Hey, what's cookin', good lookin'?" Christian said as he headed for the kitchen and stopped as Scout looked at me and whined.

"Hey, boy, what's wrong? You hungry?" Christian asked as Scout continued to whimper.

Now I knew he could see me! Or he knew I was there! I stood perfectly still. Panic hit me again. I felt like an intruder in someone's home.

"That's strange. I've never seen him act that way before." Fran's mother was worried.

Just then, a big black Lincoln pulled up in front of the store and two well-dressed hoods opened the car door for Mr. Big.

"Well, that explains it!" Mother said with disgust.

"Looks like we got some business. Christian, get your father and take Scout upstairs. Fran, get back in the kitchen!"

"Oh, Mother!" Fran said angrily but did as she was told.

The doorbell tinkled again and in walked Mr. Big.

Granny's words echoed in my mind, "His real name was Bigelow and he wasn't very big either, about five-ten and one hundred and fifty pounds soaking wet."

I was surprised to see that he looked somewhat like Humphrey Bogart. Dark hair and complexion, slight build that belied his nickname. He wore a striped double-breasted suit and the typical hat of the day. He took the hat off with his left hand leaving his right hand free to shake a hand or draw a gun. His two "associates" stayed outside, one on the steps and the other with his foot on the running board. That way they could watch both directions.

Fran had hurried into the kitchen and her mother behind the cash register. Partly to protect it and partly for the security it gave her. Mr. Peterson stepped out from behind the meat counter, wiping his hands as he approached.

"Good afternoon, Mr. Bigelow. What can I do for you?" Fran's father was only half smiling, wary of their guest.

"Mr. Peterson! Pleasure to see you and your fine family again! Just stopped by for some of the best sweet rolls this side of the Mississippi! Gotta' keep the boys happy you know! Mrs. Peterson, if you'd be so kind as to have your lovely daughter wrap up a dozen or so..."

Fran's mother was eager to comply and hid her nervousness as she went into the kitchen to help Fran with the rolls. She wanted this customer out of her shop as soon as possible!

While she was in back, Mr. Big talked to Fran's father about the real reason he stopped.

"Everything going all right about the Grand Opening of The Resort?" He asked.

"Yes, of course. All the food preparations are made."

"Good. See that we don't run out of steaks! There will be some very important people present, myself included. And of course, you and your lovely family will be there, won't you?" Was it a question or a threat?

"Why, we wouldn't miss it for the world! You are our biggest customer. The contract we have with The Resort is very important to us."

"Tell you what, if you handle this well I'll see to it that you have the exclusive as long as The Resort is in existence. Could even help you send Fran to Paris."

Mr. Big was pleased at the look of surprise on Peterson's face.

"How do you know about that? You leave my children out of this! Your business is with me. We take care of our own!" Fran's father looked dangerous now!

"I like that, "we take care of our own", that's what I'm trying to tell you. As far as how I know, I make it my business to know. Your business is my business. Like family." Mr. Big was smiling now, knowing he had the upper hand.

Mr. Peterson struggled to quell his emotions. He returned to a business-like attitude.

"Of course. We pride ourselves on service. We'll take care of all the details."

Fran's mother returned to the register with the sweet rolls. She rang the keys and broke the spell. Of course she pretended that she hadn't heard a thing.

Mr. Big stepped to the cash register and paid for the rolls.

"Mmmm, could smell them bakin' a block away! The boys will be happy." He smiled his best Humphrey Bogart smile at Fran as she stood in the doorway of the kitchen.

Raising his left hand he tipped his hat in reverse and turned for the door. As the bell tinkled his exit he stopped and turned around.

"By the way, say hi to Christian for me. Fine young man! Wish I had more like him!"

They watched as the man on the steps stood up, sniffing at the bag of rolls like a hungry dog. Mr. Big led him to the car and the three "Businessmen" drove off down the street.

Mr. Peterson looked at Fran. The same question was on everyone's lips including mine.

"How did he know about Paris?"

FIFTY

Fran saw the looks on everyone's faces. "Every body knows about Paris! I've only told every person that would listen in this town! I'm sure Mr. Big knows about every person here! Don't look at me that way, Daddy!"

"I'm sorry, sweetheart. You're right. I just don't like those gangsters! I'm not buying into their lies. Some people in this town think they are Robin Hoods. Well, that's just what they are — robbin' hoods!"

"Seems to me that you're doing business with them, Dad." Christian spoke up as he walked back into the room.

Mr. Peterson flashed a look of anger at his son. "I'm doing what I have to do to protect my family!"

"Well, it's still a good piece of business, isn't it?" Christian stabbed again.

"That's enough, you two!" Fran's mother was angry now. "I told you they'd be the death of this family! Since we can't keep them away we are all going to have to rely on our own values and judgments. This is a test for all of us. Don't let them tear us apart!"

Mother's words calmed the group but each person had drawn an inch away from the others, retreating to their own opinions.

Scout barked upstairs and Christian left to let him out. My own trance was broken and I followed up the stairs.

Christian's room was small. Whitewashed plaster and flat board woodwork, it was simple and clean. Enough room for the single metal bed and cotton-stuffed mattress, a small chest of drawers and a lamp. Two boards across upended crates formed a desk and a place to store the few books and treasures he owned.

The single window overlooking the street was graced with handmade curtains from his mother. A picture of Catherine, sketched by Fran was the only decoration hung on the walls. Aside from the blue chenille bedspread the only color in the room was the braided rug that Scout laid on next to the bed.

Scout whined, his eyes following me as I crossed the small room and stood by the makeshift desk.

"I don't know, Scout," Christian said as the dog sat up and rested his head on his lap. "Everybody thinks I'm so good, but sometimes I don't feel like it! They all expect me take over the store and spend the rest of my life in this town. It's Dad's big dream and he tells everyone about it!

"But I don't know what I want! I need to get out into the world and see other choices! Mr. Big says I could join his organization. He makes it sound so good! Money, travel, excitement! But the price...I don't know. I love Catherine but I'll never have enough money for her father. Mr. Big offers me lots of money, but Catherine would hate me! She's trapped too, you know! Her parents expect her to marry into society and be the rich girl! All she wants to do is write and find her own place in the world. Maybe if we go through with the elopement we'll both find our place together!"

Scout just whined, and Mother called up the stairs. "Supper's on!"

My stomach growled in reply and I wondered again if I could eat. As Christian sighed and stood up, I decided to leave.

Just thinking about the Zimmerman house brought me back there and I found myself in the dining room listening to the same piano music I had heard before.

Catherine was at the keyboard. The sheet music in front of her was titled *Rose of My Heart*. Though it was open, she was not reading it. She had memorized the song and her fingers played automatically.

"Did I tell you that your father and I fell in love to this song? We were at a recital at the University..."

"Yes, Mother. I hear the story every time you have me play it! Every time you are upset with Dad you make me play this infernal song!"

Catherine's fingers were pounding on the keys now, her anger showing. The music reflected her mood and the gentle love song had become a vendetta.

"Well! You don't have to ruin it!"

"I'm sorry, Mother." Catherine's tone softened and so did the music. Now she played to soothe her mother's feelings.

Rose smiled again and retreated to her memories as she set the table for dinner.

"I want things to be nice when your father comes home," she said to no one in particular.

The table was covered in fine linen and her best china and silverware. The house was filled with the aroma of pot roast and potatoes. Two tall candles graced the table in their silver holders.

The notes on the piano ended in *Rose of My Heart* and Catherine closed the keyboard.

"Did you and Dad fight today, Mother?"

"No, not exactly. We had a business discussion."

"I'll bet that Henrietta was causing trouble again!" Catherine knew how jealous Henrietta was of her mother.

"Sometimes I'm afraid I'll lose him..." Rose confessed.

"Oh, Mother! He would never leave you! And me."

Rose smiled. "I know, dear. It's just something I think we all go through. So many men run around and I don't trust Henrietta! Why does she have to work there?"

"You have to trust Dad. This is a small town. If anything were going on you would hear about it. Besides, Mr. Big did not give Dad much choice. He's going to get his way and he insisted that Henrietta leave her job at the library and work at the bank. She's his spy and Dad knows it."

"But he's a man. Mr. Big throws his money at him and offers him women. Then he threatens us with his goons..."

"Us? He threatened us?" Catherine was mortified. Rose had said too much.

"He told Dad if he did not go through with the deal on The Resort that his men would do things to us..."

"Oh, no! Mother, we have to leave! Call the authorities! They are cracking down on crime, they can arrest him." Fear was rising up in Catherine.

"No. Mr. Big has a plan in place to ruin your father. Besides, half the people in this town like Mr. Big. He's bought them. The other half already hates us for doing business with him. As if we had a choice!"

"Why can't we leave and move to Florida?"

"Not until The Resort is open. There are gangsters there, too."

"I know, so what can we do?"

"Your Dad swore to his father that he'd never let this land go and he would do anything to keep it. He has his own plan and I'd rather you didn't know."

"You mean the things he's been hiding away in my closet? I've heard him come in late at night when he thought I was sleeping. I know when he's been there in the daytime too. I caught him one day and he told me he was planning a safe to keep my inheritance in."

Rose was astonished. "I didn't know he was hiding the money in your room!"

"I didn't know it was money. There is a strong box on the shelf, though."

"I've wondered what he was doing some nights..."

"Mother! I can't believe you would think that of Dad!"

"I'm sorry. I don't really. I've just been so worried since the gangsters arrived."

"But, how does Dad think the money will help?"

"Well, if anything goes wrong, your father will say that Mr. Big has been skimming from his bosses and he'll show them the books. They'll take care of Mr. Big and we'll escape with the money if things go bad."

"That's crazy! What makes him think they won't kill us, too?"

"Too much attention. Like you said, they are cracking down on the gangsters."

The sound of a car pulling into the drive made them both jump.

"Your father's home! I'd better get the roast! Catherine, meet him at the door! I don't want him to know we've been talking."

Rose hurried into the kitchen and Catherine went to the front door. Hand poised on the knob she put on a smile and waited for her father to come up the steps.

FIFTY-ONE

Catherine held her hand on the knob and the smile on her face. Ears straining, she listened for the first footstep to fall on the steps.

When it did, she flung open the door, "Hi Daddy!" on her lips. She never got beyond "Hi, D..."

The man on the steps was not her father.

"Evening, Miss," he said as he crossed the porch, stopped by the half open door and blocked by Catherine.

He was a young man, early twenties and "dressed to the nines". Pinstripe suit and custom bent hat. He stopped uncomfortably close to Catherine's face.

Catherine peered around him. There was another man sitting in the car. The car was a black 1934 Lincoln.

"Yes?" Catherine said as if talking to a traveling salesman. She was desperate not to show her fear.

"Got a message from your father. He won't be home for supper."

"When will he be home?"

"Later. Business meeting with Mr. Big. Say, something sure smells good! What is it?"

"Roast beef." Catherine's fear was mixed with anger. Her mother's story and the mention of threats had put her on her defenses. Seeing the young hood and the message from her father brought a flush of rage to her face.

"Listen, kid, since your father won't be home for supper how about me and my friend help you eat it?"

"How about you and your friend drive into the lake!" I smiled at Catherine's spirit.

The hood smiled too. "I like a dame with a sense of humor. I think maybe you don't get it. My friend and I are coming in. Maybe have some desert, too."

"What did you say your name was?" Catherine asked icily.

"Joe. And that there is Pauly," he turned and motioned for Pauly to come up.

Pauly opened the car door and brushed the long, black, greasy hair from his forehead, hiding it under his hat.

"Well, "Joe", your manners are totally absent. Your hearing ain't so good, neither. I said you and your friend should drive into the lake. You ain't eatin' here. Now, leave."

"Listen, sister, you still don't get it. We got another message to deliver. You cooperate or else."

Pauly joined Joe on the porch and looked at Catherine. The unmistakable look of lust on his face.

"Yeah," Pauly echoed. "You cooperate or else."

As their hands reached out to push the door open, Catherine stepped back swinging the door a little wider as if to let them in.

Lowering their hands and looking at each other, they shrugged. The tough guy act had worked.

But Catherine just wanted a wider swing on the door! She flung it back with all her might, slamming it shut on both their faces.

The blow knocked the hats from their heads and sent them both to their backsides on the painted boards. Pauly continued to slide and went halfway down the porch steps before catching one of the posts for the railing.

Now they were angry! "No dame's gonna' push us around!" Joe said getting to his feet and putting on his hat.

He reached under his arm and drew his gun, using the butt of it to pound on the heavy wooden door.

As Pauly got to his feet he drew his gun also, ready to start shooting.

The door swung open again and this time they were met by Rose.

There's something about a lady in an evening dress holding a double barrel shotgun.

"You boys have a hearing problem. My daughter told you to leave. Unless your guns are bigger than mine, I'd suggest you listen." The gun was cocked and ready.

Pauly got cold feet. "Hey, Joe, I'm not that hungry anyway."

"Yeah, Pauly. Probably lousy cooks anyway. We delivered the message."

"Yeah, we got your message. Now you send my husband home in one piece the way I left him or the deal is off! And you know Mr. Big won't like his plans spoiled. You tell him *he* better cooperate!"

"Okay, lady. Settle down. See, we're puttin' our guns away. Let's go Pauly."

Rose and Catherine stood in the now wide open door and watched the two would- be dinner guests back out of the driveway.

When the car was on the road, Rose lifted the gun and pulled the trigger.

The blast from the gun took away any dignity the thugs had left and the mighty Lincoln spun its tires like a getaway car.

I laughed out loud.

"Come on, Catherine. Let's have some of that roast!" Rose said as they closed the door, laughing and hugging their way to the table.

FIFTY-TWO

I couldn't stay around and watch them eat. My stomach was rumbling and I wondered how long it would be before I was back in my own time. The first thing I would do would be raid Mooney's Chicken Shack...

To take my mind off the hunger I wondered where Albert was and it wasn't long before I got the answer. I found myself standing in the dining room of the not-yet-opened Last Resort.

Dinnertime everywhere! Just what I needed! There were Albert and Mr. Big sitting at one of the side tables by the windows overlooking the lake. Albert was nervous and looked like an unwilling guest. He sat across from Mr. Big and an attractive woman I had not seen before.

I moved across the dance floor to listen in.

"Really, Mr. Bigelow, I must be getting home. Rose and Catherine will be worried..."

"Relax, Al. I sent a couple of boys over to your house to let them know you'd be tied up awhile."

"Yeah, relax, Al. I'm sure Rose would understand you were out on business with Mr. Bigelow and your secretary."

"You should listen to Henrietta, Al. She knows what's good for you," Mr. Big smiled as one of the waiters in training brought out the dinners. He dug in, cutting the medium rare steak one piece at a time. Between bites he continued talking.

"I know you said not to order for you, but I took the liberty." He was speaking to Henrietta.

I never would have recognized her! The tight bun of her hair was gone, replaced with long, flowing falls of auburn that lay on her shoulders. A red strapless gown replaced the stodgy gray suit she usually wore. Gone too were the glasses. She looked ten years younger.

Albert could not get over it, either.

"Henrietta, I have never seen you looking so…attractive, but why are you here?"

"Mr. Big wanted me to deliver a message too. You know, Al, all these years you could have had me! Way back in grade school I told you how I felt. But no, you had to marry Rose! Well, I'm as good as she is! Now that the project is almost finished I thought I should let you know a few things. I've been on Mr. Bigelow's payroll for a long time. Ever since the project was started almost two years ago. I've been keeping an eye on things for Mr. Big. He wants to make sure nothing goes wrong this last week."

"Al, you're not eating! Come on, were the first customers! Don't you like the steak?" Mr. Big smiled as Albert picked up his fork and knife.

"Now listen, Al," he continued, "I want to make sure the Grand Opening goes like clockwork. The entertainment's all lined up. The invitations are sent. Henrietta's done a great job. My associate, Carlisle will be overseeing the opening night. Some of his ladies will be here to entertain the boys. Speaking of the boys, here's a couple of them now. What's the report, Joe?"

I wasn't too surprised when Joe and Pauly walked up to the table. "Hey, Boss. We gave them your message. They had a roast in the oven but when we told them Albert wouldn't be home for dinner they wouldn't let us in."

"Yeah, Boss. They got rude too. Slammed the door in our faces..." Pauly started but was silenced by a kick from Joe.

"Did you send these goons to my house?" Albert was angry.

"Like I said, Al, I don't want any problems this last week. Just thought a subtle message was in order."

"Subtle? Scaring my family? Up to now your boys have been on good behavior out here. Half the people in this town think you are on the level. Why mess that up?"

"See that it stays that way. The message was for you and your family, Al. I've heard some disturbing things from Henrietta lately. Maybe things aren't what they seem? Besides, I told Joe and Pauly to be polite."

"Yeah, we was polite, but that didn't stop your daughter from knocking us on our..." Pauly started again only to be silenced by another kick from Joe.

Albert was smiling now. "Knocked you on your butts, eh? My daughter?"

"Yeah and your wife was no picnic neither." One more kick for Pauly.

Now Mr. Big was laughing! Soon they were all laughing. Until Mr. Big slammed his fist on the table.

"Coupla' dames knocked you on your butts, eh? What kind of tough guys are you anyway? And I thought I told you to be subtle! No strong-arm stuff! What did you do to get them mad?"

"Nothing boss. We was hungry, that's all." Joe was sweating now.

"Well then you must still be hungry. Come here."

Mr. Big stood up and motioned Joe into his chair. Joe sat down, sweat rolling off his forehead.

"Go on, finish my plate. You boys deserve it."

Again Mr. Big smiled as Joe picked up the fork and reluctantly stabbed at the mashed potatoes.

When he bent to take the first forkful, a big hand slammed his face into the plate and held it there. Gravy flew on Henrietta's dress and she jumped to her feet.

"Sit down!" Mr. Big barked.

Joe was having trouble breathing now. Gravy went up his nose and he was sputtering. Pauly turned white.

"Now, this is subtle, see? From here on out it gets worse. All of you follow my instructions to the letter or you'll get a new kind of subtle! Mess this up and the boys from Chicago will have us all for lunch!"

Albert had stopped eating and I wasn't hungry anymore.

Finally, Mr. Big let Joe up.

"Now, do we all understand each other? Good. Now let's have some desert!"

I hung around until Albert was dismissed and followed him to his car.

FIFTY-THREE

By boat The Resort wasn't far from the house. Just a short ride across the lake. From the house you could see the lights from the windows of the main dining room and the lights on the dock cast long, silvery reflections almost like a painting.

By car it was longer ride. You had to drive halfway around the lake and the picturesque view was interrupted by clumps of trees, many bent and twisted at grotesque angles as they struggled for sunlight. Eerie at night and punctuated by occasional cabins and small houses hidden in darkness. Who knew what went on in those dark places?

Albert's mind seemed just as dark and twisted. I couldn't read his thoughts and he wasn't talking. In all of Fran's stories, he was the one I heard least about. I could guess though.

Right now he must be wondering if Rose and Catherine were okay. What had really happened with the two thugs? Had they scared them? Had they gotten physical? If they had touched either of them...!

Beyond that was the deal with Mr. Big. Was Albert entirely unwilling? Was the money his motive for doing business with known hoods? Was he worried about his public image? His standing in the community?

And what of the money? Did Henrietta know he was skimming from Mr. Big just like Bigelow was skimming from the mob? Had she told him? Was it really an "insurance policy" as he had told Rose?

What good would it do if they were dead?

I wanted to reach out and touch his shoulder. I wanted to tell him what was coming! I was as helpless as the night the car took Marianne. Only I hadn't seen that coming...

What good was it to be here in 1934 if I couldn't change anything?

All I could do was tell the story. At least the truth would be known and Rose and Catherine could rest. Scout, too, perhaps.

Did Albert feel helpless? Trapped by circumstances so that the ones he really wanted to help, the ones he cared for the most, were the ones he was powerless to protect?

Oh yes, I knew that feeling.

The car took the wrong turn. Instead of turning toward the house it turned toward town. I wondered where he was going.

The wrought iron fence of the cemetery loomed like a shadow in the lights of the car and I followed as Albert parked outside the gate and walked through the moonlight past the silent headstones.

Even the crickets had stopped their chatter as the soft ground muffled Albert's steps and he floated silently to the largest stone.

His father's.

All of my quotes had left me. My famous sense of humor as dead as the residents of this place. I had not reconciled that death was part of living. I hadn't wanted to. Doing so would have put a finality to Marianne that I was not ready to live with. I had been avoiding it for two years, watching it pull the life out of me.

Perhaps that was what I really wanted. To join her again on the other side. To stop being angry with God for giving her to me only to take her away again.

Albert looked around at all the headstones of his relatives, gathered around his father's as if at a family meeting. He looked for a place to sit and finally settled on his haunches.

"You know, Dad," he said to the stone, "the last time we talked I was lying in my bed reading. It was a summer night just like this. I could hear the trains in the distance and the crickets outside my window. Some people say I fell asleep and sometimes I think I must have been dreaming, but we know better. You were calling me to your side from somewhere far away. I remember the cold rocky plateau you were laying on. The fire was dying out and so were you. Your eyes were dim as I approached and your mouth was moving though no sound was coming from it. I did not even wonder how I got there. I was trying to hear your message. And though you couldn't speak, I understood. "Don't let go of the land! Keep it in the family; don't let your brothers sell! Don't throw away the legacy of generations who settled the farms around the lake. Don't let me die alone in this dream.""

"Then I was back in my room. The warm summer night and the sound of the trains returned. And I was left with sadness, knowing you had died. Of all your sons, I was the one you sent to college. I was the one you chose. I was the one saddled with your dream! Oh yes, I wanted it too. I thought my dream was yours. Now I know that I had pushed my own dream back and replaced it. You haunted me before you died! Now I must finish this task before I can start on my own."

Albert stood up, knees cracking. He walked around the other stones, reading each one. Then he stopped in front of his father's again and spoke.

"You know, we have a life in Florida. There are lots of people there. Lots of life and happiness. They are not surrounded by old ghosts! Catherine wants to be a writer and I think she'll be a good one. Her mother wants her to be a society girl. Maybe she can do both. Maybe she can balance our dreams for her with her own, the way I thought I could. Of course I know she is in love with Christian. I wish it were someone else. And Rose and I will someday be able to travel together. She loves her trips to the Orient and decorates the house with them. I missed so many with her. Business, you know. Must take care of the business.

"Well, The Resort is almost finished and Mr. Big will have his legacy. I'm sorry it's tangled with yours, but what could I do? When this is finished we'll move for good. The land will always stay in the family whether they want it or not! You see; it's tied to The Resort. So, here's my completion and my revenge, Father. No doubt our stones will be here someday, too. I won't be seeing you again before then."

Albert Zimmerman was quiet again. He had said his piece and made his peace. I understood him better now.

I stayed in the cemetery as he drove away, a ghost among the ghosts.

FIFTY-FOUR

I don't know how long I stayed there. Time seemed suspended in the unmoving headstones. I felt drawn in to nothingness. It would be so easy to stay here where nothing happens. No demands. No thoughts. Just lie down...

I had to break the spell. A cold wind blew through the cemetery, rustling the treetops. I couldn't feel it but I could see it and hear it. It was so strange to be here and not be here. Perhaps I would see Marianne.

No. I had something to do. My tasks were not done. I felt power returning to my will. I still wanted to live!

It was dark. An eerie darkness that was not quite real. A tinge of electric purple outlined the gravestones and trees. I heard a bark.

"Scout!" I thought. "Here, boy! I'm here."

The barking grew louder as I moved toward it. I hadn't moved my feet at all but somehow I was being propelled through the gates and out onto the road.

I watched the dog running towards me as if he were in slow motion.

The bark had changed and was no longer friendly but menacing. The dog flying through the air at me looked more like a hungry wolf.

Fangs bared, salivating, ribs protruding it lunged at me as if it were death itself!

I knew I had stayed too long among the dead.

Thinking, wishing, remembering Franny's muffins I was transported just before the apparition would have torn my throat!

I knew if I died here I would die in my world, too.

But where was I now?

"Back on The Bridge," Catherine's voice drifted to me.

The darkness I found myself in left as I opened my eyes.

"You cannot die here, Christopher. We need you. You strayed too far in my world and death almost found you. You must have direction. Go where I tell you. Let Scout guide you."

We were standing on some kind of bridge in the dark. I could see points of light like stars in the sky. But it wasn't the sky I knew. Catherine was standing in front of me, holding my arm as if I might float away.

"Who was that dog?" I asked.

"A hound of Hell. If you dwell in death too long they will find you."

"Why am I here?"

"I pulled you back. The living are not meant to see this world. You must understand what really happened in my time and bring back the proof of my mother's innocence. Let me direct your path and Scout will show you what you need to know."

"Why can't you just show me?" I pleaded, tired of this place.

"I can only go where I've been and see what I have seen. You can roam through the world in my mind. Your spirit is free of my body. Scout can guard you from the devil dog."

She let go of my arm.

I felt dizzy. The bridge drifted away in space. Catherine's face faded into the darkness.

I felt the strong neck of Scout under my hand. There was feeling here! His thick fur seemed very much alive.

Like a service dog for the blind he led me to solid ground.

There was light here.

It was daylight. I looked down at Scout.

"Where to, friend?"

He sat.

"Are we supposed to wait here? What are we waiting for?" I said.

But Scout could not answer. He couldn't talk; he could only lead me.

We were on a road; or rather, the side of a road.

I recognized it. This was the road that went around the lake. We were on the West side, toward the north, just past the Zimmerman house.

Scout's ears perked up. I listened as the sound of a car's motor reached us from around the bend.

Then I heard the tires crunching on the gravel and a loud *bang*! It sounded like a gunshot. Instinctively I dove for cover.

The car came limping into view, engine revving down, wheels digging into the dirt.

It was a big, black Lincoln. Inside were Mr. Big and his henchmen.

"What was that? Someone shootin' at us?" Mr. Big said from the back seat.

"No, Boss. We blew a tire. Old dirt road..."

The driver set the parking brake and got out to look at the blown rear tire.

"Looks bad," he said.

"Well, can you fix it? We'll be late to the Grand Opening!" Mr. Big was angry.

The driver opened the trunk.

"No tools, Boss." He said matter-of-factly.

"What d'ya mean, 'no tools'? Mr. Big's angry voice shouted back.

"I mean, there ain't no tools to get the spare off the fender. We can't fix the flat." The driver explained.

"You're kiddin' me. We got this car from Mooney! Wait till I get my hands on him!"

"Yeah, I'll fix him good! I'll give *him* a flat tire!" The other goon said.

"Hey, we gotta' get around the lake. Didn't we just pass Albert's house?" Mr. Big asked.

"Yeah, back around the last bend!" the man next to him said as the driver got back in the car, slamming the door.

"Then get out and walk back to the house. Find a phone and call the garage." Mr. Big ordered.

Reluctantly, the man did as he was told.

"What'll we do now, Boss?" The driver asked as his crony walked away looking out of place in a double-breasted suit on an old dirt road.

"What else? We wait." Came the reply.

We waited, too. Hiding in the grass even though we couldn't be seen.

The late afternoon sun sat lower behind us and dusk was falling by the time we heard the sound of truck coming up the road.

"Hey Boss! I'm back!" The well-dressed hood said as he jumped from the old flatbed pickup truck and brushed the dust from his pants.

It was a service station truck from the gas station next to Mooney's car lot.

Wearing striped overalls and a black cap with the logo on the front, the driver of the truck wasted no time.

Without a word he jumped out and started removing the spare tire from the fender.

"I'll have to jack it up. You folks mind getting' out?" He asked.

Mr. Big practically launched himself out of the back seat.

"Don't mind a bit. Been sittin' so long my legs are cramped."

"Well, we'll have you goin' in no time," the serviceman said as he placed the jack on an old board and pumped the handle. The car started to rise and soon the flat wheel was suspended in air. He spun in with his hand and watched the caved in bottom of the tire go around as he set the lug wrench and began to spin them off.

It wasn't long before the tire was changed and the car was being lowered.

"Any trouble finding the phone?" Mr. Big asked the hood.

"Naw. Just a long walk. No one home when I got there, but there was a truck in the driveway. A carpenter."

"A carpenter?" Mr. Big asked.

"Yeah, said he was doing some work for Albert. He let me in to use the phone."

"What kind of work?"

"I don't know. Didn't ask. I was just glad to get to the phone."

"All done. Where do you want the old tire?" The man from the garage asked, wiping his hands on a shop rag and stuffing it into his back pocket.

"Just throw it in the trunk. Pay the man, Pete."

Pete was the driver. He opened the trunk and the serviceman stopped in his tracks. He had never seen so many guns!

He threw in the tire anyway, suddenly nervous.

"Here you go," Pete said, handing the man a $100 bill.

"Gee, thanks, but I don't have change..." the serviceman started to refuse the large bill.

"Keep it." Pete said.

"I better get going. Dinnertime," the man said climbing back into the service truck before Pete could change his mind.

"Yeah. You better get goin'." Pete said as he climbed back into the car.

Mr. Big smiled as the motor started.

The Lincoln rolled forward and the pickup rolled backward down the road to a turn-around spot.

I wondered why Scout and I had been led here.

Just then another truck approached on the old road.

It was the carpenter.

What were you working on back at the house? I wondered.

FIFTY-FIVE

Scout stood up as the cars drove out of sight and I realized that since he was part of this world, he could be seen even if I could not.

I stood up too, feeling naked and very visible even though I knew I wasn't.

Looking back at me, he started down the road towards the Zimmerman house. I followed.

"Shouldn't this be the other way around, boy? Shouldn't you be following me?"

He didn't answer.

I looked around as we walked. I could see the lake on my left and the small dot of The Resort on the other side. The blue water shimmered in the summer sun.

"I'm a Yankee doodle dandy..." I started to sing under my breath as we walked. This was the Fourth of July! There was some activity by The Resort and some on the other side where they must be setting up the fireworks display for the Grand Opening.

But this wasn't the big lake. Pleasant Lake was closest to town and had the nicest beach. Another celebration was being set up there. A small carnival with rides and food stands. I knew people were arriving there, laying out their blankets and choosing their spots for the big celebration. Prohibition had ended, too and whatever law enforcement they had would be there to watch the crowd, probably on horseback.

"All the better for Mr. Big and his bunch." I said out loud as we trekked along.

I watched the puffs of dirt rise up under the pads of Scouts' feet as he walked ahead of me and realized my own feet left no marks. It was an eerie feeling. I could hear birds and the occasional rustle of the trees; I could even feel a breeze now and then.

But I couldn't feel my own feet.

"I'll never get used to this, Scout." I said as we rounded the bend and came upon the familiar hedges of the Zimmerman driveway.

I wondered why we had to walk the whole way. Why we hadn't just thought of where we wanted to go and then just be there. Then I remembered that Scout was here and I was not. Alone I could have done that.

I looked for my little 'Merc in the driveway and remembered it would not be here for a long time yet.

Now we were on the porch and I wondered how we would open the front door.

It opened for us.

The house was quiet but with a silence that held the sounds of life. The buzz of recent activity was still in the air.

There was a new smell, too. The smell of just-cut wood and sawdust. We followed it up the stairs to Catherine's room.

Nothing looked out of place or different.

"What were you working on, Mr. Carpenter?" I wondered.

Scout sat in front of the closet.

"The closet?" I wondered out loud.

Maybe she had needed a new clothes rod or some shelves I thought as the door opened for us again.

"I'll never get used to this," I repeated, feeling a chill in my spine. Catherine must be opening the doors for us. I had been in the closet before and nothing looked out of place. Still, the scent of cut wood was strong and I reached up to part the clothes, pleasantly surprised when I could feel them in my hands.

I can move things here!

Now I was looking at the wall behind the clothes. The sunlight through the white lace curtains providing just enough illumination to examine it.

This wall was paneled, not plastered. I ran my hand across the surface until I found a fine, horizontal cut, almost invisible.

I gave a slight push and a small section of the panel opened before me.

"So this is what you were doing, Mr. Carpenter!" I said to myself.

I was looking at a safe!

It looked brand new and I knew what was going in it! The money Albert had been skimming from Mr. Big! Probably a copy of the contract between them too. The money that had never been found. The reason for all the holes in the walls when I first got here.

Who would ever think to look in his daughter's closet?

"Well, Scout! Now I know why we are here," I said turning from the closet as he thumped his tail on the floor.

But how would this clear Rose of the charges? There must be more to the story, I thought.

I closed the panel and pulled the clothes back across the pole.

"Funny, how can I move things if I'm the ghost? Maybe I've been here too long-maybe I'm becoming a part of Catherine's world…"

It was suddenly very quiet. The thumping from Scout's tail had stopped. A chill went through me.

Backing out of the closet, I turned to Scout.

He was gone!

I stood alone in Catherine's bedroom, feeling like an intruder. I listened to the summer breeze through the open window. The white lace curtains rustled and suddenly billowed out toward me.

There were butterflies in my stomach. The day seemed menacing now.

"Scout! Where are you, boy?" I called out.

I backed out of the room into the hallway.

"Scout! Come here, boy!"

No reply.

I walked around the house. The life I had felt here before was gone. It seemed more like a museum now.

The air was too still. There was no more buzz. The light was fading, too.

Time was passing too fast. The day was gone and now I stood in darkness.

Standing in the dining room I watched as the white lace curtains there billowed outward just like the ones in the bedroom had done.

But the windows were closed!

I felt a presence.

"Scout?" I called out hopefully. "Is that you?"

The gnawing in my stomach told me it wasn't.

From out of the darkness came a growl. Though it did not show itself I knew what it was! I had stayed too long! I tried not to turn my back on it. I tried not to run, but before I knew it I was flying up the steps away from the snapping jaws that nipped at my legs as I ran.

Too close! Too close! I'm a goner...my mind raced as I reached the top of the stairs and flew into Catherine's room!

I slammed the door behind me and dove for Catherine's bed!

"Made it!" I said, not wanting to roll over and look behind me.

I had shut him out!

A shutout, ladies and gentlemen! Christopher Evans has just pitched a shutout game to the Hounds of Hell! My mind celebrated the victory.

The celebration was short lived!

Behind my back came the now familiar growl.

I was trapped! There was no place to go!

I felt the hot breath on my neck. I knew if I turned around I would see the salivating jaws and the blood-stained fangs that would rip me to pieces!

I curled up into a little ball. I remembered how I would never face the room when I slept as a child. I felt safer when I buried my face into the couch or the wall. Sure, my back was cold and vulnerable but if I couldn't see the danger it couldn't really hurt me.

Or could it?

The snapping jaws and hot breath felt very real! I wasn't a child anymore and this wasn't Kansas, Toto!

I started a prayer, hoping I could finish it before the hound took my soul!

FIFTY-SIX

Paralyzed by fear, I couldn't even think the words! I realized that most of us pray when it's too late.

"Better late than never!" I said to the wall.

The walls are listening. Somebody said that once, probably to traumatize little kids.

And something in this wall was!

I watched as a woman's arm came through the wall and grabbed mine! I didn't know what scared me more, the Hounds of Hell, or the ghostly arm coming through the wall!

I didn't have time to think about it, though. Before I knew it, I was on the other side. The other side of what, though?

This side looked the same as the one I had just left! Except it was still light out and there was no Hound of Hell in the room.

I was still in 1934, still in Catherine's room and still on the bed.

But Catherine wasn't there.

I knew she had pulled me through, though. Away from the snapping jaws of darkness I had somehow slipped into.

Scout wasn't there either and I still had no idea where he went.

I laid on the bed for a long time without closing my eyes. I did not know if I was awake or asleep, and I didn't want to find out.

But I knew I was safe. Somehow in the universe of Catherine's mind she was watching over me.

The curtains blowing in the wind no longer seemed menacing and I tried to form a plan.

I did not want to spend any more time here than necessary! Finding the safe was a big one but still did not explain what had really happened to Christian and Catherine's family.

Being on the road with Scout today led me to believe I should be at the Grand Opening tonight. What I had seen before was only part of what happened. Tonight I would be at the actual event as it happened!

I sat up on the bed. I wanted to get there before dark, for sure!

And I was.

Without Scout I could once again float through this world like a ghost. Thinking about The Resort and the Grand Opening brought me there with a speed I had never had before. I felt a sense of power at being able to transcend time and space! But this sense of power was short-lived, too.

FIFTY-SEVEN

I found myself in the boathouse at The Resort, as Christian and Tom were preparing the launches for tonight's event.

"What do you think, Tom? Should I take Mr. Big up on his offer?"

"Look at me, Christian. Don't you see my cast? My bruises? Do you really think I fell off a horse? That's the story they told. I can't be at the party tonight even though I've been working for Mr. Big all this time," Tom said as he tied the now polished boat to its berth with his one good arm.

"Mr. Big do that?" Christian asked.

"Yeah. Him and his boys were hitting somebody when I happened to walk in on them."

"Who was it?" Christian asked.

"Someone they caught skimming from the operation. Had him tied to a chair, beating him to death while the others watched. An example of what could happen to them if they double-crossed the boss. I walked in to pick up the deposit for the bank like I always do and saw the man die in the chair. Mr. Big smiled when he died. Then he saw me!"

"What did you do?" Christian was white as a ghost now.

"I froze. Shock I guess. People out here think of him as a kind of Robin Hood. I did too. He is though; a Robbin' Hood! Mr. Big said *'Get him!'* and two of his boys grabbed me and threw *me* in the chair. I was so scared I wet my pants! He laughed. 'Hello, Tom,' he said. 'You ain't gonna' tell anyone what you saw are you?'

'No, Mr. Big, I ain't gonna' tell a soul!' I said.

'What did you call me?'

'Mr. Big...'

'I hate that name! You call me Mr. *Bigelow*! You got that?'

"Before I could answer, he smashed me in the face with his fist. Then he told me to raise my left hand. He grabbed it and twisted it until it broke."

"Now, take the money and get out of here! I've spent two years building this Resort and a reputation in your town and you ain't gonna ruin it for me, are you?"

"No sir," I blubbered, "I ain't gonna' tell no one nothing!"

"Good boy," he said. "If I find out you do, I'll kill you and them!"

"Jesus, Tom! Why are you telling me?" Christian asked.

"Because you're my friend and I don't want to see it happen to you!"

"But now we could both die...if someone found out or even suspected..."

"Who will know? Unless you tell them!" Tom suddenly backed up from Christian.

"Relax, I'll never tell." Christian reassured him. "But tonight Mr. Big wants my decision. He knows I want to marry Catherine and he's offered me a job in the city. It could be my chance to get out of here."

"Is that the life you really want, Christian? Is that how you want to raise your kids? He's not the nice man people think he is. The people in town that don't like him know what he really is. They've been around. The others all think the gangsters live in St. Paul and that Minneapolis is a respectable town. Don't be fooled like I was. There are other ways. Even the Army is better."

"Catherine wants to know, too. Her father knows how we feel about each other. He knows we want to elope. He also knows I don't have any money and times are hard. He's been working with Mr. Big. I know it bothers him to know I've been talking to him. Soon, they will be leaving for Florida and the nice young banker Mr. Zimmerman has lined up for Catherine. I'll lose her forever."

"Better than her losing you!" Tom said.

Putting the caps on the bottles of polish, the two friends looked at each other.

"Listen, Christian. Bigelow's made a deal with Fran to send her to Paris. You know she wants to go to art school there..." Tom said.

"What kind of deal?" Christian was afraid to ask.

"All she has to do is have his baby and give it up." Tom continued.

"What?" The shock on Christian's face drained the remaining blood from his already white skin. Then it came back with rage!

"That's incredible! How do you know that?"

"I listen." Tom said. "Do you still want to work for him?"

"Work for him? I want to kill him!" Christian said and turned for the door.

"Wait! You'll get us all killed!" Tom reached out with his good arm and grabbed Christian's shirt.

"But I've got to warn Fran..." Christian pulled away from Ray's grasp.

"She already knows the deal. She doesn't have a choice! None of us do. He'll get what he wants or kill us all!" Tom let go of the shirt.

"There must be a way to stop him." Christian said.

"There isn't. Believe me. I've seen more of his operation than anyone here."

"What about the Feds?" Christian asked hopefully.

"You mean the ones he hasn't paid off? They got nuthin' on him. He even pays his taxes."

"What can we do?" Christian sounded hopeless, drained.

"We can stay alive!" Tom answered.

The feeling of power I had gotten from being a ghost left me now. For the second time in my life I felt completely powerless. I knew what was going to happen and all I could do was watch. Just like when that car slammed into us and took Marianne.

Yes, I could relate to Christian.

FIFTY-EIGHT

One of Mr. Big's cronies shuffled up to the boathouse. The black tuxedo he wore looking out of place with his scarred face and crooked nose. The notch in his right ear highlighted by the light behind him.

"Hey, you guys! You got them boats ready?" The man yelled out. "Mr. Bigelow wants a ride around the lake and he wants Christian to pick up the Zimmermans."

"Yeah, they're ready!" Tom answered bitingly.

"What did you say, punk?" The hood asked.

"Yes, *sir*, the boats are ready." Tom answered with a touch of sarcasm.

"You'd *better* say, Sir, and do it with respect. A smile, too!" The thug demanded.

Tom smiled.

"That's better, kid. Now get goin'! You're driving the boat for Mr. Bigelow."

I watched as the two boats chugged out of the boathouse and wished I could do something to help but all I could do was watch.

I wondered what was going on inside the Resort.

It didn't take long to find out! Before I knew it I was standing in the dining room surrounded by bustling waiters in short white jackets as they went from table to table checking the settings and the place cards to make sure every V.I.P. would be seated correctly.

Each table was set in custom-made china imprinted with the words Last Resort. I shook my head at the message the words inadvertently gave.

Mr. Big had insisted on the name for a number of reasons. One was his view of advertising and the slogan he was so proud of - The Last Resort you'll ever need to find!

Meant to imply that this was the be-all and end-all of resort getaways!

He didn't hear the jokes the staff told out of earshot from the management. Things like, 'The Last Resort I'd ever want to stay at!' and 'I'd eat there but only as a Last Resort!'

He also did not let on The Resort's other purpose-a place where his 'boys' could lay low for a while.

But spooked investors and his own reputation shrank his vision of a plush getaway. He may have fooled some of the townspeople, but not all. Many people traveled to the city and knew what was going on. They knew Mr. Bigelow as the notorious 'Mr. Big' and argued against The Resort at town meetings.

Then, too, the Annandale Hotel had long been host to celebrities and wealthy sportsmen and was not anxious to share the business.

All these things had combined to put Albert Zimmerman in a very awkward position. Under pressure from Mr. Big to press on, he had at first dipped into his wife's account for the matching funds he had promised Bigelow. Soon, questions from Rose had caused him to form a more desperate plan.

After replacing Rose's money, he began skimming from Mr. Big. Using his own money and the money from the investors, he began to scale down the size of The Resort; falsifying cost estimates and citing lack of investors he convinced Mr. Big that the reductions were necessary. The money that Ray picked up from Mr. Big every week was destined for the safe I had found in Catherine's bedroom. Pure cash, untraceable and with no ties to Mr. Big.

Soon, there would be a fortune hidden in the closet.

Bigelow was skimming from the Mob to raise the extra money to build The Resort. The last thing he needed was to make too much noise about it. Keeping his name secret on the contract was not only necessary for the investors, but the big boys in Chicago, too.

Even if he suspected Albert of double-crossing him he would let him be for a while. He needed him. He needed a legitimate front for The Resort as well as a management company and guarantees that he could pass the business on to his future heir. An heir that Fran would provide.

All these things went through my mind as I stood there watching the waiters.

I turned to the windows overlooking the lake and watched the launch with Mr. Big and his cronies skip across the water.

Now, two years of deception were about to unfold. Tonight would be the spark that would set off the fireworks that would forever change the lives of all the people who came into contact with The Resort and the Zimmermans.

Extra help had been brought in for the Grand Opening. There were three chefs in the kitchen instead of just one. How Bigelow managed to get them to work together I did not want to know! One chef was temperamental enough from what I had always heard!

Maybe the tough looking goon in the tux standing by the swinging doors to the kitchen was all the incentive they needed!

Over by the main entrance, the hatcheck girl and the cigarette girls were checking each other's costumes. Uniforms, I mean. The white-ruffled, short black skirts and fishnet stockings were classic of the big-time nightclubs of the day.

The band had arrived also. Orchestra was more like it. They took up the small stage area, adjusting their chairs to the space and began warming up.

While the big lake in town would be hosting a small carnival and fireworks for the annual Fourth of July celebration, The Resort would be hosting a big band celebration for invited guests only. There would be no polka music here, no mounted police, no kids and cotton candy.

The only cotton here would be on the tables.

Soon, the Zimmermans would be arriving on the boat with Christian. The rest of the guests would follow promptly at six.

I had already seen some of tonight's events through Granny's story and my dinner with Mary Lou.

I intended to see the rest of the story tonight.

FIFTY-NINE

Like everything else in this ghostly world, it did not take long to get to dinner. All I had to do was think of it and suddenly the dining room was full.

Time was different here, probably because I had entered this world through Catherine's mind.

Dream, dream, dream... I heard the Everly Brothers song in my head. *All I have to do is dream...*

"Good evening, ladies and gentlemen and welcome to the Grand Opening of The Last Resort!"

Mr. Mooney's voice interrupted my thoughts.

"Each of you has been invited here to celebrate Independence Day with us. As Mayor of Annandale I'm pleased to be your host tonight. I believe this resort will be a boon to our growing economy and make our town an even better place to live. I invite you now to listen to the music of Mr. Duke Ellington and his orchestra as you enjoy your dinner."

There was a round of applause as Mooney left the stage and I could not decide if the audience was applauding because he left or welcoming the entertainment. I had to admit, though, that Mooney was not a bad MC.

Mooney returned to his table, taking his seat next to Rose who sat beside Albert who sat beside Mr. Big. The man with the notch in his ear sat on the other side of Mr. Big.

Mr. Big's table was one of three at the edge of the dance floor directly in front of the microphone. Catherine and Fran were seated at one table along with Henrietta and Fran's parents.

Other business owners, the realtor and lawyer who held the documents for The Resort and the contract between Albert and Mr. Big attended the other table.

Apparently, the other tables were seated according to the importance of the people in the community in hopes of their favorable influence for The Resort.

But the only other table that interested me was the one that Carlisle and his girls sat at. They looked a little out of place surrounded by the well-dressed society they were in. But Carlisle was there to see that his girls kept everyone happy through the night.

A big, fat man, Carlisle was remarkably light on his feet and throughout the evening he and his ladies always got the dancing started.

But back at the beginning of the night the conversation at the tables was very interesting indeed! It was very strange to stand and listen and not be seen as the waiters came and went taking orders and filling drinks.

Christian was there, too. Having changed into his waiter's jacket after picking up the Zimmermans in the boat.

He made sure he took care of Catherine's table.

There was a mix of excitement on his face. On the one hand, happy to see the girl he loved and on the other hand afraid for his sister and what would happen tonight.

He was aware of two sets of eyes drilling into the back of his head. Albert, the protective father and Mr. Big, who was anxious to recruit him into his organization. Then there was the matter of he and Catherine eloping! As if the pressure of working a Grand Opening was not enough!

But he did a remarkable job of keeping his composure. He was polite and smiled at all the right times, though he struggled with wanting to talk to Fran!

At Mr. Big's table the talk was on FDR and the WPA.

"I think it will do a world of good for the country!" Mr. Big said.

"Yes, I believe you are right." Albert agreed.

Rose would not be left out of a conversation, political or not.

"Yes, Catherine is excited about all the opportunities in writing these days. The President's support of the arts is unprecedented!" She smiled as she picked up her drink, happy to have swerved the conversation.

"Yes, the influx of artists fleeing Germany and Europe has had quite an effect on the whole country," Mr. Big countered, letting Rose know that he was up on the arts, also.

I turned toward Catherine's table.

"Did you know that they have just created an office of Poet Laureate in Minnesota? Margaret Ball Dickerson has been nominated! I haven't read any of her work yet, but I intend to!" Catherine said to Fran.

"I'm so excited for you! I have always liked your writing!" Fran replied as she sipped the laced soda Mr. Big had provided for her.

The girls were too young to be drinking, even on the Fourth of July but Fran had told Bigelow that she would need some help unwinding.

"I want you sober tonight!" He had told her. "But then again, I can't have you freeze up on me now, can I?"

He had decided to have Carlisle supervise Fran's beverages personally. Carlisle knew what a young lady could handle.

Fran tasted the vodka in her soda and said nothing.

"And you, Fran! Going to Paris to study art! When do you leave?" Rose asked.

"In two days. The Silver Streak is set to stop here in Annandale on the way to New York. They say it's the fastest train ever built! From there I will take a ship to France."

"All those artists coming here from Europe must have really inspired you!" Rose continued.

"Well, why not? You're leaving for Florida aren't you? What will I do when you're gone?" Fran frowned.

"I have a present for you." Catherine said as she reached into her handbag and drew out a small box.

Fran unwrapped the little package with tears in her eyes.

"A locket!" She said.

"Open it." Catherine prodded.

Standing there, unseen, my heart was beating as I witnessed the scene. Inside the locket were the two small pictures of her and Fran.

Dinner was served and the dancing began as dusk fell on the lake. I looked out the tall windows that formed the outer wall.

Soon the fireworks would start!

I jumped ahead again. Now I was with Christian as he confronted Mr. Big behind the doors to the stairway.

"Well, Christian! Have you made up your mind?" Mr. Big was saying.

"Yes I have. No thanks." Christian said as he tried to pass by Mr. Big.

"What do you mean 'no thanks?'"

"I mean no thanks. I've got other plans." Christian repeated as Mr. Big blocked his path again.

I could see there was more he wanted to say but for the sake of his friends and family he held his tongue.

"Well, if I were you I would change my mind. I'm not used to taking no for an answer." Mr. Big used a friendlier tone now, but there was an edge on his voice.

"I'm not gonna change my mind!" Christian's voice was rising. He struggled to keep from blowing his cool.

Mr. Big could see there was something else on his mind.

"Has someone been talking to you?" He asked, not so friendly now.

"No. I just have other plans, that's all." But his nervousness betrayed him.

"Okay, Christian. It's your choice." Mr. Big said flatly.

That was it. End of conversation. Bigelow turned and let Christian pass into the kitchen. When he was gone Mr. Big smiled to himself and went up the stairs to the suites.

I did not want to witness what was about to happen again.

The band played on and I was suddenly on the dock in front of the road across from the Zimmerman house.

I was watching a boat approach the dock while the fireworks lit the sky behind it.

Christian piloted the launch to the side of the dock and tied it fast. Then he helped the ladies out and they said goodnight as they walked across the road to the house.

Albert had stayed behind to talk to Christian.

"So, are you still planning to run off with my daughter?" Albert was direct, his rage fueled by alcohol and fatherly pride.

"What if I am?" Christian said, defiantly. He had a belly full of so-called adults tonight.

"How do you plan to support her? I understand you turned down an offer from Mr. Bigelow." Albert searched Christian's eyes.

"And I understand you are in league with a gangster! You would have me work for one? You would bring your daughter into the world of crime?" Christian's eyes flashed back.

"I'm doing my best to protect my family! Sometimes we don't have much choice..." Albert was suddenly on the defensive.

"I had a choice! I told him no! But that makes you happy doesn't it? Because now you'll drag Catherine to Florida and make her marry your hand picked bank manager."

Both men were heated up pretty good. The louder their voices got, the louder the fireworks sounded.

Albert raised his hand, ready to punch Christian.

Suddenly, Christian arched his back and lost his balance, hitting his head on the side of the boat as he fell into the lake.

Albert had not touched him. In shock, he kneeled on the dock calling his name, and reaching into the water to fish him out.

From where I stood I could see Christian had been shot! The sound was masked by the noise of the finale to the pyrotechnics display.

Where had the shot come from?

In an instant I was there watching the man with the notched ear lower the rifle. He had shot him from the boathouse.

I roared in rage and frustration. I lunged for the killer but felt nothing in my hands. I was not really there.

I wanted to sit and cry, knowing that Christian was dead and that upstairs Fran was sacrificing herself to the man who just ordered her brother's execution!

SIXTY

I flew back to the dock in a rage! This was a nightmare! I wanted to wake up but I couldn't! I knew that these things had already happened and I could not change them!

Albert was lying on the wet dock. He pulled his empty hand out of the water, sobbing.

"What have I done? What have I done? Christian...come back!"

My emotions were strained to the limit! My analytical mind had left me. The sense of detachment I had come to rely on since Marianne had died was gone now, too.

Finally, in shock, Albert stood up on shaky legs. He turned and walked, zombie-like to the road and up the driveway to his house.

He did not want to think of telling Catherine and Rose what had just happened.

"My fault, my fault..." he kept saying over and over.

The fireworks had died and the night sky was finally quiet again. There was a shrill sound of silence in the summer air.

In his daze he did not notice the shadows that ran across the windows of the house.

Inside, another tragedy was in motion. Another nightmare was about to shatter what was left of his mind.

"Get your filthy hands off me you beast!" Catherine was at the top of the stairs fighting off Joe.

"C'mon, you know you want it!" He said as he pushed her back against the wall next to her bedroom door.

"My father will be here any minute!" Catherine yelled in his ear.

"Good! Let him come! He won't stop us. We're gonna do him too!"

"Animals! I'll tell Mr. Big!" Catherine threatened.

"Ha! Go ahead!" Joe taunted. "He sent us! He got the word tonight that everything was set. He doesn't need your father anymore!"

"Mother! Help me!" Catherine cried in desperation.

But her mother couldn't. She was being pursued by Pauly.

"C'mon, Missus!" Pauly said. "Make it easy on yourself! At least have a little pleasure before you die! I'll do you while we watch Joe rape your daughter!"

"I'll kill you both!" Rose swore as she twisted out of his grip in the kitchen and ran to the stairs.

"That's funny, we came here to kill you!" Pauly said, chasing her through the room.

At that moment, Catherine had escaped Joe's clutches at the top of the stairs.

In anger, he lunged forward, pushing her off the top step.

She bounced down the stairs like a giant rag doll and came to rest in a twisted, grotesque position at the bottom, still in her light blue party dress, eyes open staring at a horrified Rose.

Rose screamed!

Pauly stopped, momentarily, then lunged for her again as she turned and ran for the door. Tripping over Catherine he scrambled to free himself from her twisted corpse. In his mind he was sure she had come to life and was holding him by the feet.

Albert was just climbing the porch steps when Rose burst out of the door, knocking him over.

She ran past him, down the steps. Her eyes wild, she was headed toward the tool shed.

Albert stood and watched as she opened the door and went inside, emerging with an axe!

"What?" Was all he could say. Rose was running his way, axe held high in the air!

Bewildered, he opened the door just as Pauly was about to come through it.

The door knocked the hood off his feet sending him backward into Joe.

Both men fell backwards as Albert got a glimpse of his dead daughter lying at the bottom of the stairs!

Before the scene could register, Rose was on the porch with the axe!

Desperately, Albert ran for the sliding doors to his office. Joe and Pauly scrambled back into the kitchen.

Seeing the office doors closed, Rose concluded the killers were behind them!

The fine hardwood panels ripped savagely as the axe drove through them time after time.

Finally, the blade held fast! She had hit something!

There was a slumping sound, like a body sliding to the floor.

A look of satisfaction crossed Rose's face. Exhausted and spent, she left the axe in the door, slumping into a heap on the floor.

She did not know whom she had struck; did not know where the other one was or even remember seeing Albert on the porch.

The battle was over, she thought.

I was in total shock. "No more. No more, please." I said.

But there was more!

In the kitchen, Joe and Pauly heard the silence. Like rats in the dark they slid from their lair.

Stepping around Catherine they walked slowly up behind Rose.

"Rose! Watch out!" I yelled.

But she couldn't hear me!

Rose sat in Albert's blood as it oozed from under the door. Slowly the shock was wearing off. She started to push herself away from the door.

Only to meet Pauly's arm as it wrapped around her neck!

She froze.

"Well now, if it ain't the Missus!" Pauly whispered in her ear.

Joe just stood and watched, a sick smile on his face.

"We can still make this nice, whad'ya say?"

"Bastards! I'll kill you both! I'll see you in hell!" Rose was defiant to the end.

"You know, we can't stay here all night." Pauly said, taking out his gun and putting it to her head.

"Go ahead, shoot!" Rose mocked him.

"No, that would be too easy. No fun in that. You're gonna do it for me." Pauly was beginning to drool.

"Yes, give me the gun..." Rose taunted.

"Oh, I will, but I'm gonna help you hold it." He said.

"I'll never do anything you want me too!" Rose said as she spat in his face.

"Would you rather watch us have sex with your dead daughter?" Joe put in.

Rose believed that they would.

"Now, take the gun." Pauly repeated.

Spirit broken, mind in shock, her family dead, Rose took the gun with Pauly's hand on it.

She let him put his finger on hers as she caressed the trigger.

"No Rose..." I whispered.

The gun went off, one more bang in the night, unheard across the lake.

SIXTY-ONE

I couldn't look at Rose or Catherine or the blood of Albert oozing out from under the door. Shock turned to rage and I wished I could attack the killers!

But, again I was helpless.

"Hey, Pauly! We got 'em back good for kicking us out before, eh?"

"Yeah. Serves 'em right for not inviting us in for the roast beef!"

I felt sick to my stomach though it really wasn't here.

"Remember what Mr. Big said, we can't leave nuthin' here to link us to it. Let's get busy and blow this place."

I watched as Pauly checked the scene. He had wiped his prints from the gun he had forced Rose to take. Only her fingerprints would be on the gun. He was satisfied it looked like a suicide.

"Not a bad piece of work, if I do say so myself." He said.

"You're an artist, Pauly!" Joe complimented him.

They walked around the house, dusting places where they had been, making sure there were no fingerprints to find.

They were thorough, their coldness amplifying the horror I had seen.

"Looks to me like the Missus found out what was going on with Albert and Henrietta! Not only that, but her daughter! Poor woman lost it! Went crazy, killed her family then shot herself." Joe reported.

"Case closed," Pauly said. "Now, you take the car and I'll take the boat and we'll go back to The Resort. Remember to walk in separately and not together." Pauly took control now, remembering the kicks from Joe after their last visit here.

"Okay. I got it." Joe started for the front door then stopped and took one more look at Catherine. "Would have been sweet, though!"

They left the lights inside the house on as they had been all the while. There was little traffic on this road anyway. No one would notice anything unusual, maybe for days.

Plenty of time for Mr. Big and the boys to return to the city like nothing had happened.

They had parked the car around back. Catherine and Rose had no idea anyone was waiting inside when they walked in.

Joe started the car and drove around to the driveway with the lights off.

Pauly walked up the driveway and crossed the road, reaching the dock and climbing into the boat. I hoped Christian's body was clear of the hull and propeller.

Pauly knew Christian's body was near, though. He had been there when Mr. Big set up the hit. Now that everything was in place he would tie up all of his loose ends.

I returned to the house as the two killers went their separate ways.

Something moved behind me! I turned slowly from the window, daring myself to look!

Rose's eyes had squeezed shut just before the gun went off. Now they were open! Though her body did not move, I saw her ghost rise up out of it! "I'll kill you both!" She had said.

I watched as she walked right through the front door, her blood-stained dress now clean as snow, her head undamaged. In the moonlight she caught up with the moving car as it turned onto the road.

I could only imagine what Rose would do inside the car. But if I could see her, maybe Joe could too! I was standing in the driveway now, knowing that Rose had come back for revenge!

He must have seen her in the seat beside him because the car swerved suddenly and drove into the lake, accelerating as it flew down the short embankment and into the water!

The car sank out of sight, Joe still behind the wheel.

Pauly had started the boat and was busy heading it into the open water. The noise of the motor blocking out the sound of the splash the car made.

From where I stood I could see that now he was not alone in the launch. Rose's wild hair flew in the breeze and I thought I heard her laugh as the boat turned back around.

Full throttle the boat aimed straight for the dock, slamming into it so fast that it completely shattered!

Pauly's body shattered also, flying in pieces with the wood and sinking into the watery grave.

I didn't feel sorry for either one of them. Mr. Big would probably not miss them until tomorrow. No one else would miss them at all!

Rose flew past me and into the house. Catherine had risen, too. She looked down at her crumpled body, as if leaving it behind. Her dress unwrinkled, her hair in place as she walked to the window as if waiting for her date.

Still standing in the driveway I looked back at the window.

Catherine and Rose stood side by side as they looked out at me.

And waved.

SIXTY-TWO

The hot summer night had no effect on me. Temperature was nothing in this world since I was not really here. But I felt a chill anyway. I wanted to turn and run, if only emotionally, from the horror of this world, as I had done so many times before.

Still thinking about what was happening back at The Resort with Fran and Mr. Big, I tried to project myself there.

But something was wrong. I did not go anywhere.

I concentrated again but still did not move. I began to walk up the driveway. Maybe from the dock I could make the jump.

The night was strangely quiet. The fireworks had stopped. Even the occasional back yard pyros had ceased with their bottle rockets.

The crickets had stopped, also. All the little background noises that we don't notice until they are gone. There seemed to be a velvet blanket over my ears.

I stood on the dock, what was left of it. One end was mangled where the boat had hit. It dipped into the water, hanging by its twisted ropes.

The water was still. Too still. Nothing moved here. The moonlight itself seemed frozen.

I turned around and faced the road. The house stood in the distance, lights on just as I had left it.

Behind me, from the end of the shattered dock, I heard a sound!

It was a growl! A savage growl that I had heard before! And there were two of them!

"The Hounds of Hell!" I thought as I broke into a run, my feet not touching the slippery wet boards as I tried to escape.

Will power brought me to the road, the Hounds biting at my back, their hot breath chilling me again, raising the hairs on the back of my neck.

I was a goner! I knew I couldn't make it across the road and all of the way into the house!

Something else was moving also!

To my left was a pair of floating lights! A truck was coming down the road! Looking at it had slowed me enough for the Hounds to catch me! I was gone!

In the middle of the road, I stood in the path of the truck. I knew it couldn't hurt me though, because I was not really here! At least I hoped it couldn't! But, if it couldn't hurt me it wouldn't hurt the Hounds either!

There was another growl! This one was different and followed by a menacing bark. Scout!

From the driveway, Scout had run into the road to defend me!

The truck swerved, startled by Scout's sudden appearance. It hit a tree on the side of the road, the driver knocked unconscious.

On the door of the cab was a logo, Al's Cartage Company. I didn't realize it then but it was the same name as on the truck that had killed Marianne.

Scout was still in the road, snarling and barking in a savage fight with the two hellish hounds. I crossed over to the other side and stood in the driveway of The Zimmerman House as Scout continued his defense.

Backing up slowly an inch at a time he eventually stood in the driveway by my side.

The Hounds backed off, still snarling, red eyes burning into us in the dark, as if to say, 'this is our territory'.

Then they were gone.

It took quite a while for my heart to stop pounding. I stood there petting Scout until I could feel his taut muscles relaxing under my hand.

Now that things were quiet again, I tried to understand what had just happened.

The reason I could not project myself anywhere else was because this was the limit of Catherine's mind. This was the end of her life in this world of 1934. She was bound to this place and the brief life she had here. This was the only place she had any power.

There was only one place I could go now. There was nothing else I could learn here. These were all the clues that could be found.

Scout picked up his ears.

"What is it boy?" I tried to say, but no words came out. My voice was gone.

I knew I would be gone soon, too. I had to get back in the house and back to my own time.

Scout ran off, disappearing into the inky blackness that was spreading all around us.

I had stayed among the dead too long! The blackness was closing in and I knew the Hounds would be in it!

Now I was running again, to the porch, opening the door and slamming it behind me to shut out the evil fog.

Slam! The door shut with an unnatural velocity, smashing the silence of the house like an explosion from the fireworks display.

I backed up from the sound, stumbling on Rose's body, and tried to regain my balance. I spun around too late and fell over Catherine, hitting my head on the banister post at the end of the stairway.

I fell again, slumping to the floor as the velvet blackness of unconsciousness crept in.

SIXTY-THREE

The house looked different when I woke up. The bodies were gone. The sliding doors with the axe were gone. The blood was gone too!

"Thank God!" I said as I realized I was back in my own time! Here was a world I knew. Here was a world where I could be seen and heard. A place I could feel and touch!

I stood up, groggy and sore. How long had I lain here like that?

"I want a Coke!" I said just to hear my own voice.

I turned toward the kitchen enjoying the sunlight that shined through the new white lace drapes Betty Lou had made.

It was warm in the house. I could feel the July heat! I was feeling better all ready!

Inside the kitchen I noticed how clean everything looked. The refrigerator was running quiet and smooth. All of my senses seemed sharper now.

I opened the door of the fridge and reached for an ice-cold can.

I enjoyed the *pop*! of the can as I opened it and walked past the bathroom into the family room and headed for my desk.

Sitting down at the computer I decided to check the e-mail. I did not want to think about what I had just been through. Not yet.

Had I been paying more attention I would have noticed the manuscript stacked neatly on the right hand corner was considerably thicker than it had been when I left it last.

But my mind was not on the story. It was on the ordinary. E-mail was a great way to return to the 'real' world.

It took a while for the pages to load but finally I was typing in my password.

All of the usual spam was there along with the junk mail and letters from fans. There were notes from the publisher, too. Sales people were always after me through my writing.

Usually annoyed, I smiled this time, grateful for the problems I had.

One by one I deleted them all except the necessary ones.

Doing the chores on the computer helped me phase back in to my own time. I threw myself into the task, resisting the urge to open a few of the sexy links.

I smiled at myself for doing it.

"What the heck, why not?" I said to myself as I clicked on the one remaining link.

I sat back and had another sip of the coke as the page loaded.

Sure enough, a full-size sexy picture began to load and I stared at the screen totally absorbed, oblivious to everything else.

"Caught you!" The voice behind me startled me right out of my skin!

I jumped up out of the chair, whacking my knee on the edge of the desk and spilling the Coke right out of the can.

"I just get back shopping and I find you in front of the computer like you're in a trance!" Marianne's voice shocked me to the core.

Again I couldn't speak!

"Christopher? What's the matter? You look like you've seen a ghost!"

I passed out.

And woke up again at the foot of the stairs.

"I don't think I can take any more shocks." I said, my hand over my heart.

The phone rang sending me into another one!

"Hello," I answered cautiously, not knowing what to expect.

"Chris? It's Betty Lou. Are you okay?"

"Yeah, I'm okay," I lied.

"Well, tonight's the Grand Re-Opening. You are going to be there, aren't you?"

"Uh, yeah, I guess I am."

"Well, Raymond is counting on it! He wants to know if you'll do a book signing tomorrow."

"Sure. Anything. What time should I be there tonight?"

"I? Don't you mean we?"

"Why? Am I going with you?"

"No, silly. You and Marianne! What time are you guys going to be there?"

"Uh, six I guess..."

"Okay! See you then!"

She hung up and I dropped the phone.

"Could it be?" I asked myself.

There were too many questions in my mind. I ignored them all as my heart started beating faster and faster!

"Marianne?" I smiled, and then started to laugh as I ran through the house.

"Marianne! Where are you?"

I searched from top to bottom but still got no answer.

In the master bedroom I stopped short.

There was a new double bed, nicely made and clothes in the drawer.

The closet was neat and held two wardrobes.

I recognized Marianne's jewelry on the dresser.

I went into Catherine's room. It was just as I left it.

The curtains were new, though and matched the ones downstairs.

I parted the curtain and looked outside.

A royal blue Jaguar pulled into the drive.

The door opened.

It was *Marianne*!

SIXTY-FOUR

But it wasn't Marianne!

It was a dream. I was back in darkness again on The Bridge. Catherine floated before me.

"*Christopher...Christopher...*" her ghostly whisper pulled me away from my beautiful dream.

"Why? Why are you doing this to me?" I shouted.

"You are caught between worlds. You could be lost forever in your dream."

"What would be wrong with that?" I cried.

"The real world needs you. It is not your time to leave."

"But I'm tired and it all seemed so real..."

"Do you really want to stay a ghost? Unable to be seen, heard, or felt? You have had a taste of it. Did you like it so much?"

I thought about what she said. "No. It's worse than being a prisoner."

"Then you must really go back."

"But did I find what I needed here? How can I help clear Rose? What was I sent here for? I couldn't stop anything! I saw it all happen and I could do nothing!"

"I have shown you the limits of my world. My time was short and you could only go as far as the edge of my mind. You must take whatever you found and apply it in your time. You will find a way. If it wasn't possible, none of this would have happened."

I nodded. Catherine was right and I knew it. I had experienced things I never thought possible. I needed to keep an open mind and look for a way.

Catherine was drifting away! She rose from The Bridge and began to waver and fade into the darkness.

"Catherine! Wait! Come back! I have so many questions."

"You must find the answers within yourself."

"But how will I get back without you?"

"Concentrate. That's all you have to do," Her voice was growing fainter.

I became aware of a sound beneath me. Something I hadn't noticed before.

"What is that sound? What does this bridge cross?" I was growing fearful now.

"Something you have and I don't." Catherine's fading voice answered.

"What?"

"Time, Christopher. That is the River of Time.

And she was gone.

"Where?" I wondered. "Where did she go?"

Concentrate, she had said. Concentrate on what? Or is it when? Or where?

An old song came to mind. *It seems we stood and talked like this before...but I can't remember where or when...*

Maybe I wasn't ready to go back. Like in my dream. Maybe I didn't want to face the truth about my real heritage and myself.

My whole world had been uprooted! My comfortable beliefs were gone! The family I had researched was not my blood family! Every one I had ever loved was dead.

And maybe the worst thing of all—my grandfather was a gangster and a murderer!

How could I go back to a world I only thought I knew?

What would happen if people found out who I really was?

Did I have those murderous genes in me, too?

Here I was on The Bridge over the River of Time. What would happen if I jumped?

It would be so easy. But...

I would be a coward for eternity!

The Hounds of Hell would be a better fate!

The rushing of the River grew louder now. As if to pull me in! Soon the noise was unbearable!

I held my ears and shouted!

"NO! No-o-o-o-."

The water lapped at my feet. The bridge swung back and forth. I couldn't keep my balance!

I was going over!

I began to concentrate. Was it too late?

SIXTY-FIVE

It wasn't too late! I found myself at the foot of the stairs, my head on the hardwood floor.

I looked at my watch. It was the same time and date I had left. I sat up, one hand feeling for a knot on the back of my head, my back registering pain and stiffness.

Slowly, I got to my feet and stretched, relieving some of the pressure on my back.

I was still in one piece!

Happy I did not jump off The Bridge, I stood, looking around the house.

I was really here, this time! I could feel it.

The house was quiet. But it was a normal quiet. Not like the one I had experienced back in time. Occasional gusts of wind lifted the curtains that hung on open windows.

There was a storm brewing.

I felt a drop in temperature and knew we'd get rain tonight.

I no longer knew what the house was supposed to look like. It had been changing since I arrived. I could no longer sort out what was new and what had appeared.

There were pictures hung on the stairway wall and the ones I had found in the china cabinets were still there. The holes in the plaster were gone, as they had been before. Here and there were the signs of age, though. It was as if the house was caught between two times.

I listened some more.

There was no sign of Catherine or Rose but from above I heard the creak of a floorboard.

Someone was here! Someone real, someone with some weight.

"Marianne?" I thought hopefully, remembering the dream I had on The Bridge.

I refrained from asking out loud, the hairs on the back of my neck warning me to be quiet.

Carefully, I slipped off my shoes and stood in my stocking feet. Setting the shoes on the third step I tiptoed to the front window grateful to be able to feel the floor.

I looked out at the drive. The day had turned dark with the clouds from the building storm. The temperature continued to drop and in the distance I could hear the rolling thunder.

Nothing there but my little 'Merc. No Jaguar, no Marianne.

From above another floorboard creaked.

Someone else must be in their sock feet! I heard no shoes.

Whoever was up there must have seen me lying here and stepped right over me! This would not be someone who was worried about my health!

I could not imagine who it would be.

I began to wonder if the Hounds had followed me back again.

Turning from the window I looked up the stairway.

"Well, you're up, finally!" Came a man's voice from the landing.

I froze as his stocking feet appeared and began to come down the steps one by one.

Finally, his face came into view.

"Phil! For God's sake, you scared the life out of me!" I said.

"Well, you must be a ghost then! They say this house is haunted."

He was down the steps now.

I looked at his shoeless feet.

"You're wondering why I have my shoes off?" He asked, smiling.

"Seems like a good question." I answered.

"Well, I knocked on the door but there was no answer. I saw your car out front and walked around the house looking for you. Finally, I looked through the curtains from the porch window and saw you lying at the bottom of the stairs. I used my key to let myself in to see if you were all right. I saw you weren't dead and wondered if someone had pushed you down the stairs. So, I took my shoes off and went upstairs to investigate."

Phil's story sounded true, but I wondered why he hadn't tried to bring me around or call an ambulance. I looked for his shoes but they were nowhere in sight. Something told me I could not trust him.

"Did you find anyone?" I asked.

"Nope. Figured you must have slipped. Had one too many Cokes, did you?"

I smiled at the sarcasm. "What brings you out here, Phil?"

"Well, to tell you the truth, I was hoping we could have a little man to man talk. I'm very curious about what is going on out here. I have not seen or heard of anyone sent out here to work on the house except for Betty Lou and the curtains. Where is all of this coming from?"

"You wouldn't believe me if I told you." I said, turning for the front door to signal the end of our 'visit'.

"Try me." He said, pulling a gun from his suit jacket and pointing it right at me!

"What's that for, Phil? Why don't you tell me what you are really doing here? I don't see your shoes anywhere. Were you hoping I was dead? If I had needed medical attention would you have called anyone? You're still looking for the money aren't you? Vandals didn't put the holes in the walls, you did!"

It was risky confronting him with that gun, but maybe if I could get him talking I would have a better chance of getting out of this alive!

"Okay, you got me. So what?" Phil said. "I know that money is here and it belongs to me! I have a right to it!"

"Why, Phil? Why do you have a right to it?"

"Because Robert Bigelow was my grandfather!"

Now I was shocked! How could that be? I was sure my greatest fear had come true and that I was the son of Fran's baby girl by Mr. Big!

"What?" Was all I could say.

"Yeah, don't look so shocked, Christopher! I saw the letter from Mrs. Bigelow."

"Letter from Mrs. Bigelow? What letter?" I had no clue what he was talking about.

"The letter on your desk over there. The one sent by her estate after she died. The one where she releases her dead husband's papers and names you as Fran's grandson. The letter that gives you sole inheritance to The Resort and the house! The letter that sent you out here in the first place!"

Something was wrong. Something had changed! I thought back. Of course! The delivery truck! It had crashed to avoid Scout, who had run onto the road to defend me! Something that would not have happened before! I kept this to myself as I answered Phil.

"That's not what happened, Phil. My publisher called you because he was worried I wouldn't finish my contract and deliver the last book. You called me, remember?"

"Hey, what are you trying to pull? Are you trying to confuse me? Well, it won't work! Everything was going great until you showed up! No one paid any attention to this place and I would have found that secret safe eventually. Then you came in waving that letter and saying how you were the one who owned this place!"

"You didn't want the property for a bed and breakfast?" I asked.

"That was just a cover story. All I wanted was the loot that old man Albert had siphoned from Mr. Big. I know he stashed it somewhere in this house. The records show a carpenter was here in 1934 and installed a hidden safe. Company policy prohibited recording the location of it though."

"What else did that letter say? How are you Bigelow's grandson?"

"Didn't you read the thing? Or did you hit your head harder than I thought? My grandmother was Henrietta. She did everything for Mr. Big! Everything! Since she couldn't have Albert, she figured he'd reward her for spying on him at the bank. She's the one who told Mr. Big about Fran. She told him everything he wanted to know about everybody! She made it all possible, checking the bills for the materials etc. She tipped him off to Albert. And she got nothing for it. Except pregnant!"

I was listening so intently that I forgot about the gun.

"What happened?" I asked, knowing he'd tell me the whole story!

SIXTY-SIX

"He dumped her, like everyone else. Right after the Grand Opening! Right after she followed him upstairs to celebrate and caught him with Fran! Oh, I heard the story many times! She told it every time she got drunk. At the bar or when she was babysitting me!"

"What happened to her, Phil?"

"She died. Cirrhoses of the liver. She became an alcoholic. After he dumped her she tried to contact him but was warned to stay away or he'd kill her. Then, Rose's family took over the bank after they all mysteriously died. They fired everyone! Seems Rose had talked about Henrietta to them once or twice! She got a job at the bar in town; same one Pete hangs out at. Drunk all the time, chasing bikers; had my mother and raised her telling the same story. My mother grew up forced to entertain the men Grandma brought home when she passed out. She got pregnant by some drifter and had me. She's gone now too."

"Does Fran know all this?"

"Fran? Yeah, she knew. Saw Henrietta in the doorway the night of the Grand Opening of the resort. She was half Grandma's age and Henrietta hated her for it. She told her once that at least *she* hadn't had to give up her baby! Fran was never in love with Mr. Big. My Grandmother was! So you see, that money is rightfully mine!"

The gun had lowered while he talked. Now he raised it again.

"What would you do with it, Phil? It's blood money."

"Who cares? It's sitting there doing nothing! No one ever looked for it! They never found any record of it at either bank. It's not written down on any documents. No one will miss it!"

He was becoming more agitated now

"Listen, Phil; We're cousins now. If you shoot me you'll never find it! Then you'll have to explain what happened to me!"

"Shut up, 'Cuz'! Why don't you just tell me where it is and I'll take my wife and blow this town! Won't have to keep living on her money. She never liked it here anyway. Always the outsider! Just like Rose!"

The hair was standing up on the back of my neck again. I knew something was going to happen!

"What makes you think I know where it is?" I asked, looking around nervously. The air was full of static now.

"I checked your bank records. Your book is still selling well, but none of your money is coming out here! Now the house is being restored and no one has seen anything."

"Doesn't that tell you something, Phil? Do you really think I could do all that writing and restore this house at the same time? This house is moving back in time. It is restoring itself!"

Now Phil could feel the charged air. He started to act even more nervous and agitated.

"Enough talk! You're trying to scare me! Just take me to the damn safe..."

Just then the storm outside broke with a sudden clap of thunder that made us both jump!

The gun went off in Phil's hand! Unprepared, his arm flew up and the bullet fired wildly. I used the surprise to jump him and knock it out of his grip.

I kicked it away as Phil doubled his fist and went for my breadbasket!

I pulled back, lightening the blow and reached for his neck hoping to get him off balance.

His feet slipped on the hardwood floor and we wrestled to the ground, turning and rolling towards the staircase.

I was on top but only for a moment!

His stocking feet came up and knocked me back on the steps. I grabbed the banister and ran up the steps, forcing him to follow.

He was on my heels like the Hounds of Hell!

I reached the top and bolted for Catherine's door.

It wouldn't open! I turned to face the crazed Phil.

But he wasn't there!

He had run back downstairs and found his gun!

A shot rang out, splintering the wood in the doorframe by my head!

"So, that's where the safe is! Of course! Catherine's room! The only room that stayed intact all these years! Daddy's little rich girl!"

I tried to move but another shot held me in place.

"Just stay there, Christopher! You're going in with me!"

Advancing up the stairs he kept the gun aimed at me. My heart was pounding and I tried to think of something to say.

"Phil, stop! You don't want to go in there!"

The thunder continued to boom and crack with the fury of the summer storm. The house looked eerie, illuminated by flashes of lightning as the rain pelted the roof.

"Oh, try your ghost stuff on me some more! You had me going for a while with the static in the air, but it's just the storm! Do you think I'm a little kid? I was never a kid. I grew up with the stories of gangsters and bitter women!

Now, you go first or I'll shoot you and push you through the door!"

I remembered a recurring nightmare I had as a child. It went on for years until I was fifteen. In this nightmare I'd be running through a big old house from something I could not see. I'd run and climb every stairway trying to get away until I came to the very top and the last door. I'd fling the door open and come face to face with a wild-eyed woman wielding an axe over her head and looking right at me!

The power of that memory caused me to dive at Phil's legs, dodging the next bullet and driving him back against the railing. I rolled and got to my feet.

"Forget it! I'm going in!" He said.

Raising his foot, he kicked the door open just as a loud crack and a flash of lightning lit up the top floor.

The door flew open and Phil came face to face with a wild-eyed Rose and the axe held over her head!

The blood drained from his face as he staggered backwards to escape the descending blade! He hit the railing a little too hard and it gave way, sending him to the floor below. I watched the blood pool around his head as the storm began to subside.

SIXTY-SEVEN

The low rumble of the fading thunder seemed to coincide with the events in the house.

I looked at the shattered banister that had almost given way as Phil crashed into it. Here and there the spindles had snapped, jutting out into angry, vicious points that could pierce any vampire!

Phil had grabbed one as he rolled down the stairs. Now it lay under him, the source of the pooling blood. I wondered if he was still alive.

A low moan from the bottom of the steps told me he was. I started down the stairs, my back sliding along the wall to avoid the weakened railing. The darkness had lightened some as the storm moved away, but the power was still out. The room was a murky gray and it was still hard to see.

As I reached the lowest step I heard the rumble of the thunder again and with it another rumble that I knew all too well!

"The Hounds are here!" My own voice whispered to me and I froze on the step. In the half-light I saw one of them standing over Phil, waiting for him to die!

He must be on The Bridge! I thought. "But I'm not, *am I?*" A growl from the top of the stairs told me I was too. "Damn things always travel in packs!" I said.

There was no time to try and figure it out! I reached out and tore one of the spindles from the ruined banister.

Turning my back on the one at the top of the stairs I raised it at the hound standing over Phil.

The red eyes of the hound glared at me. Its lips were curled back over the hellish canines and I thought about the sharp points of the spindles. Maybe they were something like werewolves! I raised it threateningly again.

Growling savagely, the hound held its place. I knew I held some power! But as I advanced toward Phil, the hound leapt over his body and straight at me!

I scrambled back up the steps toward the one at the top, narrowly avoiding the snapping jaws one more time!

The relentless hound charged again!

Bracing myself against the wall I took the spindle and rammed it into the snapping jaws! The spindle broke his charge and I used it to throw him backwards over the twisted railing.

Back at the bottom, the hellhound shook the railing from its jaws and headed back up the stairs again!

I ran up the steps! There was no time to yank another weapon from the railing! I would have to deal with the one at the top when I got there!

As if I were living my nightmare the steps seemed longer and longer. I seemed to be running in slow motion. Like an eddy in the river, time seemed to be caught in a swirl.

I looked up at the hound that waited and back at the one that chased me. There did not seem any way to cheat Death this time.

But I didn't feel like dying today! Reaching out again, I tore another spindle from its socket and turned on the demon behind me! I brought it down like a club on its head, stunning him and stopping his attack! Before he could shake it off I pulled it back and aimed the sharp point at his heart and drove it home!

A hellish blast roared out of him, tearing through the house like the sound of a tornado as he fell back on the steps, erupting into a ball of fire and then vanishing in a howl of agony!

Now there was only one to face!

The smell of brimstone permeated the air as I started up the steps again, staring into the red eyes of the waiting Hell Hound! I didn't flinch. I was through running!

"Come on!" I yelled, a wild sound in my voice.

But these things live on fear and seeing none in me the hound vanished!

"Ha! Can't face me, eh?" I gloated at my victory.

Just as I began to celebrate a low rumble came up the steps behind me! The hound had vanished only to attack me from behind!

The noise at my back told me I had only seconds to run! I ran up the remaining stairs only to come face to face with the wild-eyed Rose, her axe held high above her head, her eyes looking right through me! The axe was about to fall!

I closed my eyes as the axe came down!

Right into the head of the charging demon! There was a soft, sickening sound as the blade sliced through the skull and stopped in the soft gray matter of the brain.

I slumped at the top of the stairs sure I was dead.

The hellish howl of the hound tore through the house once more as the second demon gave up its ghost and burst into flame behind me!

I realized the axe was not meant for me!

Rose had been aiming at the hound!

I was alive!

SIXTY-EIGHT

The sheriff had a few questions for me as they loaded Phil into the ambulance.

"He'll live," he told me. "Now tell me what really happened."

"Like I said, he had a little too much to drink. Came out here all upset about my book and started a fight."

"And in self defense you pushed him down the stairs?"

"No, we were scuffling at the top of the stairs. I threw him off and he crashed into the railing and fell down the stairs, grabbing one of the spindles on the way down. The storm had knocked out the phone and I had to use the cell phone in his jacket to call the ambulance."

"What about the bullet holes in the door frame? Someone was shooting."

"Oh, those were here when I got here. Probably from some vandals a long time ago."

"Okay, Mr. Evans. We'll check your story with Phil when he's able to talk. In the meantime, stick around. You will be at the Grand Re-Opening of The Resort tomorrow, won't you?"

"Of course. Ray is counting on it." I said.

I could not wait for everyone to leave. Finally it was quiet and I was alone in the house.

I went to my desk and found the letter from Mrs. Bigelow.

"Dear Mr. Evans,

You don't know me but this letter is being delivered to you as part of my last will and testament. On behalf of my late husband, Robert Bigelow I fulfill his last request..."

The letter told the whole story. In it was Mr. Big's confession, the whole story of The Resort and his plan to create an heir to leave it to. The letter confirmed that Fran was my grandmother and Mr. Big was my grandfather! It also served as proof of ownership for The Resort and the house that was tied to it. Mrs. Bigelow revealed the name of my mother's adopted family-one of Mrs. Bigelow's sisters, the wife of a dentist. Mr. Big had provided for our care and we were never told. I was to inherit The Resort when I was twenty-one, but something had gone wrong!

Still struggling with her husband's infidelity and jealous of his plan, Mrs. Bigelow was torn with spiting her husband and fulfilling his last request. She decided to wait until she died also.

Mr. Bigelow died in 1951 while riding in his chauffeured limousine. He had avoided the purge of the gangsters in the Thirties and with his wife's help had stayed clear of the authorities and the Mob for seventeen years! On October 6, his driver was surprised by a large German shepherd who appeared suddenly in the road as they returned from a trip to the resort. The car went off the road, smashing into a tree and pitching Mr. Big into the glass between him and the driver. He died instantly. The driver died later.

Mrs. Bigelow had a lot to lose besides her husband. She lived on in her mansion in St. Paul, the well-connected lady of high society.

The letter also named Joe and Pauly as the killers of Albert, Catherine, and Rose; and Carlisle, the man with the scarred face and chipped ear as the assassin of Christian. The big man with the ladies was also a killer.

My mother had waited until thirty-five to have me, the first male heir of Mr. Big. Well, not counting Phil.

Included in the letter were the documents to support the claim, including titles signed by Ray's grandfather, who was the City Attorney at the time and also the owner of the real estate management company who controlled The Resort.

I sat for a long time pondering all that I had read and all that had happened before I drifted off to an exhausted sleep.

What to do with all this information?

The banging on the front door woke me from my sleep. I stretched and realized I had fallen asleep in the chair behind the desk.

"Okay, okay, I'm coming!" I growled as the banging continued.

Tucking in my wayward shirt I reached for the knob and opened the door.

"Pete!" I was surprised to see him.

"Hey, Chris! Been trying to call but the phone's out. Heard the Sheriff was here last night and Phil's in the hospital! Came to see if you're okay."

"Yeah, I'm okay. Come on in."

Pete stepped in.

"Want some coffee?" I asked.

"Uh, beer'll do. Good Lord! What happened here?" He was pointing to the broken banister.

"Had a little trouble last night. Want a job?"

"Man, I don't know if I can fix that." Pete stroked his chin.

"Tell you what, Pete, how about the whole place? I'd like to restore it."

"Probably need some help. I've got some friends with me." He smiled.

"Friends? What friends?"

Pete walked over to the front door and swung it open. The whole driveway was filled with custom bikes and cars from Mooney's car club. Betty Lou waved at me from her Corvette.

"We came by to tell you we'll all be at the Grand Opening tonight if you'll have us." Pete said hopefully.

"Well, I wouldn't have it any other way!" I smiled back.

Whatever beer I had in the fridge was passed around and we spent the morning listening to the oldies until they all drove off.

There was one more thing I had to do before I left for the party.

Carefully climbing the shattered staircase I stood in front of Catherine's door.

I tried the handle. It was locked.

I don't know why I knocked. It just seemed like the thing to do.

"Come in." A quiet, cheerful voice said.

I tried the door again. This time it opened.

SIXTY-NINE

The door opened to the pristine bedroom that had been Catherine's domain for so many years.

All anyone ever had to do was knock.

The sunlight shone bright through the lace curtains and a cooling breeze billowed them into the room.

Seated on the bed were Catherine and Rose, dressed in the gowns they had worn that night of the Grand Opening so many years before.

There was no blood, no sign of any trauma.

They smiled at me.

"Well, we must be going." Rose spoke up. "Catherine and I are leaving for our trip. We'll be meeting up with Albert and Christian and I doubt we'll be back this way."

I stood quiet, not knowing what to say.

"I have something to leave you with, Christopher." Catherine said as she handed me a yellowed page from her dresser top.

It was a poem.

JOHN E. CARSON

SUMMER'S GHOSTS

The summer gathers
In the fall
Blown upon
The garden wall

Paintings of
The former days
The browns and reds
And golden maize...

Oh, how fast
The season's flown
Oh how short
The time I've known!

Faded echoes
Of summer life
Cut short now
By winters knife.

To fall so fast
And near the tree
No wandering wind
To carry me!

Oh, hurry while
The color shows-
Feel the youth
Before it goes!

You who walk
Along the lane
You who think
That you'll remain...

When we were
High upon the tree
Shouting out-
Look at me!

May stop and rest
Late in the fall
And brush the ghosts
From the garden wall.

Catherine Zimmerman

When I looked up from the page they were gone. As I
stood in the empty room I heard a whisper...
"Thank You!"

Somehow I knew that they were now at rest. I sat on the bed for a long time then opened the closet and found the safe.

It wasn't locked.

It was empty, except for some personal possessions meant for Catherine.

"Of course! Albert never had a chance to put anything into it!" I said out loud.

The safe had just been installed! All the money that he had skimmed from Mr. Big had been put back into The Resort to replace the money pulled out from the skittish investors! The safety net Albert had planned on had to go right where it was supposed to go. The scaling down of The Resort was an absolute necessity and so was Mr. Big's money.

When Ray's grandfather had assured Mr. Big that all was in place and his plan was secure, Bigelow decided that the rumors Henrietta had told him about Albert were true and that it was time to part with Albert and his family even though he would have liked to get to know Catherine and Rose better!

When the tire had gone flat on the road and his driver told him about the carpenter, he took that as all the proof he needed! But Albert had put it all back!

I laughed as I went down the steps, holding the railing of the beautiful banister in the fine old house that Albert had built in 1932.

It still looked brand new!

EPILOGUE

A fine young man in a white jacket opened the door of my little 'Merc as I pulled up in front of The Last Resort.

"Good evening, Mr. Evans. I'll park your car for you." He smiled.

"Thank you." I said, taking the locket from the mirror as I got out.

I walked up the steps to the double front doors and swung them open.

Ray was there to greet me.

"Christopher! I was worried you wouldn't make it! Everyone is waiting!"

Ray hustled me into the dining room. The tables were all full and the room was a buzz of conversation.

There was a band on stage. The same band I had seen in New York at the Best Seller celebration for *Stepping Stones*.

Before I could look around, I was ushered into my seat at the front table.

"Good evening, ladies and gentlemen!" Ray's voice boomed out from the microphone in front of me.

"The Last Resort is proud to welcome you to our Re-grand Opening! Tonight not only marks a new millennium but the end of an era, too. There will be fireworks later and dancing to the sounds of the Big Band just as there was in 1934. We are pleased to announce the expansion of The

Resort to its originally planned opulence thanks to the generous support of the new owners. Now, please give the waiters your attention as they take your orders for dinner."

During the dinner that followed, the reporter, Julie Ackerman came over and asked me about the new book I was working on.

"Well, I think it will be a hit. Its called *Stepping Stones 2-The River of Time.*"

"I've heard you are planning another project also," she was fishing.

"Well, as a matter of fact, I am."

"Well, what is it?" She persisted.

"A poetry collection."

"Poetry? You write poetry, too?"

"Well, it's not mine."

"Whose is it, then?"

"Okay, I'll give you an exclusive. It's the collected works of Catherine Zimmerman. A local writer."

"Zimmerman? Of the Zimmerman House? The daughter was a writer?"

"A poet." I corrected her. "She is a poet."

"Is? You talk about her like she's still alive."

"Tell you what, you can read all about it when my book comes out."

Shaking her head, she thanked me and left the table.

I sat there; watching the sun fade and seeing the reflections appear in the tall windows overlooking the lake.

The Big Band began warming up and the room grew a little quieter in anticipation of the music.

Still looking out the window I noticed a young woman in a blue gown appear in the glass.

"Catherine?" I thought, remembering her ghostly appearance earlier in the day.

A pair of hands covered my eyes.

"Boo!" A voice I hadn't heard for a long time startled me.

"Sorry, I'm late! Fourth of July traffic at the airport!"

I looked up to see Marianne!

"Ladies and Gentlemen! The Last Resort and The Big Band are pleased to present the owners of The Resort and the authors of the best selling book *Stepping Stones,* Christopher and Marianne Evans! Would you please help me welcome them to the Spotlight Dance of the evening!"

Before I could even react I was in Marianne's arms again! The band was playing *You Belong To Me.*

"How..." I started to say, and then remembered how things had changed when Scout ran into the road defending me from the Hounds of Hell.

Marianne put a finger to my lips and smiled.

"Remember what you said in New York?" She said as we swayed to the music, "We started this together and we'll finish it together!"

After the fireworks all my questions were answered.

John E. Carson has been writing since the age of 14. One of ten children he went to work at an early age to help his struggling parents.

Now, after forty years, he has realized his life long dream of becoming a published author.

Beginning in 1999, with his song, *Deep of the Night*, recorded by singer/entertainer, Charlie Roth, John has continued publishing poems and stories, reaching an ever widening audience and breaking into national print in Ideals Books in 2005 with his poem, *Painting in Thread* and in 2006 with his first novel, *Ramblin' Rose and The Internet Newsletter*, published by Aspirations Media Inc. (AMI). More novels are in the works.

A father and grandfather, John lives with his wife and co-author, Marlene Rose in Monticello, Minnesota.

Visit John on the web at **www.readjohncarson.com** for all the latest updates and insights into the various projects and events in and with his works.

We hope you enjoyed this book. Your comments and thoughts concerning this book or AMI are welcome.

www.aspirationsmediainc.com

If you're a writer or know of one who has a work that they'd love to see in print – then send it our way. We're always looking for great manuscripts that meet our guidelines. Aspirations Media is looking forward to hearing from you and/or any others you may refer to us.

Thank you for purchasing this
Aspirations Media publication.